Jack sat unmoving, ~~moments after Suz~~

Every instinct in hi~~m~~ tail on fire. What the hell had she drawn? Why did she bury her last card without showing it? Who really won the hand, and who lost?

She'd folded a winning pair. Jack knew it as sure as he knew his own name. But why? What did she have to gain by offering herself as a stake in a poker game, then deliberately losing the hand? She had to have known that he intended to collect the debt she now owed him. He'd put it as plain as he could without saying the words outright. He wanted the payment they talked about back at Ten Mile Station. He wanted *her*. He couldn't breathe without craving her so bad he hurt.

She had to have known what she was wagering. She had to know what she'd just lost.

Abruptly he shoved his chair back. He was done with trying to figure out the woman. Done with wondering just what crazy ideas were swirling around under the mass of silky brown hair. For whatever reason, she'd played her hand the way she'd wanted to, and Jack was going to claim his winnings.

Merline Lovelace "writes with humor and passion."
                                          —*Publishers Weekly*

Dear Reader,

Are you as fascinated by the old West as I am? Given my military background, I've always been particularly interested in the army's role on the frontier. One of my all-time favorite trips was a swing my husband and I took through Wyoming, Montana and the Dakotas. I don't think we missed a single restored fort, battlefield or roadside marker.

One marker especially intrigued me. On a lonely stretch of dirt road near present-day Lusk, Wyoming, we found a slab of pink granite surrounded by a metal-pipe fence. The wind-worn stone marked the grave of Mother Featherlegs Shephard, murdered in 1879 for her money.

Of course, I was hooked. My research into her life and times turned up a host of other fascinating real-life characters, including George "Big Nose" Parrott. They're both here in *The Colonel's Daughter,* along with the determined colonel's daughter and a man seeking his own brand of justice in a wild, untamed land.

So curl up, keep warm and enjoy this tale of times past. And if you enjoy this book, be sure to watch for *The Captain's Woman,* the next book in the Garrett family saga. When war fever sweeps the country, Lieutenant Sam Garrett joins Teddy Roosevelt and the Rough Riders— much to the dismay of the girl who decides she *won't* be left behind. Coming from MIRA Books in January 2003.

Best wishes,

Merline Lovelace

Merline Lovelace

The Colonel's Daughter

MIRA

If you purchased this book without a cover you should be aware
that this book is stolen property. It was reported as "unsold and
destroyed" to the publisher, and neither the author nor the
publisher has received any payment for this "stripped book."

ISBN 1-55166-871-8

THE COLONEL'S DAUGHTER

Copyright © 2002 by Merline Lovelace.

All rights reserved. Except for use in any review, the reproduction or
utilization of this work in whole or in part in any form by any electronic,
mechanical or other means, now known or hereafter invented, including
xerography, photocopying and recording, or in any information storage or
retrieval system, is forbidden without the written permission of the publisher,
MIRA Books, 225 Duncan Mill Road, Don Mills, Ontario, Canada M3B 3K9.

All characters in this book have no existence outside the imagination of the
author and have no relation whatsoever to anyone bearing the same name
or names. They are not even distantly inspired by any individual known or
unknown to the author, and all incidents are pure invention.

MIRA and the Star Colophon are trademarks used under license and registered
in Australia, New Zealand, Philippines, United States Patent and Trademark
Office and in other countries.

Visit us at www.mirabooks.com

Printed in U.S.A.

This book is for my own handsome hero
of thirty-plus years, who makes exploring Badlands
and historic old ruins such grand adventures.

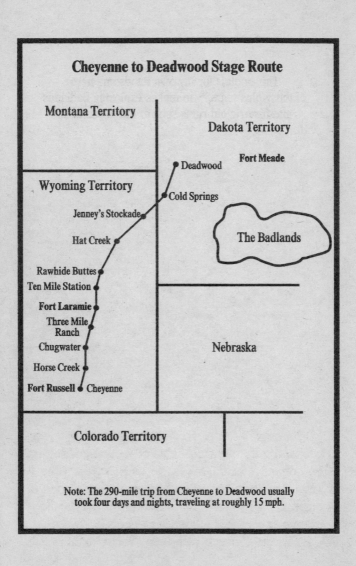

Cheyenne to Deadwood Stage Route

Montana Territory

Dakota Territory

Fort Meade

Deadwood

Wyoming Territory

Cold Springs

Jenney's Stockade

The Badlands

Hat Creek

Rawhide Buttes

Ten Mile Station

Fort Laramie

Three Mile
Ranch

Nebraska

Chugwater

Horse Creek

Fort Russell Cheyenne

Colorado Territory

Note: The 290-mile trip from Cheyenne to Deadwood usually
took four days and nights, traveling at roughly 15 mph.

1

Wyoming Territory
September, 1879

The sharp pop roused Suzanne Bonneaux from a fitful doze. She jerked upright, her spine snapping into a line every bit as straight and stiff as the Misses Merriweather could have wished during Suzanne's two years at their Academy for Select Young Ladies.

With a shake of her head, she tried to clear the haze caused by dust, the unseasonable September heat and two days and nights of jouncing along in one of the Black Hills Stage and Express Line's great, lumbering coaches. Frowning, she darted a quick glance from under the brim of her feather-trimmed hat at her fellow passengers.

The portly watch salesman facing her on the

middle seat grasped his merchandise case to his chest. With eight people jammed inside the coach, two of them sentenced to the agony of the backless middle bench, there was no room between the other passengers' legs to store his goods. At each stop the driver had tried to convince the salesman to relinquish the case so it could be stored in the boot, but the merchant insisted on using it as a pillow in a futile attempt to sleep.

He wasn't sleeping now, however. Like Suzanne, the sharp crack had jarred him into full wakefulness.

"Did we snap a trace?" he asked nervously.

"Might have," the blacksmith wedged between two other men on the rear-facing seat replied. "Hard to tell, with all these creaks and groans."

Like the dust that swirled in through the windows, noise was a constant companion to the passengers traveling aboard the Cheyenne to Deadwood stage. The leather springs on the massive, red-and-gold-painted coach creaked at every turn. Its wheels thumped at each jarring rut. After the first few hours, Suzanne had learned to separate the pop of the driver's whip from the slap of the reins. Very soon after that she'd stopped listening.

"Didn't sound like no trace to me," the ranch hand next to Suzanne muttered. Unsteadily, he shoved the cork into the bottle he'd been guzzling from for the past two hours, ever since he'd stumbled out of the saloon at the Ten Mile way station and climbed aboard the stage.

"I'm gonna take a look."

Leaning right across her, he stuck his head out the window. His knees knocked Suzanne's thigh, and the stench of raw whiskey and stale sweat rose up to penetrate the road dust clogging her nostrils. Drawing her dangling, beaded purse onto her lap and out of his way, she scrunched into the corner.

"There's riders strung across the road up ahead," he reported. "Must be a half dozen of them."

"Could be one of them wants to board the stage," the traveling salesman suggested hopefully.

"More like they want to rob it," the wrangler muttered, pulling back inside.

Instant alarm swept through the coach. The watch peddler wrapped his arms tight around his merchandise case, as if to protect his goods from the ruthless predators who preyed upon the stage lines like vultures. Next to him, the youth on his way to the Black Hills gold fields turned as pale as a bedsheet under his round-brimmed hat. He threw a worried look at Suzanne, the only female on the coach, as did the barrel-chested blacksmith.

"You just sit tight, miss," the smithy rumbled. "We won't let anyone hurt you."

"Thank you."

The calm reply would have done the Misses Merriweather proud, given the unusual circumstances. Despite her unruffled demeanor, however, Suzanne had no intention of trusting her fate to her fellow passengers. She'd been taught to protect herself by someone far more skilled at survival than her elderly preceptresses. Slipping a hand into the side slit of her navy serge traveling skirt, she gripped her two-shot derringer while the other travelers inside the stage hastened to echo the blacksmith's reassurances.

"Don't worry, ma'am. If they are robbers, they're most likely after cash 'n gold. Even Sam Bass and his gang never kilt no passengers, jest a couple of drivers."

"That's right, miss."

Only one of the other passengers voiced no opinion. He remained slouched on the seat opposite Suzanne. Arms crossed over his leather vest, his flat-crowned black hat pulled down almost to the bridge of his nose, he paid no more attention to the commotion than he had to the shocked titillation of fellow travelers when he'd boarded the stage.

His name was Jack Sloan. Nervous whispers about him had circulated among the other passengers from the moment he stashed his saddle in the coach's boot and climbed aboard. His hand-tooled boots, button-over blue shirt and sorrel leather vest weren't remarkable in themselves, but the long-barreled Colt strapped to his thigh had drawn every gaze. He wore it low on his hip, butt forward in the way of the plainsmen. The weapon was old, as was its worn, double-looped leather holster, but none of the passengers doubted its efficiency.

Suzanne had heard of the man, of course. The army troops she'd grown up around were always repeating—and exaggerating stories about the colorful figures who populated the West. She'd met a number of them, including the flamboyant Bill Hickok and Wyatt Earp, who'd spent some months riding shotgun for gold shipments being transported on the Cheyenne-Deadwood stage. Her own stepfather, Colonel Andrew Garrett, had also gained something of a reputation as both Indian fighter and peacemaker on the plains.

In recent years another legend had sprung up. The lurid penny presses and dime novels that fed easterners' fascination with the Wild West had described Black Jack Sloan as a genuine shootist. If just half the sensational tales written about him were true, he'd killed his first man before his beard had started to come in and had gunned down a dozen more in the years since.

The glimpse Suzanne had caught of his cold gray eyes before he'd stretched out his legs, pulled down his hat and proceeded to ignore his fellow passengers suggested the sensational reports held at least a grain of truth. Even in his long-legged slouch, he gave off the sinister aura of a diamondback dozing in the sun. Still, a gunman might be a handy person to have aboard the coach at this particular moment. Assuming he woke up enough to take an interest in what was happening, Suzanne thought tartly.

Another crack split the air, eliminating all doubt among the passengers. To a round of curses from the driver, the lumbering vehicle began to slow.

Suzanne's heart thumped under her braid-trimmed navy serge half jacket and high-collared white blouse. Given that the Black Hills Stage and Express Line carried the mail, passengers and strongboxes stuffed with cash and gold dust, the stage company employed highly experienced drivers and guards to ride shotgun. If this particular driver was reining in, she could only conclude that he couldn't maneuver around or fight his way past the outlaws.

Her grip tightened on the derringer. A most unladylike trickle of sweat dampened the valley between her breasts. She should have listened to her mother, she thought ruefully. Julia Bonneaux Garrett had urged Suzanne to wait for her stepfather's return before departing Cheyenne. The colonel would have arranged a military escort. Or, more likely, would have accompanied Suzanne himself on her urgent quest to find her longtime friend,

Bright Water, once known by the childhood name of Little Hen.

After fifteen years of military service at frontier posts, Andrew Garrett understood better than most the impact of last year's order directing the Arapaho onto the Shoshone reservation at Wind River. Bright Water's band was among the last to make the arduous trek to the distant reservation. If Suzanne didn't reach her friend in time and convince her to at least consider the offer she'd brought back from Philadelphia, Bright Water might disappear forever among the distant mountains and swirling snows.

As Suzanne had explained to her mother, she couldn't wait for the colonel's return. She simply *couldn't*. At which point her younger brother, Sam, had remarked that two years of schooling back East hadn't replaced the vinegar in Suzanne's veins with sugar. Scratch her surface and she still showed the temperament of an army mule.

She was drawing on that stubborn streak to give her courage when the drunken wrangler fumbled for his revolver and thumbed the hammer.

"Here, man!" the blacksmith objected sharply. "Don't fire that!"

"I ain't lettin' no stinkin' road agents take my roll."

"The guard hasn't fired a shot. You'd better—"

The smithy never finished his protest. A light-

ning-swift kick from a hand-tooled boot knocked
the revolver out of the cowboy's hand. The Smith
& Wesson banged against the side of the coach
and landed on the floor beside Suzanne's tan kid
boots.

Cursing, the ranch hand turned on the man
sprawled across from him. "What the hell you do
that for?"

Sloan pushed up his hat with the tip of his forefinger. Steel-gray eyes stabbed into the angry
wrangler.

"A man shouldn't draw iron unless he's in a
condition to use it. Or prepared to die."

"You oughta know," the cowboy sneered with
whiskey-induced bravado. "Considerin' the times
you done pulled out that Colt, you must be over-
ready for plantin'."

"Some think so."

The flat reply sent a ripple down Suzanne's
spine. Half fascinated, half repulsed, she stared at
Sloan's face. Lean and hard-jawed, it was shadowed by black stubble. The facilities at the way
stations where they'd stopped to change horses and
grab a hasty meal hadn't run to luxuries like hot
water for washing or shaving.

"You in the coach!"

The roar came from just outside the window,
eliciting various expressions of alarm from several
passengers and a startled yelp from Suzanne.

RUSH me the issue
that you have reserved
in my name!

BUSINESS REPLY MAIL

FIRST-CLASS MAIL   PERMIT NO. 24   BIG SANDY TX

POSTAGE WILL BE PAID BY ADDRESSEE

GOOD · OLD · DAYS®
PO BOX 9008
BIG SANDY TX 75755-9879

NO POSTAGE
NECESSARY
IF MAILED
IN THE
UNITED STATES

Great Deal!

Bask in the warm glow of
golden memories from yesteryear.

1 Year
ONLY
$15.97
+ $2.98 delivery

Send No Money
Now—We'll Bill
You Later!

GOOD·OLD·DAYS®

☐ **YES!** I want to try a year (6 big issues) of America's favorite nostalgia
magazine for only $15.97 (+$2.98 delivery)
Outside USA $15.97 + $9.98 delivery and add GST/HST if needed. U.S. funds only.

☐ **SAVE EVEN MORE!** Send me 2 years (12 big issues) for only $29.97 ppd!
Outside USA $29.97 + $9.98 delivery

BONUS! Never any renewal notices! See Continuous Service Guarantee below.

NAME (PLEASE PRINT)

ADDRESS

CITY/STATE/ZIP   IBDGDGD   EXP 10/16

EMAIL ADDRESS—To receive subscription information   GD-SC065
and special offers from *Good Old Days* and Annie's.

CONTINUOUS SERVICE GUARANTEE—We promise to continue sending your magazines without inter-
ruption unless you tell us otherwise. We'll bill you for your renewal at the then-current rate at the time
of your next subscription anniversary. Never any renewal notices, and you may cancel at any time and
receive a prompt refund on any unmailed issues.
Please allow 4–6 weeks for delivery. *Good Old Days* is published six times a year, single-copy price is $5.99 per issue.
If the post office alerts us that your magazine is undeliverable, we have no further obligation unless we receive a
corrected address within two years.

"Put yer hands up and keep 'em up!"

Wedging around on the seat, she came face-to-face with the outlaw peering through the window. Or more correctly, nose-to-nose. The man possessed the most prominent beak she'd ever encountered on another human! Fleshy and red-veined, it hooked like a great, oversize wedge above his bushy black mustache.

While Suzanne stared in amazement, the robber's avid gaze skimmed past her, lingered on the case still clutched to the watch salesman's chest, then took in the other passengers.

"Well, well!" A huge grin split his face. "Lookee here, boys. It's Black Jack hisself."

Several of the outlaws now ringing the stage crowded closer. One adorned in crossed bandoliers and a wide-brimmed hat trimmed with silver conchos peered through the window on the other side.

"*Hola,* Jack."

"Hello, Alejandro."

The leader of the band winked at Sloan. "Looks like we done found us some ripe pickin's here."

His conspiratorial tone raised a decidedly unpleasant suspicion in Suzanne's breast. Frowning, she cast her fellow passenger a swift look. Was Black Jack Sloan in league with these ruffians?

It was a well-known fact that unscrupulous ticket clerks often "marked" coaches carrying wealthy passengers or particularly rich cargoes.

Sharp-eyed watchers at way stations along the route would note the marked coaches and ride hell for leather to alert their cohorts. Various gangs had even been known to plant one of their own aboard the coaches, with instructions to disarm the passengers—as Sloan had just done to the drunken cowboy.

While doubts swirled in Suzanne's mind, the leader of the band appeared ready to carry on an amiable conversation. "Ain't seen you since we stood back-to-back in that saloon shoot-out down to Pecos, Jack."

"Too bad I didn't know then you were going to take up robbing trains and stages, Big Nose. I wouldn't have covered you."

Sloan's comment went some way to mollifying Suzanne's suspicion, but elicited an excited exclamation from the gangly youth wedged next to the watch salesman.

"Big Nose? Are you Big Nose George Parrott?"

"Know anyone else with a bill like this one, boy?"

"I heard about you clear back in Ohio!"

"You don't say!" Hugely pleased by his notoriety, Parrott's grin broadened. "Well, haul yer hindquarters outta the coach and you kin tell me what folks are saying about me back in Ohio while you dump yer pockets. You climb out, too, miss, and the rest of you."

With the inside of the coach just a little more than four feet in width and height, it took some untangling of arms and legs before the passengers could alight. The watch salesman scrambled out first, clutching his precious case. The gangly would-be miner followed. Sloan emerged next, swinging down with a sinister, sinuous grace.

Their descent gave Suzanne enough room to maneuver. Twitching her heavy skirts into decorous folds, she reached for the door frame.

"I'll take that."

Before she could protest, one of the outlaws yanked her drawstring purse right off her wrist.

"Hobbs!" Parrott roared. "Mind yer manners! Let the lady climb down before you relieve her of her trinkets."

Treating the robber to a frosty glare, she ducked through the opening. She had one dainty half boot on the step when all hell broke loose.

"I ain't handin' my poke to those bastards!"

She heard a chink of metal against wood, and a chorus of alarmed protests from the passengers still inside the coach. Caught half in and half out of the coach, she froze.

"Dammit!"

The furious oath exploded behind her. A hard yank on her bustle tumbled her backward at the same instant gunfire blazed from the window of the stage.

Suzanne slammed into a hard object, bounced off and hit the sun-baked earth on bent knees and splayed hands. A half second later, what felt like a mountain landed on her back. She flattened like a flapjack as every ounce of air whooshed out of her lungs.

She couldn't breathe, couldn't see past the feathers on the hat that had fallen down on her forehead. The dead weight on her back ground her into the dirt. The bone stays in her corset gouged her breasts. Through the ringing in her ears, she heard more gunfire, shouts, the rattle of wooden crossbars and hardened oak wheels, but the desperate need to draw air into her lungs drove all other considerations out of her mind.

Lifting her head, she gulped desperately. A rough hand yoked her neck and pushed her face back into the dirt.

"Keep down!"

Red spots danced on her tight-squeezed lids. Choking, wheezing, Suzanne bucked frantically. Whoever lay atop her was obviously trying to protect her from the bullets flying above their heads, but he might very well suffocate her in the process.

"Get...off...me!"

"Keep down, I said!"

He hooked a thigh over her flailing legs, pinioned her arms at her sides. Dizzy and now distinctly faint, Suzanne pushed out a desperate plea.

"Get...off. *Please!* I can't...breathe!"

The spots had become a whirling kaleidoscope of scarlet and black when the weight finally rolled off Suzanne's limp form. She lay sprawled in the dirt, her mouth popping open and closed like that of a landed trout.

"Miss! Miss, are you all right?"

She dragged in several precious gulps of air before raising her head. Her hat tilted crazily over her eyes, its decorative quail feathers tickling her chin. With a shaky hand, she shoved it back into place and met the worried gaze of the youthful prospector.

"I'm...a...bit...winded."

The big, gawky boy reached down anxiously. "Grab holt of my hand and I'll help you up."

She struggled to her feet, still shaken but recovering swiftly. Pulling in another deep breath, she looked up just in time to see the red-and-gold-painted coach disappear around a bend in the road. Big Nose Parrott and his cohorts galloped after it in wild pursuit.

Only then did Suzanne's whirling mind comprehend what had happened. That idiot of a wrangler had sparked a shoot-out and spooked the horses. Either the driver hadn't been able to halt them, or he'd decided to take advantage of the situation and make a run for it.

Biting back the unladylike curse that leapt to her

lips, she righted her hat, dusted her gloved hands down the front of her skirt and managed a wobbly smile for her protector.

"You have my gratitude, sir, for shielding me the way you did."

A furious blush started at the open neck of his rough-spun shirt and rushed into his cheeks. "I, uh, er..."

"What's your name?"

Dragging off his round-brimmed brown hat, he clutched it between hands the size of small plows. His face glowed beet red beneath a thatch of gold-bright hair.

"Mathias, ma'am, Mathias Butts. My mam and pa call me Matt. But you needn't be thankin' me. It weren't me what jumped on you."

"It wasn't?"

"No, ma'am." He hooked a thumb over his shoulder. "It was Mr. Sloan."

"Mr. Sloan?"

She glanced beyond the boy to the two men some yards away. The rotund traveling salesman was vigorously brushing off his pea-green suit. Sloan was dusting himself off as well. A series of sharp whacks filled the air as he slapped his hat against his vest and shirt. His hair, Suzanne noted, was thick and unruly and every bit as black as the prickly whiskers on his unshaven cheeks.

As much as it pained Suzanne to be indebted to

a man like Sloan, he *had* thrown himself on top of her, after all. Pulling out the silver filigree stickpin that anchored her hat, she repositioned the feathery confection and stabbed the lethal sixteen-inch pin back through the heavy, upswept mass of her honey-brown hair. After a quick swipe of her cheeks with her handkerchief, she was ready to express her appreciation.

To her consternation, Sloan had apparently decided no expressions of any sort were required. Without so much as a word to her or the other two passengers, he'd turned on his heel and was striding back down the road they'd just traveled.

2

Well, for pity's sake!

Folding her arms across her dust-streaked bodice, Suzanne called out to the departing gunman.

"Mr. Sloan!"

He didn't turn, didn't so much as check his long-limbed stride.

Annoyed now, she infused her voice with a hint of the steely command her stepfather used so effectively with his troops. "Mr. Sloan! I should like a word with you, if you please."

The imperious call caught his attention. He swung around, his eyes unfriendly under the brim of his flat-crowned black hat.

"And if I don't please?"

She ignored his rudeness. "May I inquire where you're going?"

The scornful glance he aimed her way said she

could have figured that out by herself if she'd put half a mind to it.

"Back to the last stage stop."

"But that must be a good four or five miles."

"I make it closer to six."

Putting up a hand to shield her eyes, Suzanne squinted through the shimmering heat at the road behind Sloan. Narrow and rutted, the dirt track cut across shallow gullies, over undulating hills and around the buttes that jutted up out of the prairie grasses like great red boils. The Laramie Mountains formed a purple smudge against the far horizon. Already dusted with snow, Laramie Peak towered above the rest. A few puffy clouds dropped gray shadows on the grass, and a hawk circled the otherwise empty skies. There wasn't a curl of smoke to be seen, and certainly no sight of the sod shanty that constituted Ten Mile Station.

Suzanne spun back around. The Cheyenne-Deadwood stage road ran along the eastern edge of Wyoming Territory and on up into the rugged Black Hills of Dakota Territory. The hills were some distance yet, with many miles of rolling, windswept prairie yet to cross before they reached the rocky crags and deep gulches of Dakota.

Her destination lay to the north, where the Arapaho camped at a bend of the Cheyenne River. The need to reach her old friend pulled at Suzanne with urgent fingers. With every instinct she possessed, she knew that Bright Water must cross the barrier between red and white now, before it was too late. She had to reach the Arapaho camp on the Cheyenne River before Bright Water's band began its march to the Shoshone Reservation far to the west, had to convince her friend to take the other path that had been offered her. Suzanne hated to delay her journey. Hated even more the thought of retracing her way south, when her destination lay to the north. Frowning, she swung back to Sloan.

"Wouldn't it make more sense to wait here until help arrives?"

"You can do whatever strikes your fancy, lady."

"Really, Mr. Sloan, you know very well there's greater safety in numbers. Surely you don't intend to just walk off and leave the three of us to fend for ourselves."

His gaze shifted from Suzanne to the other two men. "They're not my responsibility. Neither," he added with a careless shrug, "are you."

"If you feel that way, perhaps you'll explain why you shoved me into the dirt and covered my body with yours?"

His mouth twisted. In another man, that sardonic half curve might have been mistaken for a smile. On Sloan, it didn't come close.

"I wasn't being noble, if that's what's buzzing around under those feathers. I tend to get nervous when bullets start flying, and just wanted you out of my line of fire.''

''I see,'' she said in a tone of polite disbelief.

''I don't think you do. The fact is, your rump hit me square in the chest when you tumbled off the step. You took me down with you.''

''I see,'' she said again, more stiffly this time.

A nasty glint entered his eyes. ''You might look like a good gust of wind would blow you halfway across the plains, lady, but you pack a decent weight under that bustle of yours.''

His deliberately provocative remarks didn't faze Suzanne. Before going back East to school, she'd spent most of her youth at a succession of frontier army posts. The experience had exposed her to all manner of men, from rough-and-tumble troopers to the homesteaders, gold seekers, gamblers and railroaders who pushed westward to claim the continent. She'd long ago learned to recognize this particular species of rogue male. Sloan was the type wise men went out of their way to avoid and fools were fascinated by.

Suzanne was no fool. Nor was she particularly intimidated by Black Jack Sloan. She decided it was time to apprise him of that fact.

''If you think to discompose me with your crude comments about my person,'' she said coolly, ''your aim is off the mark.''

The glint disappeared. His expression went as

flat and cold as a tombstone. "My aim is never off the mark."

"Do, please, spare me these dramatics. They neither frighten nor impress me."

Hooking his thumbs in his gun belt, Sloan rocked back on his heels. His iron-gray eyes made a slow descent from her hat to her hem. Just as slowly, they rode back up again, pausing for what Suzanne considered an unnecessarily prolonged time in the vicinity of her bosom.

"Has anyone ever told you that you've got a tongue on you, lady?"

"Yes, any number of people. And you may stop referring to me as 'lady' in that sneering way. My name is Suzanne Bonneaux. *Miss* Bonneaux, if you please."

Christ Almighty! Just listen to her! Jack couldn't quite believe he was standing under a hot sun, bandying words with a dab of a female in bent quail feathers and a high-collared blouse buttoned clear up to her ears. Did she think poking her chin up in the air like that would take him down a peg?

Jack had never backed down from a challenge in his life, but chances are he would have walked away from this one if his blood hadn't still been pumping from the bungled robbery attempt and subsequent shoot-out. Unhooking his thumbs, he sauntered forward.

"Well, *Miss* Bonneaux, I don't give two hoots in hell whether you're impressed or not, but you'd be smart to be afraid."

Damned if her chin didn't tip up another notch.

"Of you?"

"Of me."

"I'm sorry to disappoint you, but—oh!"

Quick as a sidewinder, Jack whipped an arm around her waist. One tug tumbled her against his chest.

A puff of trail dust billowed up between them, along with a tantalizing whiff of lavender, starched linen and female. He could feel the ribs of her corset under her layers of clothing. Feel, too, the soft breasts plumped against his chest.

He expected her to screech or claw at his face or even faint. He *didn't* expect the flash of curiosity that brightened her doe-brown eyes before an expression of polite boredom blanked them.

"Really, Mr. Sloan, you're becoming rather tedious."

Tedious? Folks had hung any number of labels on Jack over the years, but this was the first time anyone had ever dished that one out.

"Maybe I should liven things up a bit."

His smile mocking, he tightened his arm. She tilted back to avoid more intimate contact between her shirtfront and his chest. The movement canted her hips against his, with results as unexpected to him as they were startling.

Heat fired in his belly, hot and swift and fierce. In two beats of his heart, he went hard.

Christ! He hadn't been exaggerating when he said she packed some weight under her bustle. Despite her small size and delicate appearance, she carried a potent set of curves. Damned if she didn't fit against him exactly the way a woman should.

She stared up at him, her eyes wide, her mouth pursed tight as a prune. Her lips were so close, so damned close. For an insane moment Jack actually considered dipping his head and taking a taste of her.

She must have read his intent in his eyes. Red surged into her cheeks. Anger had her stiffening up like a poker in his arms. Jack had just about decided the game was over when she slipped a hand into her skirt pocket. The sixth sense that had saved his life more times than he could count tensed his muscles. He knew what was coming, could have prevented it by grabbing her wrist and twisting it up behind her back. Instead, he merely smiled when she shoved a good inch of steel into his ribs.

Their eyes locked, his steely gray, hers a warm brown flecked with gold, like cinnamon sticks dipped in honey. He didn't see fear in them, only a combination of determination and disdain.

"I wonder if you have the guts to pull the trigger," he mused.

"You'll find out if you don't release me in the next five seconds."

He was tempted. Damn, he was tempted! He could wrestle the gun away from her easy enough. She'd fight him, but she wouldn't struggle for long. He wasn't the only one whose blood was pumping. He'd seen the flash of surprise in her eyes, the all-too-brief curiosity. She'd wanted to taste forbidden fruit. Had thought about it for a second or two. Just long enough to stir up a fire in Jack and send hunger knifing into his gut.

He hadn't felt that kind of hunger in a long, long time. He shouldn't be feeling it now. Not with this woman, anyway. Hell, not with any woman. A man who pulled on his boots each morning fully prepared to hear harps or smell brimstone by nightfall had no business standing in an empty road like this, with no cover, while he contemplated kissing Miss Suzanne Bonneaux all to hell and back.

Stupid, Sloan. Real stupid.

His only consolation was that he'd made his point. The woman would think twice before she issued another mocking challenge.

Or so he thought until he released her.

Uncocking the neat little pearl-handled Remington, she slipped the derringer back into her skirt pocket. Two spots of color rode high in her cheeks, but her voice was as cool as summer ice. "Have you quite finished making an ass of yourself, Mr. Sloan?"

She didn't ruffle easy. He'd give her that.

"Near about," he drawled.

"Good."

With a flounce of her lace-trimmed petticoats, she turned to the two men observing the proceedings with slack jaws.

"Mr. Butts, have you a weapon on your person?"

The youthful farmer-turned-prospector gulped. "No, ma'am."

"How about you, Mr....?"

"Greenleaf," the salesman supplied. With a nervous glance at Sloan, he tipped his dust-covered bowler. "Benjamin Greenleaf, at your service, Miss Bonneaux."

"Are you armed, Mr. Greenleaf?"

"No, ma'am, I'm not. All I carry on my travels is my case of goods."

"Then I'd better take the point." She swung back to Jack, all brisk business now. "The Colt strapped to your thigh carries considerably more firepower than my Remington, Mr. Sloan. I suggest you bring up the rear, in case your friends do decide to return."

"I don't call Parrott and his band of cutthroats my friends."

"Do you not? Parrott certainly seemed to count you among his boon companions."

Chin high, she swept past him and started down the dirt track.

Suzanne set a brisk pace, but was soon silently cursing her goatskin half boots. Cut in the latest style, they were designed to display a lady's high arches and dainty toes. They were *not* designed for traipsing across the prairie.

She would have traded her shoes and every piece of the fashionable wardrobe she'd brought back from Philadelphia for some well-worn riding boots and a split-legged buckskin riding skirt. And a hat! A decent hat to shield her eyes and face! Her little puff of feathers might have come right from one of Goody's Fashion plates, but what Suzanne needed was the shovel-brimmed cavalry cap she'd worn as a child.

Her pinched toes and unshaded eyes didn't bother her half as much as the irritating way her thoughts kept returning to Jack Sloan, however. The man annoyed her intensely, and fascinated her completely. Really, when he'd narrowed his eyes and advanced on her with such deliberation, her heart had thumped quite painfully. And when he'd swept her into his arms....

Honesty compelled her to admit that he'd given her plenty of opportunity to retreat. Yet her instincts had shouted at her to stand her ground, that the only way to deal with a man like Black Jack Sloan was to meet him head-to-head. Or in this case, she thought with a little shiver, belly-to-belly.

The shivery sensation puzzled her almost as much as the man who'd caused it. Granted, he was handsome as sin, but Suzanne knew enough to judge a man by his actions, not the set of his shoulders. Unfortunately, Sloan's actions during their brief association gave her no clear measure by which to judge him. She didn't believe his assertion that he was just trying to get her out of his line of fire when he yanked her off the stage step. If that was indeed the case, he needn't have thrown himself on top of her.

On the other hand, there was his reputation to consider. And the fact that he'd fully intended to walk off and leave his three fellow passengers stranded on the open prairie. He hadn't liked being taken to task for that, she thought, or having his actions questioned.

Which brought her back to that moment in the middle of the road, when she'd looked up into his gray eyes and seen herself reflected in them. Another shiver danced down Suzanne's spine, followed immediately by a ripple of irritation. Really, she didn't understand this fascination with the man. Or the thrill that had raced through her when she'd thought he intended to kiss her.

She'd been kissed before. A rather respectable number of times, as a matter of fact. A banker's son back East had coaxed her out into the moonlight on several occasions. Lieutenant Carruthers, who claimed to have fallen instantly under Suzanne's spell when she'd rejoined her parents at Fort Russell a few weeks ago, had proven himself quite adept in that department, as well.

But none of those *boys* had sparked anything close to the heat that jumped along her nerves when she'd looked up into Sloan's glittering gray eyes. Something deep inside her told Suzanne his kiss would be different from any she'd ever experienced.

A wild need to touch the fire, to taste the danger, had raced through her. For an instant, just an instant, she'd teetered on the edge. Common sense had pulled her back. Yet common sense didn't account for the sting of regret she still couldn't shake. Tipping her feathers down another few degrees to shade her face from the burning sun as best she could, Suzanne plodded along.

With each thud of his boots on the dirt road, Jack tried to ignore the trim, neat figure encased in blue serge some yards in front of him. He was no more successful at that than he was at shaking off the memory of the curves buried under her layers of whalebone and stiffening.

Not for the first time since he had boarded the stage, claimed a corner seat and assessed his fellow passengers through half-closed eyes, he wondered why the devil this brown-eyed bit of fluff was traveling alone. She could have been shot in that bungled holdup attempt, for God's sake, or savaged by Parrott and his gang. Although the bluff, seemingly good-natured outlaw insisted on hailing Jack as a friend since the night they'd covered each other in a saloon shoot-out, Parrot sported a mean streak as wide as the lump of flesh on his face.

The knot that formed in Jack's gut at the thought of his traveling companion in Big Nose Parrott's hands annoyed him intensely. He'd stated nothing but the truth a while ago. She wasn't his responsibility, dammit. He had only one responsibility, one that rode his shoulders day and night, and it didn't have anything to do with honey-eyed, neat-figured females.

She wasn't even the kind of woman whose company he preferred. By choice as well as necessity, Jack limited his contacts with females to those who made their living servicing men's needs. The crib girls, parlor women and hurdy-gurdy dancers in these parts knew exactly how to pleasure a man without a lot of fuss or botheration.

That was the way Jack wanted things, the way he intended to keep things. He lived his life a day at a time, with no ties to anyone. Nor was he look-

ing to play nursemaid. If *Miss* Bonneaux's father
or brother or fiancé were fool enough to let her
climb aboard the Deadwood stage without escort,
they were the ones to shoulder the blame for whatever happened to her along the way.

Tugging his hat lower on his brow, he kept his
eyes narrowed against the sun's glare, his senses
alert for any sounds or signs of riders, and his gun
hand swinging loose. Heat shimmered blue-green
above the rutted road. Horseflies swarmed like
bees. The watch salesman began to pant and
shifted his heavy case from hand to hand.

Jack wasn't surprised when the woman ahead of
him began to limp, but she didn't voice a com-
plaint or slow her pace, even when the limp grew
into a noticeable hobble. As the afternoon wore on
and the heat beat down with unrelenting ferocity,
Jack had to admit the woman had more sand in her
than common sense.

He wasn't the only one who noticed the limp.
The young cawker fretted over her like a mother
bear over her cub.

"You look like them boots is hurting you,
ma'am."

"They're a bit uncomfortable," she admitted
with a stiff little smile, "but I'll manage."

"You could, uh, lean on me if you was wishin'
to."

Her smile softened, spread across her face. In

the blink of an eye, she went from a well-looking if somewhat prissy young female to a warm, full-blooded woman.

"Thank you, Mr. Butts. I shall certainly do so if I find it necessary."

The boy's face turned as red as a Pennsylvania outhouse. "I, er... That is..." He swallowed convulsively. "You're welcome, ma'am."

Jack sucked in a swift breath, as surprised as the kid at the transformation. If the woman had unpinched her lips long enough to give Jack a look like that when he'd taken her in his arms, he'd have bent her over his arm for sure. Annoyed by the lust that licked through him at the thought, he issued a brusque order.

"Either take the kid's help or don't, but keep moving."

Three faces swung around to his. One was tight with dislike, one still brick-red but disapproving. Even the roly-poly watch salesman managed to forget his fears enough to scowl.

"I'm not planning to sleep under the stars tonight," Jack stated bluntly.

"I have no particular wish to sleep on the ground, either, Mr. Sloan," she replied.

"Then hustle your bustle, *Miss* Bonneaux."

Bright spots of color appeared in her cheeks again. With a swish of lace-trimmed petticoats, she whirled and started off once more.

The boy shot Jack a frown and followed in her wake. Shifting his merchandise case to his other hand, the perspiring salesman swiped at his forehead with his handkerchief and trotted after them.

Jack shrugged aside their accusing looks. There wasn't a whole lot he could do about the woman's limp. Cutting off that silly excuse for a boot would only make matters worse for her. A person didn't sashay barefoot through rattlesnake and scorpion country. If there was a stick of wood to be found on these rolling, treeless plains, Jack might have fashioned her a crutch or a cane. If her limp got much worse, he supposed he'd have to carry her.

The prospect raised a tight smile. He suspected Miss Bonneaux would like being slung over his shoulder about as much as she'd welcome a petticoat full of fleas.

3

The sun was hanging lazily in the sky when the travelers spotted the feathery green cottonwoods surrounding Ten Mile Station. Suzanne had never been so glad to see anything in her life as that distant copse. She felt as though her outrageously expensive, delicately fashionable boots had raised blisters on every one of her toes.

Grinding her back teeth against the pain, she picked her way along the rutted dirt track. Young Matt Butts trudged close behind her. So close behind her, in fact, that his worried face had bobbed into view each time Suzanne drew in a tired breath or reached up to blot the perspiration on her cheeks or neck.

"Looks like it's still 'bout a half mile," he estimated, squinting through the late afternoon haze. "Maybe you should sit here on this rock and rest while I go fetch a wagon for you."

"I'm too hot and thirsty to sit here in the sun. I can walk another half mile."

"I can see you're hurtin' bad. If you don't want to wait here, I could..." He gulped. "I could carry you."

His cornflower-blue eyes were kind under his shock of sun-bleached hair, and she found his shy manners endearing. Despite his size, he was really very sweet. And rather handsome when one looked past the obvious. His big hands protruded like hams from his shirtsleeves, and his boots were the size of barn doors, but when he finished growing into his skin, she suspected Mathias Butts would set more than one woman's heart to fluttering.

"That's very chivalrous of you, Mr. Butts. If I find I can't put another foot forward, I'll take you up on the offer. You might regret it, though." A dry note crept into her voice. "According to Mr. Sloan, I pack more weight than appearances would indicate."

"I'm sure he didn't mean it the way it come out," her young gallant protested.

Sloan's derisive snort indicated that he'd intended it *exactly* the way it had come out. The boy shot a reproachful glance over his shoulder before earnestly assuring Suzanne she'd be no burden.

"My pa raised hogs for market. You couldn't weigh more than the pig carcasses I used to haul to the wagon."

Another snort came from behind them, this one marked by an unmistakable hint of amusement. Suzanne bit down on the inside of her lip to hide her own smile.

"The end of our trek is in sight, Mr. Butts. I'll walk the rest of the way."

She made it, but not without experiencing some serious regrets. Gritting her teeth, she limped toward the sod shanty set in the shade of the cottonwoods.

The larger way stations strung every fifty miles or so along the stage line usually included stables, a granary, a blacksmith and repair shop, as well as overnight accommodations for passengers, and the inevitable saloon or two. Smaller swing stations like this boasted only sod or cedar-log huts with a barn and corral large enough to handle twelve or fifteen horses. As Suzanne knew from their previous stop some hours back, Ten Mile Station consisted of a single-room hut, dark and smelling of old smoke. A tattered muslin partition separated the kitchen from the sleeping area. More muslin covered the walls in a futile attempt to keep the crumbling sod from sifting down on everything inside.

As crude as the place was, Suzanne couldn't wait to reach it. All she wanted was a basin of water to soak her toes, followed in quick order by some of the bitter coffee and cold beans the station manager had offered the travelers during their earlier stop. Clamping her jaw down against the pain in her toes, she limped up to the door. She'd just reached for the iron latch when it swung open.

The bandy-legged station manager stopped on the threshold. His whiskered jaw sagged in surprise as he took in the dust-covered travelers. "What in thunderation happened to you folks?"

"Road agents," Sloan said succinctly. "Big Nose Parrott and his gang were waiting for the stage just past Three Mule Creek."

"Well, shee-it!"

Snatching off his hat, the manager threw it down and stomped the battered felt.

"Pardon my Chinese, ma'am, but that's twice this month we been holt up! Damned bushwhackers oughta be strung up from the nearest tree."

"I couldn't agree with you more," she said as he stood back to allow them entry.

Inside, Suzanne sank gratefully onto one of the hand-hewn wooden benches drawn up to the table. The others followed, with the station manager popping questions like firecrackers on the Fourth of July.

"Was anyone hurt? Where's Jim Billups, the driver? What about the rest of the passengers? And the strongbox? Did Parrott get the strongbox?"

"We don't know." Plunking his merchandise

case onto a table, Benjamin Greenleaf collapsed onto the bench opposite Suzanne. "The three of us had just climbed out of the coach when someone started shooting. Last we saw of the stage, it was tearing lickety-split around the bend with Big Nose Parrott and his men chasing after it."

"Well, I'll be damned! I'd better get my partner and saddle up to go lookin' for it. You folks take your ease until we get back."

"Hold on!"

Sloan's preemptory command stopped the man in his tracks.

"When's the next stage to Deadwood?"

The manager hooked a thumb at a yellowed waybill tacked to the wall. "Thursday, if they hold to the schedule."

"Four days from now? That's not good enough. I've got business in Deadwood that can't wait. How much for a horse and saddle?"

"Sixty-five dollars for the horse. They're turned out to graze in the flats behind the barn. Take your pick of any wearing the Express Line brand. As for the saddle, we keep a few spares in the barn. Twenty dollars ought to cover the cost."

"Done." Digging a roll of greenbacks from the pocket of his leather vest, Sloan peeled off several bills. "I'll be heading out in the morning."

"Suit yourself. The rest of you folks make yourself to home. There's beer in the barrel and a slab of salted bacon on the shelf. I'll be back soon's I can.''

He stomped to the door, his boot heels thudding on the floorboards. Sloan paused only long enough to lift the lid off the wooden ale keg, swish a tin-handled dipper around and guzzle down several long swallows before he, too, strode out.

The door banged shut behind him.

''Well, how do you like that?'' Greenleaf muttered, staring at the closed door. ''Off he goes again, without so much as a tip-de-doo or fare-thee-well.''

Suzanne tapped a finger on the table. The oddest sensations swirled in her chest. Annoyance, mostly, edged with a stinging little nip of regret. Really, why should Sloan's abrupt departure surprise or disappoint her? He'd certainly made it plain that he didn't care what happened to her or the others. After his sarcastic suggestion that she hustle her bustle, the man hadn't spoken ten words to her during the long trek back to Ten Mile Station.

Yet there was that moment, when he'd held Suzanne locked against him...

The Misses Merriweather would faint dead away if they knew how desperately their star pupil had wanted to rise up on her toes and take a taste of Black Jack Sloan's hard, unsmiling mouth.

Her mother would understand, though. Julia

Bonneaux Garrett looked, spoke and acted like the proper officer's wife she was, but she loved the colonel with all the passion of her French-Creole heritage.

A heritage Suzanne evidently shared more than she'd realized. None of the embraces of her various beaux had fired her blood like those few moments in Sloan's arms. The fact that she could still feel a little spurt of heat deepened the crease between her brows.

Thoughtfully, she removed her gloves and hat and placed them beside the merchant's case. The battered case recalled Suzanne to the fact that her own grip was still aboard the coach...and that another stage wasn't due in until Thursday.

Well, she certainly didn't intend to sit idly at this isolated way station for four days. Like Sloan, she had pressing business elsewhere.

"I could string up a blanket."

With a wrench, she brought her whirling thoughts back to the young man standing before her.

"I beg your pardon?"

"I could string up a blanket, so's you could take off your boots and, uh, stockings." The inevitable red climbed into his cheeks. "You'd better soak your feet before your blisters fester."

"Thank you, Mr. Butts. I'll do so immediately."

"Please, ma'am," he pleaded with an embar-

rassed smile, "could you see yourself clear to cal-
lin' me Matt? I just can't get used to hearin' a
'mister' hung ahead of my name."

"Very well, Matt it is. If you'll string up that
blanket, I'll see if I can find a basin and the station
manager's supply of medicines."

She located a dented tin wash bowl readily
enough, but soon discovered that the on-hand medicinal supplies were limited to horse liniment, tur-
pentine and a half-empty bottle of Dr. Harvey's
Rheumatic Tonic and Dyspeptic. After one whiff
of the tonic, Suzanne decided to place her faith in
the simple remedies Bright Water had taught her
over the years.

"I saw some agrimony growing among the
weeds by the corral," she said to Matt. "Would
you be so kind as to fetch me a few stalks?"

"I would if I knew what it was."

"It's a tall, spiky plant with yellow flowers."

Grabbing his hat from the table, he jammed it
onto his thatch of straw-colored curls. "You sit
down and rest. I'll fetch them flowers and be right
back."

"Not just the flowers," Suzanne called after
him. "I need the whole stalk."

Deciding to visit the necessity out behind the
shanty, Mr. Greenleaf asked Suzanne if she'd look
after his case. He, too, departed, giving her a few
moments of badly needed privacy to slip out of her

jacket, unbutton her blouse and wash away the accumulated dust and grime. She had herself back together again and had put a kettle of water on the hob to boil when Matt returned with an armload of sticky-leafed stalks.

"I always thought these were just weeds."

"Most people do, but I have a good friend who taught me something of the medicinal properties of these plants."

"Is he a sawbones?"

"No, a Northern Arapaho medicine woman."

Matt's blue eyes widened. It was obvious he found it exceedingly odd that a lady like Suzanne would call an Arapaho friend.

"I've never come across any Arapahos. We got some Miami settled in Ohio, and once a band of thievin' Shawnee broke into our smokehouse in the middle of the night. Pa and my brothers and me run 'em off. I heard about the Arapaho, though." His face twisted in mingled disgust and curiosity. "Don't they cut up their enemies and carry bits and pieces of 'em in their medicine bags?"

"They carry whatever their visions tell them they should."

Long experience had taught Suzanne that few whites shared either her insights or her sentiments regarding Bright Water's people. She decided not to attempt an explanation of the complex coming-of-age ritual that included seven days of fasting

and prayer before a warrior determined what would
go into his medicine bag. Instead, she steered the
conversation into less controversial channels.

"What did your pa think of you leaving the farm
to go prospecting?"

"He wasn't too happy 'bout it. My mam 'bout
cried up a storm, too. I'm the last of her brood,"
he confessed. "All the rest, they claimed their forty
acres and settled down close to home."

"But not you."

"Not me. I skinned enough hogs and planted
enough corn to see me through the rest of my
years."

Hunkering down on the bench opposite Suzanne, he reached for one of the stalks. His big
hands stripped the leaves with easy, swift pulls.

"I aim to make my fortune in the gold fields up
around Deadwood," he confided, "then head for
San Francisco. I hear a man with a poke of gold
in his pocket can see some real fancy sights in San
Francisco."

Suzanne bit her lip. Her real father had been a
riverboat gambler. The handsome, dashing Philip
Bonneaux had lost at the gaming tables what little
remained of her mother's inheritance after the War
Between the States. He'd planned to recoup the
family fortunes in the gold fields of Montana Territory, but, like so many lured West by the promise
of riches, he'd died penniless. Suzanne had loved

the irrepressible, irresponsible gambler with all her childish heart and still regretted losing him.

"Not everyone strikes it rich in the gold fields," she warned her young friend gently.

"Maybe not." A stubborn look settled around his mouth. "But a man's gotta find his own way...no matter *what* some bit of gingham and sass might say."

"What's her name?" Suzanne asked with a smile. "This bit of gingham and sass?"

"Rebecca. Becky."

"And Becky didn't want you to leave Ohio?"

"Ha! Not so's I could tell! She said the hoity-toity ladies of San Francisco was welcome to me...if they had a hankerin' for overgrown jack-asses with empty pockets and an even emptier brainbox."

"She sounds like a plainspoken woman."

"When she's got her wind up, she sounds more like a cat with her tail caught in the barn door."

Thoroughly disgruntled, he reached for another stalk and twirled it between his big hands.

"She didn't used to be so bad. I can't count all the nights we went down to the river to gig frogs together. She knew just how to whack my pa's ole mule between the eyes, too, when he got ornery and started tryin' to take a bite out of us. Then she went and put up her braids and there's been no talkin' any sense to her."

"When a girl puts up her braids, she doesn't always want to hear sensible kinds of things."

"Becky sure doesn't."

Glumly, Matt stared at the shredded leaf in his hand for a moment or two before lifting his gaze to Suzanne.

"She's a lot like you, Miss Bonneaux. Bigger, maybe, and a bit broader across the..." He made a gesture with the leaf. "The, er..."

"The front?"

"And back," he agreed sheepishly. "But, like you, she's not afraid to look a man in the eye."

He hesitated, uncomfortable with the personal turn of the conversation but clearly wanting advice.

"If you don't mind me askin', what kinds of things do you want to hear from a man who comes courtin'?"

Her thoughts drifted to the dashing young lieutenant under her stepfather's command. Richard Carruthers had taken one look at Suzanne after she'd arrived home from school and beaten a path to his superior's front door every night after tattoo. The handsome young officer had a way with words and knew just how to delight a woman with them...unlike a certain crude shootist.

"We like to hear all kinds of silly, nonsensical things," she told Matt.

"Like what?"

"Oh, I don't know. That our eyes shine like diamonds, perhaps. Or our sighs pierce your heart like one of Cupid's darts."

"Cupid? Isn't he that fat little angel?"

"I believe he's usually depicted as a cherub."

"I never could see what's so romantic about a mean little bugger who goes around shootin' arrows into folks."

Put that way, Suzanne didn't, either.

"All right. Forget Cupid. Just tell your ladylove that you'll fashion a bed of roses for her to lie on, and you'll shower her with the petals."

"Why would I want her to lay down on roses? The thorns would prick her all over."

A little desperate now, Suzanne fell back on her favorite playwright. "Well, perhaps you might quote Shakespeare to her.

The brightness in her cheek
would shame the stars
As daylight does a lamp..."

Matt looked dubious. "I'm supposed to say she's red-faced as an oil lamp? That doesn't sound so romantical to me."

"Those lines are from *Romeo and Juliet,*" his adviser informed him. "A good many people believe that's one of the bard's greatest plays."

"If you say so."

"Trust me. Try that verse on your Becky next time you see her."

The steam went out of him. His shoulders slumping, he reached for another stalk.

"That might be sooner than either of us figured on. If Big Nose and his gang caught up with the stage and cleaned it out, all I've got to my name is the handful of coins in my pocket. They won't buy what I'll need to get through the winter at Deadwood."

Judging by her father's experiences in the Montana gold fields, Suzanne couldn't help but think losing his stake and being forced to return home to his Becky might be the best thing that could happen to Matt. But she said nothing as he scooped up an armful of the stripped stalks and headed for the now-steaming kettle.

"I'll put these on to boil for you."

Twenty minutes later Suzanne sat down on a bunk, propped both hands behind her on its coarse blanket and dipped her feet into the tin washbasin.

"Oo-o-oh."

Instant relief washed through her. Her head fell back against the muslin-draped sod wall behind her. Eyes closed, she let Bright Water's remedy work its magic.

A spoonful or two of mashed agrimony in a cup of water also made for a good mouthwash, she remembered hazily. A couple of swishes would take away the taste of trail dust and the slightly rancid beans she and Matt had downed while waiting for the concoction to boil. She should wash her hair, too, she thought. The heavy mass was coated with dust and slipping out of its pins again. She'd put herself back together, she decided, when her footbath cooled and she could gather enough energy to move.

She had no idea how long she lolled against the bumpy wall, eyes closed, petticoats tucked up around her knees, feet immersed. But when she blinked awake, the interior of the way station was dark and Jack Sloan stood at the end of her bunk.

4

Jack's fingers fisted on the coarse blanket someone had strung up for a curtain. The kid, probably.
Young Butts was so awed by the prim, prissy Miss
Suzanne Bonneaux he could hardly put one foot in
front of the other without tripping all over himself.

She didn't look particularly prim or prissy now,
though. Startled from sleep, she looked rumpled
and confused and all too enticingly female. His
glance lingered on the warm-brown hair spilling
over her shoulders. The hint of soft curves where
she'd unbuttoned her high-necked blouse. The
rucked-up skirt that bared pale, shapely legs.

With a sudden clenching in his gut, Jack imagined those legs locked around his. He could almost
hear her hoarse pants. Almost feel her bare heels
digging into his calves as he spread her wide,
found the slit in her drawers, surged into her slick,
hot flesh.

"Mr. Sloan!"

Feeling like a bucking, twisting mustang brought up hard and short at the end of a forty-foot snubbing line, Jack jerked his gaze to her face. She struggled upright on the bunk and blinked the last of the sleep from her eyes.

"What are you doing?"

"Enjoying the show."

Flushing, she tossed down her skirts and yanked her feet from the basin. "I don't suppose it occurred to you that I might wish for a little privacy?"

"It occurred to me. It also occurred to me that I forgot to tell the station manager what to do with the gear I stashed in the stage boot. Ask him to sell the saddle, would you? He can forward whatever he gets for it along with my bags to me in care of the Express Office in Deadwood."

Judging by the expression on her face, she itched to tell him precisely what he could do with his saddle, saddlebags and instructions to the station manager. A contrary disappointment rippled through Jack when she bit back the tart reply he'd come to expect of her.

"Very well."

With a nod, he dragged the mattress off the bunk above her and hauled it into the kitchen. Butts and Greenleaf had claimed the other two bunks. Jack would bed down by the fire and be on his way at first light.

Not that he'd get much sleep. He was too edgy, too frustrated by the unexpected delay. That was what came of selling his horse and jumping on a damned stage. He'd be lucky now to reach Deadwood before Charlie Dawes got wind Jack was after him and took off again.

The possibility burned a hole in his gut. Dawes was the last one. The only one still alive. Jack had been hunting him for two years now. The idea that he was so close, only a few days' ride away, had Jack flexing his gun hand. Dawes wouldn't get away this time.

Memories crowded in on him. Of another night, another sod hut. Even after all these years, he could still hear the screams. Still feel the anguish. And the rage. It knotted his muscles, wrapped around his chest, buried its fangs in his throat.

Cold, hard certainty settled in his gut. Dawes wouldn't escape him this time.

Shaking himself like a dog to chase away the memories, he unbuckled his gun belt and hooked it over the back of the closest chair. He was about to drop onto the straw mattress when he spotted a half-full bucket beside the fire. Evidently *Miss* Bonneaux hadn't appropriated all the water in the place to soak her dainty feet.

Giving in to the urge to remove a few layers of

road dirt, he swung the bucket onto the table and shrugged out of his leather vest. His shirt followed the vest onto a chair. The water felt so good when Jack splashed it over his neck and shoulders, he gave himself a thorough dousing. Still bent over the bucket, he scraped a hand over his jaw. He carried a straight razor and change of clothes in his saddlebags. If the bags didn't turn up in Deadwood in a day or two, Jack would have to replace their contents.

The possibility that he might have lost everything he owned didn't particularly concern him. He traveled light, always had. Always would, he supposed, until he grew too old or too slow to outgun the next whiskeyed-up fool who drew on him.

It would happen. Probably sooner instead of later. A man with his reputation wasn't likely to die all wrinkled and shriveled up, laid out in a bed with a preacher saying words over him. He'd go down with a bullet in his chest...or in his back. Putting Black Jack Sloan in a pine box would give a man bragging rights for the rest of his life, however the deed was accomplished.

Well, he'd known what would happen when he'd first strapped on his father's old army Colt. He'd made his choice then, and would live with it, no matter.

A sudden crash shattered the stillness. Jack dived for his gun belt. In a move that was pure instinct, he whipped the Colt free of the holster, spun around and dropped into a half crouch.

Ten yards away, Suzanne froze. The tin basin that had slipped from her fingers clattered noisily at her feet. Spilled water soaked the hem of her skirt, but she didn't move, didn't dare breathe with that long, deadly barrel pointed right at her heart.

"What happened?" Benjamin Greenleaf popped upright on his bunk, blinking owlishly. "What's going on here?"

"Sloan!"

Two giant boots hit the floor with a thud. Matt sprang up and looked wildly at the man crouched beside the banked fire.

"Are you drawin' on Miss Bonneaux?"

With a muttered curse, Jack straightened and tipped up the Colt.

"I wouldn't advise you to come creeping up on a man like that," he snapped at the still-frozen woman. "The next one might be a little quicker to burn powder than I am."

"I wasn't..."

Suzanne swallowed, almost as annoyed by the squeak in her voice as she was shaken by what had just transpired.

"I wasn't creeping up on you. I was going out to empty the basin and accidentally dropped it."

It was the truth. More or less. She'd pour honey over her head and curl up on an anthill before she'd admit that the sight of Sloan sluicing himself down had stopped her dead in her tracks. Like some wide-eyed fool at a carnival, she'd gawked at his broad shoulders and corded muscles, until the blasted basin had slipped right out of her hands.

Even now she had to fight to keep her gaze from straying to his naked chest. It was wide and well-ribbed, shadowed with dark, curling hair still glistening from the water. Swallowing, Suzanne scooped up the basin.

"I'm very sorry to have awakened you gentlemen," she said to Matt and Greenleaf. "Please, go back to sleep."

They reclaimed their bunks, and Suzanne fingered the dented tin bowl while Sloan reached for his shirt. Common sense told her to keep her mouth shut, forget the proposal she'd been considering for some hours now, but common sense wouldn't get her to Bright Water.

Slowly, she moved across the room. "May I have a word with you?" she asked, keeping her voice low so as not to disturb the others again.

"You can have two," Sloan replied carelessly, "if you're quick about them."

When she didn't answer right away, he shoved his shirttails into his pants and shot her a quizzical look.

"You want something, *Miss* Bonneaux?"

"Yes." Ignoring both his deliberate sarcasm and

the little inner voice that told her she was about to grab a rattlesnake by the tail, she plunged right to the heart of the matter. "I'd like to hire you."

One black brow shot up. Whatever Sloan had expected from her, that clearly wasn't it.

"Hire me?"

"Hire your gun, if you will. I have pressing business that requires me to reach Fort Meade, in Dakota Territory, as soon as possible. Like you, I can't wait for the next stage."

"You'll have to," he said with a shrug. "I'm not for hire. Neither is my gun."

"You don't understand. It's imperative that I get to the Arapaho reservation on the banks of the Cheyenne River within the next few days. I have a friend there who..."

"I don't give two hoots in Hades who's waiting for you, lady. My business is in Deadwood, not Fort Meade."

"The fort is only a half day's ride out of your way."

"That's a half day too long," Sloan said flatly, swinging away.

"I'll make it worth your while."

He stopped, turned back, raked her with a slow, mocking glance. "One of Big Nose Parrott's boys snatched your purse. Just what kind of payment are you offering?"

"Not that kind!"

"Too bad. I might have reconsidered."

"Please don't play these games with me, Mr. Sloan. As I've already told you, I find them rather tedious."

Something flickered in the depths of his gray eyes, quickly come and just as quickly gone. He stepped forward, crowding her against the table. He was so big he blocked the rest of the room from sight, so close she could smell his damp skin.

"Just what makes you think this is a game?"

A shiver danced along her spine. It wasn't fear. Oddly, she didn't fear him, but his nearness made her nerves snap and crackle like ice too thin to bear her weight.

"I'm not a child, Mr. Sloan, nor quite the helpless female you seem to think I am. These heavy-handed threats don't frighten me."

"They damned well ought to. Do you really believe that little peashooter in your pocket would protect you if I decided to bend you over that table and flip up your skirts?"

"No," she fired back. "Nor do I believe you're the kind of man who would rape a woman, or I wouldn't have asked for your escort."

His eyes went cold. "You don't have any idea what kind of man I am."

Suzanne knew she ought to retreat before the ice broke under her and she sank in over her head. If her blood hadn't been pounding in her ears, if his nearness hadn't set her pulse to jumping, she wouldn't have countered his claim with a soft reminder.

"You dragged me down and shielded me this afternoon. That tells me something."

This time he didn't bother to deny he'd tried to protect her. "So I dragged you down? You're a fool if you think all men don't tote around equal parts good and mean. It's just a matter of which part gets scratched when."

Sloan wasn't saying anything she hadn't heard preached from the pulpit many times. What's more, her stepfather had drummed the same lesson into her. In his careful way, the colonel made sure she understood the risks of growing to womanhood surrounded by troopers who could perform the most heroic deeds or the most outrageous acts depending on the circumstances and the amount of liquor they'd consumed.

"I'll try not to scratch you the wrong way," she promised softly.

"You already have, lady."

Much as it went against her grain to beg, she made another appeal. "Please, Mr. Sloan. I must get to Fort Meade."

"Not with me," he repeated flatly. "I'm not for hire."

* * *

He rode out just before dawn.

Suzanne came awake to the thump of boots crossing the dirt floor, followed by the creak of the door hinges. She lay still for a moment, thinking of the previous night. Thinking, too, of the empty stretch of days that loomed ahead. It was the middle of September. This unseasonable heat would break any day. Overnight, the air would snap with cold. Bright Water's people were probably already taking down their teepees. If anyone but her dearest friend was camped beside the Cheyenne River, Suzanne might have curled into a tight ball and told herself she'd done her best.

Instead, she swung her feet off the bunk, combed her fingers through her tangled hair and contemplated her sadly wrinkled clothing. Before falling asleep last night, she'd removed her more uncomfortable garments, including her tight half jacket and her stays. She dangled the stiff-boned corset by its laces for a few moments before deciding to abandon it completely. Her waist was small enough that she didn't really need lacing to fit into her skirt, and if she followed through with the plan that was taking shape in her mind, she certainly wouldn't need the added discomfort.

When she emerged from her blanketed cubicle, she found the others had risen, too. Benjamin Greenleaf had gone to make a morning trip to the privy. Matt, bless him, had already stripped, mashed and boiled another handful of agrimony stalks.

Suzanne thanked him with a smile. "Your Becky's a lucky woman, whether she knows it or not."

Quickly, she bathed her feet, then tore a narrow strip from one of her petticoats. Matt eyed her doubtfully as she dipped the linen in the healing solution and bent to wrap it around her toes.

"Don't see how you're going to pull on them flimsy shoes with your toes all bundled up like that."

"I don't intend to pull on my shoes." Tucking in the ends of the bandage, she started on her other foot. "Would you be so kind as to search the barn to see if you could find me a spare pair of work boots?"

He looked surprised, as though he couldn't imagine a lady like Suzanne clumping around in borrowed boots, but clapped his hat on his head willingly enough.

"Yes, ma'am."

While he searched the barn, Suzanne put the coffee on to boil and performed another search of the kitchen shelves. Her explorations yielded a corked bottle of molasses and a small burlap sack of oats alive with weevils. Picking out the wiggling white insects with a thumb and forefinger, she flicked them into the banked fire and mashed the oats.

Boiled and sweetened with molasses, they'd make a welcome change from cold beans.

The lumpy porridge was ready when Greenleaf returned from the privy and Matt from the barn.

"I found these," he said doubtfully, holding up a scruffy pair of work boots. "I scraped the muck off best I could, but they still carry something of a stink."

"More than something!" the watch salesman protested with a grimace.

"They'll do," Suzanne said calmly. They'd have to, she thought, breathing in the rich, familiar odor of horse manure. "Put them down and have some breakfast. Then I must ask you for one more favor."

"Yes, ma'am?"

"I need you to go out to where the horses are grazing and bring in one for me to saddle."

"Miss Bonneaux!"

Matt dropped the boots with a thump. "You can't be thinking of riding to Deadwood by yourself!"

"If I must. But I expect I'll catch up with Mr. Sloan on the trail."

The two males exchanged glances.

"We couldn't help but overhear you and Sloan arguing last night," Greenleaf confessed. "He sounded like he meant it when he said he wouldn't act as your escort."

"I'm sure he meant it at the time," Suzanne replied with a show of nonchalance. "This morning, he may very well see things differently."

Greenleaf looked skeptical, Matt downright worried. "I wish you'd think hard on this, Miss Bonneaux."

"I have thought hard. I must get to Fort Meade as soon as possible, either with or without Mr. Sloan's escort. I'm not without certain skills, you know. I grew up on army posts. I can ride and shoot as well as any trooper."

Better, actually, considering the months of training it took to teach raw recruits how to handle a rifle or stay on a horse. She only wished she carried more firepower than the two-shot derringer nestled in her skirt pocket.

"Well, it's your choice," the merchant said, shaking his head. "I hope you don't come to regret it."

Suzanne sincerely hoped so, too. She dug into her breakfast, knowing she'd need energy for the hard ride ahead. Knowing, too, that her journey to Cheyenne River had taken on an added dimension, one with a deep, rough voice and eyes the color of a winter morning.

By the time she gathered a few supplies, scribbled a promissory note to the station manager for the boots and foodstuffs and sent Matt out to round up an Express Line horse, Sloan had a good hour's start on her.

She'd catch him easily enough. He'd be riding hard but couldn't push his horse in this heat or it would get the thumps and Sloan would find himself walking again. Suzanne was smaller, lighter. And, as she'd pointed out to Matt and Benjamin Greenleaf, she was army-raised. She couldn't count the number of times her mother had bundled her, her younger brother and everything they owned into an ambulance wagon for yet another move to another post. When Suzanne and Sam had grown big enough to sit a saddle, they'd made the marches on horseback.

Matt's return brought her clumping out of the way station in her borrowed boots, the burlap sack of supplies clutched in her fist. He'd brought two horses down, she saw, one a chestnut gelding with black points, the other a dappled gray. Both were saddled and bridled.

And with his particular brand of shyness and gallantry, he announced that he was going with her.

5

"Too bad Becky can't see me now."

Suzanne hid a smile as Matt squared his slumping shoulders, narrowed his eyes and tried to look bad.

"She didn't hold much with my desire to go off adventuring," the youth confided ingenuously. "Predicted I'd squeal like one of Pa's hogs on the way to the butchering block if I ever come face-to-face with one of the desperadoes I read about in dime novels."

"Like Big Nose Parrott."

He gave an embarrassed grin. "I'll admit I near about jumped outta my skin when he stuck his beak through the stagecoach window. But now here I am, escorting you across the prairie like some Pinkerton man."

"I appreciate your company," Suzanne said truthfully. Matt might not be the best rider in the world, but he did make the dusty miles seem shorter.

"After I get you safe to Fort Meade, I'll head on over to the gold fields. I'll have to work some to pull together another stake," he admitted. "I shoulda knowed better than to hide the fifty-dollar gold piece Mam slipped me inside the lining of my carpetbag. The bag's stashed in the stage boot."

"Maybe Parrott and his gang didn't catch up with the stage," Suzanne suggested. "With luck, the driver whipped the horses clear to the next way station and your bag will be waiting for you at the Express Office in Deadwood. It could be the stage line is even offering a reward for information about the men who held us up."

Matt brightened at the prospect. "I can tell them all about Big Nose Parrott. I've read up on the fellow! Did you know he's robbed as many trains as stages? And how he's rumored to hole up in the Dakota Badlands?"

"No, I didn't."

"Well, shoot fire, could be I even get my name in the papers! Mam and Pa and Becky might just read how Mr. Mathias Butts of Plainsboro, Ohio, helped capture a notorious road agent."

Clearly dazzled by the possibilities, he shrugged off the fact that he had less than a dollar in loose change jingling around in his pocket. The possibility of fame didn't appear to make up for the ache in his hindquarters, however. With each slap of the saddle Suzanne suspected he felt a little more like a raw rumpsteak.

"Do you need to rest?" she asked when he rose up in the stirrups to shift his weight.

"No, ma'am. I'll admit, though, I'm a sight more used to dragging a plow behind the two ornery mules Pa keeps at the farm than riding them. I kin hitch the pair to the wagon quicker 'n spit when it's time to haul hog carcasses into town. I never spent much time in the saddle, though."

Suzanne declined to comment on the obvious.

Clearly embarrassed that she should have caught him favoring his bottom, he tried to change the direction of her thoughts. "How'd you learn to ride and read signs the way you do?"

"Didn't I mention that I grew up on army posts? My stepfather commands the Second Cavalry regiment, currently stationed at Fort Russell, outside Cheyenne."

"Oh, a horse soldier. That explains it, then."

"The colonel put me on my first pony when I was six years old."

"No wonder you take to a saddle so easy."

"I take to one a lot better when I'm wearing a riding habit," she said ruefully.

Matt darted a look at the length of ankle and stockinged calf displayed above her borrowed boots. Her bustled-up skirt wasn't cut for riding astride.

Suzanne caught the quick glance and the wave of red that surged into his cheeks. He shifted in the saddle again, sweating profusely under his shirt.

Poor thing! He was obviously at the age where the sight of any portion of a female's anatomy would enflame him. She didn't doubt his Becky had kept him in a constant sweat.

"Did your step-pa teach you to track, too?" he asked in a rather choked voice. "You picked up Sloan's trail and have been following it like a hound on the scent of a coon for the past two hours."

"No, I learned to track from the father of the friend I told you about, the Arapaho medicine woman. Lone Eagle was an army scout. He could glance at a bent stalk of grass and tell instantly whether a two-legged or four-legged creature had crushed it and how long ago."

"You sure had me fooled. When you climbed aboard the stage at Cheyenne, I coulda sworn you'd just stepped off the train from Boston or New York or some big city like that."

"Actually, you're not far off the mark. I just returned from Philadelphia a few weeks ago. I've been at school. The Misses Merriweather's Academy for Select Young Ladies." She sent him a smile. "That's where I read *Romeo and Juliet.* It's really quite a beautiful love story."

"If you say so."

"I'll tell you what. When I get back to Cheyenne, I'll try to find a volume of Mr. Shakespeare's plays and send them to you at Deadwood."

"If I'm going to spend my free time fingerin' pages, I'd much rather be reading 'bout characters like Pecos Bill and Black Jack Sloan."

"You shouldn't believe everything you read in the penny presses, you know. I suspect Mr. Sloan's reputation is much exaggerated."

"I don't doubt we'll find out when we catch up with him! He's not going to take kindly to us tailin' him."

As they discovered a little less than an hour later, Matt had understated the case considerably. Not only did Sloan not take kindly to being tailed, he came damned close to putting a bullet right through Suzanne's heart for the second time in less than twelve hours.

Jack first sensed he was being followed when he stopped beside a sluggish stream to water his horse. Eyes narrowed, he studied the little swirl of red dust rising into the air some distance behind him. It could have been stirred up by a rabbit scurrying for his hole, chased by a kestrel diving for prey. But the sky hung cloudless and clear of circling hawks, and Jack had lived too long looking back over his shoulder to take a chance on maybes.

He was waiting, the Colt drawn, when his pursuers rounded an outcropping of rock and scrub. Disbelief pounded through his veins, followed fast and hard by fury.

"Have you gone sun loco?" he snarled, pushing out of the scrub.

"Not yet," the damned snip replied calmly, reining in her horse. "Although that's a distinct possibility. I should have borrowed a wide-brimmed hat to go along with these boots."

Her unruffled demeanor sent his fury shooting up another three or four notches. "Don't you know that tracking down on a man is a sure way to get yourself blown out of the saddle?"

"Of course I do. If I'd been tracking any other man, I wouldn't have followed so close or let you know we were behind you."

His jaw snapped shut so tight he almost heard the bones crack. What in hell did she have rattling around in her brain box? Did she figure she could follow him clear to Deadwood without his knowledge if she had a mind to? For that matter, how in blue blazes had she followed him this far?

She read his thoughts with an ease that had Jack grinding his teeth. "I told you last night I'm not the helpless female you think me."

"And I told *you* last night, I'm not for hire."

"Then I won't pay you. But there's no law that says Matt and I can't ride along behind you."

He threw a savage look at her companion. The kid sat his saddle like a sack of old potatoes. Jack would bet he was already raising saddle sores.

"Are you snake-bit, boy? Or did *Miss* Bonneaux here smile sweet-like and get you so hot and pokered up you didn't have the gumption to tell her she's crazy as two loons."

The red that rushed into his face answered Jack—not that he needed answering. Young Butts was at that age where he shot up faster than new corn if a passable female even looked at him sideways.

The fact that this particular female had made Jack himself shoot up twice now didn't exactly ease his fury. Nor did her crazy plan to tail after him clear to the turnoff to Fort Meade.

"We won't be a burden to you, Mr. Sloan, but surely you can't object if we use your reputation as a shield for the next day or two?"

"The hell I can't." He thrust the Colt into its holster. "You listen to me, lady. You'd better rid your mind of the idea I'll protect you if we run into some nervous squatters or another bunch of road agents."

"You did before."

"Dammit, you don't understand. I'm more likely to pull you into trouble than out of it.

Whether or not you believe all you've heard about me, I'm a walking target for any drunk or hothead who thinks he can prove himself a man by out-drawing me. If you and the boy ride with me, you might just become targets, too.''

Her eyes held his. ''Matt is old enough to weigh the risks and make his own decisions. So am I.''

''Well, you made the wrong ones this time. I suggest you haul your carcasses back to Ten Mile Station.'' Snagging his mount's reins, he brought it around and swung into the saddle. ''I ride alone. I always have.''

Since he was twelve years old, anyway.

His face grim, Jack spurred his mount into a gallop. With every thump of the roan's hooves on the dry earth, he repeated the litany that had kept him going all these years. The same litany he'd sung in his head since the night he'd strapped his father's Colt around his skinny hips and ridden away from the farm his folks had been trying to scratch out of a Colorado hillside.

They wouldn't escape. None of them. They wouldn't escape.

Charlie Dawes was the last. The man was hiding out in Deadwood, breathing borrowed air. The last thing Jack needed was a feather-headed female and fuzz-cheeked boy hanging on to his coattails when he cornered the bastard and blew him full of lead.

* * *

He set a punishing pace.

The Express Line mount he'd chosen covered the sun-baked road at a steady lope. The gelding was big, probably a wheeler judging from the easy way he neck-reined. Every hour or so, Jack would take him to a slower gait, then dismount and walk for ten or twenty minutes until he'd cooled.

Each time he stopped, he scanned the sun browned dips and swales behind him. And each time he spotted the two mounted figures trailing farther and farther back, he spit out another curse.

Didn't the woman have the sense God gave a crow? Didn't she know what could happen to her out here in the open, without a man to protect her? The boy didn't count. Hell, from the way young Butts flopped around on the back of his horse, he'd be lucky if he didn't fall off in a heap before another hour passed.

Not that Jack cared what happened to him. The boy was no concern of his, dammit. Neither was *Miss* Bonneaux.

He was still trying to convince himself when twilight purpled the horizon. He pushed on until night dropped like a buffalo skin over the earth, determined to let the two fools behind him reap the rewards of their folly. Unsaddling the roan, Jack ground-tied him and left him to graze.

He soon had a campfire spitting sparks. He'd

helped himself to a tin mug from the way station to boil coffee in, but sure could have used some of the cold beans he'd wolfed down for breakfast. Well, he'd gone to bed with his stomach shrunk up and rumbling often enough in the past ten years. He'd shoot a jackrabbit or a grouse tomorrow morning, he decided, and grease his insides up good.

Jack wasn't sure when he first caught the scent of frying bacon. It just tickled his nostrils at first, so faint he thought his brain was playing games with his belly. The night had cooled the air and the horse blanket he'd pulled over him for warmth provided a powerful scent of its own.

He lay still, head propped against the saddle, hat tipped back to give him a clear view of the stars. There were a million or more out tonight, bright points of silver in a sky so dark and vast it swallowed a man up whole. Nights like this, Jack was almost glad he didn't have a place to call his own or a roof to keep out the stars. Almost.

He hadn't looked back since he had ridden out of Colorado all those years ago, hadn't thought much about the homestead his folks had staked out above Rainbow Junction. Times like this, though, he had to fight a longing for...

Damn! He pushed upright, sniffing the air. That *was* bacon he smelled. The tantalizing aroma had his stomach doing a jig with his backbone. For some reason, that infuriated Jack even more than being tailed. Lock-jawed, he grabbed his rifle and stalked down the scent.

They'd set up camp just over a small rise, almost within shouting distance...which, he knew, was exactly her intent. Part of him had sensed their nearness. Another part, the ornery part, refused to acknowledge either his relief that they'd managed to stick so close or his disgust at not being able to lose them.

"Good evening, Mr. Sloan."

The blasted female was squatting beside the fire and didn't even bother to glance up.

"Would you care to join us for supper?"

Jack had a feeling his back teeth would be ground down to stumps before he shook loose of the woman. He aimed an evil glare at young Butts, who was looking about as miserable as a man could after ten hours in the saddle, and stomped into the small circle of firelight.

"I've met some stubborn fools in my time, *Miss Bonneaux*, but you're about the stubbornest."

"Thank you."

The answer was so polite and proper his teeth ached all the worse, but laughter danced in the eyes that met his across the snapping fire.

"Dinner should be ready soon. Would you like some coffee while you wait?"

Acting for all the world as if she'd just invited

him to take Sunday afternoon tea, she tipped a
stream of thick, black liquid into a tin cup and held
it out to him.

The mug hung in the air, an invitation, a challenge. Jack swallowed a curse, and came within a
breath of spinning around and stomping back to
his own campsite. Reaching out, he took the
damned cup.

"I can't figure out why someone hasn't strangled you long before now."

Her laughter spilled free. "My brother says the
same thing. Do sit down, Mr. Sloan. You're giving
me a crick in the neck."

Nursing the coffee in both hands, he planted his
backside a few feet from the boy. Matt sat cross-
legged on a saddle blanket folded three times over.
Shoulders drooping with weariness, wrists draped
loosely over his knees, he gave Jack a sheepish
glance.

"I couldn't let her ride out by herself."

"I'm guessing there wasn't a whole lot of 'let'
involved. *Miss* Bonneaux's going to do whatever
she takes it into her head to do."

The subject of their discussion poked the sizzling bacon with a stick whittled to a green point.
"Do you think it might be time you stopped referring to me as *Miss* Bonneaux in that detestable
manner?"

He considered the matter. "It might."

"Good. Well, gentlemen, I think I've got enough grease to fry up some johnnycakes."

She used a pointed stick to transfer the bacon from the skillet to a tin plate.

"I see you made yourself free with the station manager's supplies," Jack said sourly, conveniently forgetting that he was wishing he'd done the same thing just moments ago.

"I left a note promising payment."

Just like that, his stomach did another jig. She'd promised him payment, too, but not the kind he'd wanted from her.

"Matt, would you pass me the sack of oats?"

Scowling over the brim of his cup, Jack watched while the trim, dainty miss who looked like she'd melt in a good rain picked weevils from a handful of oats and flicked them into the fire. That done, she mixed a little water into the coarse-ground grain and shaped the lumpy dough into thick cakes.

The woman was one surprise after another, and Jack didn't particularly like surprises.

"Where did you learn to cook over a campfire, *Miss*..." He caught himself. "Suzanne."

The smile she sent him near about lit up the night. He gripped the tin cup so hard he felt the thin metal crease under his fingers.

"As I told Matt earlier, my stepfather is a cavalry officer. He made sure my brother and I learned all manner of necessary skills. Some," she confessed with a grin, "I had to un-learn when I went back East to school. My teachers almost fainted dead away when I demonstrated to the other students how well-dried cow dung burns in a kitchen stove."

Jack buried his face in his cup. He didn't want her to see the smile that tugged at his mouth. He wasn't ready to let down the barriers separating him from this prickly, contrary, fascinating female. Couldn't let down the barriers, he reminded himself grimly. Surging to his feet, he tossed out the dregs of his coffee.

She glanced up at the abrupt movement. Smoke from the frying dough wreathed her face. The heat had put a flush in her cheeks. Long, straggling tendrils had escaped her untidy bun to curl over her shoulder. Her eyes were dark and luminous in the firelight.

Walk away! his mind shouted. *Make dust. Now, while you still can.*

Her voice drifted to him across the crackling fire, calm and steady as a tall oak in a storm. "The johnnycakes are browning up nicely."

Ride out. Tonight. Leave her here with the boy. She'll find her way.

"We'll be ready to eat in a few minutes."

He swore a silent, savage oath. Knew damned well she'd keep on his tail whether he wanted her there or not.

"I'll take you as far as Rawhide Buttes tomorrow. After that, you're on your own."

"Very well."

At least she had sense enough not to crow. Jack gave her marks for that.

"You'd better douse your fire and retrieve your horse," she suggested with a poke at the johnnycakes. "I'll have supper dished up by the time you get back."

6

The following day, Jack ate Suzanne's dust most of the way to Rawhide Buttes.

She rode astride, as loose-backed as any cavalry trooper, skirts flapping at her calves. If the length of silk stocking showing above her borrowed boots flustered her, she sure didn't let on. She'd plucked the quail feathers off her hat and bent down the brim to shield her eyes. She'd shed her bustle, too. The rucked-up fabric at the back of her skirt sagged without the wire cage. Although the sun didn't burn with quite the same intensity it had the past few days, it generated enough heat for her to shed her jacket, tie it behind her on the saddle and undo the top few buttons of her high-necked blouse.

Yesterday, Jack would have bet his last dollar that the dainty miss seated across from him on the stage would suffocate before she'd shed any of her fancy outer layers. It bothered him that he'd read her so wrong. The glimpses he caught of the long neck and creamy skin now exposed to the breeze bothered him even more.

Deliberately, he dropped back. No sense torturing himself. Not that viewing her backside was any easier on him than viewing her front. She'd given up trying to bundle her honey-brown hair and left it down, tied back out of the way with a rawhide thong from her saddle. The long, curling tail fell down her back and swished when she moved, just like a mare's. And just like a stallion on the scent of a rut, Jack couldn't keep his eyes off her.

It didn't help that young Matt Butts appeared just as taken with the woman.

"Best not to think what you're thinking, kid."

The hog farmer wrenched his gaze away from Suzanne's legs. Cheeks crimson, he mumbled that he wasn't thinking nothing. Jack knew better. His own thoughts weren't the sort a man could take into church with him.

"That kind of female ties a man up in so many knots he can't stand up straight," Jack warned, "let alone stiffen his spine."

An unexpected flash of humor appeared in the boy's blue eyes. "Is there any other kind?"

"Been knotted up before, have you?"

"Sort of." Grimacing, the kid shifted his

weight. "I slipped free, though, to come out to the Black Hills."

"You don't think the rope will still be waiting for you when you get home?"

"I'm not going home. Not for a while, anyway. There's places I want to see, things I want to do." His voice took on an eager note. "You ever been to San Francisco?"

"Once, a few years back."

He'd tracked Obediah Chilton, the third man on his list, to San Francisco. Jack had spent weeks roaming the city's fog-shrouded streets before he discovered his quarry had moved on to the California gold fields.

"Is the city as wide-open and wild as they say?"

"It's taming down some, but a man can still buy just about anything there if he's got the cash in his pockets."

"That's the way I heard it. What about Sacramento? Have you been there, too?"

Jack's jaw locked. He'd found Chilton fifty miles west of Sacramento, in one of the hundreds of mining towns that had sprung up along the gold trail that cut north to south along the foothills of the Sierra Nevadas. The man had cried like a baby when Jack cornered him in a saloon and told him to draw or die one small piece at a time.

"I've been there."

The flat reply drew a quick glance from the kid.

He might still show some green behind the ears, but he was old enough to tread warily on another man's past. Especially a man with a past like Black Jack Sloan's. Matt's questions eased off.

But not his saddle aches.

By midafternoon, he could hardly sit upright. Whenever the travelers dismounted to walk their horses, he stumbled along on India-rubber legs. Suzanne kept the lead and slowed the pace more with each passing hour. Once or twice she'd flicked a quick glance over her shoulder at Jack, as if she sensed how much it chafed him to amble along at a slow walk.

She sensed right. Impatience bit at him like a three-fanged snake. He'd get her and the kid to Rawhide Buttes, he'd promised her that much. The station was a good size stop, not like the swing station at Ten Mile. If she was so bullheaded as to want to keep traveling from there, she could damned well sweet-talk someone else into riding shotgun for her.

She wasn't his responsibility, dammit.

The sun flamed low and orange when the massive red rock formations that gave Rawhide Buttes its name rose in the distance. As the three riders drew closer, the lively notes of "Buffalo Girls Won't You Come Out Tonight" rolled through the gathering dusk to greet them.

Like most of the major home stations strung out along the Cheyenne-Deadwood stage route, Rawhide Buttes offered the wayfarer both sustenance and sin. This particular station, Suzanne soon discovered, combined the two in one rather lively operation.

Music pumped out of a clapboard building erected in the shadow of the butte. A crude sign nailed to a porch strut identified the place as Mother Featherlegs Shephard's Saloon and Hurdy-Gurdy Parlor. Raucous laughter bellowed through the open door of the saloon, almost drowning out the wheezing notes of the hand-cranked organ.

A combination of rods and strings, the hurdy-gurdy had once graced the courts of Europe. Composers such as Haydn and Mozart had composed music for the instrument. In more recent years, its easy portability had made it so popular on the frontier that the women who worked the dance halls had become known as hurdy-girls or hurdies.

Suzanne was no stranger to hurdies, generally considered one class up from the prostitutes who serviced the troops stationed at frontier army posts. While social barriers existed in the West, just as they did in the East, the distinctions tended to blur when troopers starved for feminine attention and the comforts of their own hearth took wives wherever they could find them. One of her stepfather's top sergeants had married the most popular hurdy-

girl at the Blue Snake Saloon, just outside Fort Huachuca. Leaky Peg had made the transition from dance hall denizen and occasional whore to army wife with her ribald sense of humor and great, gusting belly laugh intact. Suzanne had found her stories fascinating, although she suspected Leaky Peg had censored them considerably before sharing them with the colonel's daughter.

Still, Suzanne probably wouldn't have chosen to enter the doors of Mother Featherlegs Shephard's parlor if it wasn't also doubling as the temporary way station for the Black Hills Stage and Express Line. The charred remains of the wooden building that had previously served as the stage stop lay just across the street from the hurdy-gurdy parlor.

The place had burned down only last month, the station manager explained. The fire almost took the barn and granary, too, but the saloon's patrons had rushed out to form a bucket brigade and saved those structures.

The station manager also gave the weary arrivals another bit of grim news. Big Nose Parrott and his gang had indeed caught up with the stage they'd been traveling on.

"They kilt the driver stone-cold dead. Gut-shot one of the passengers, too. A wrangler off the Diamond J, up to Hell's Canyon way."

The drunken cowboy. Suzanne didn't waste much sympathy on him. If the fool hadn't dived for his gun, he wouldn't have a bullet in his belly and she wouldn't be standing here in borrowed boots.

Matt slid off his horse and hooked an arm around the pommel to keep his legs from collapsing under him. "What happened to the luggage on the stage? My carpetbag was in the boot."

"Can't say for sure 'bout your grip, but Parrott and his gang took whatever was worth taking, including the strongbox. We put another driver aboard and sent the stage on to Deadwood. You folks kin claim whatever Parrott didn't make off with at the Express Office."

Matt looked so discouraged that Suzanne's heart wrenched. His grand adventure was off to a shaky start.

Well, Sloan had promised to bring them this far and he had. Now it was up to Suzanne to find another escort on to Cheyenne River and Matt the stake he needed to see him through the winter in Deadwood Gulch.

She had a far better notion of what he faced in the coming months than he did. Winters in Ohio couldn't begin to compare to those on the Great Plains. Blizzards howled like banshees from hell across these vast open stretches. Snow swept in under windowsills and piled so high against doors it took days to tunnel out. Even the more wooded, mountainous regions like the Black Hills offered little protection from the frigid blasts and smothering blankets of snow. Men trapped in the frozen gulches without adequate provisions had been known to eat their mules...and their fellow prospectors.

The sensational trial a few years ago of William O'Day was still talked about throughout the territories. As the judge noted when he sentenced the man to be hanged by the neck until dead, Carver County once had five Democrats. O'Day ate four of them.

Yes, Matt would definitely need money for a stake. And Sloan's rude response to Suzanne's offer of a promissory note in exchange for his escort suggested she would need some hard cash to hire his replacement, as well.

She tapped a toe in the dirt, annoyed by the way her stomach hollowed at the reminder that she and Black Jack Sloan would part company at Rawhide Buttes. She couldn't deny the man fascinated her. Or that he stirred urges she didn't want stirred. Urges that should have dissipated after so many hours in his gruff, unsociable company, but hadn't.

She'd now spent two days and nights with the man, yet knew little more about him than the lurid tales published in the penny presses. She was almost certain those tales had been highly embellished.

Well, now she'd never know for sure. Summoning a smile, she gave her attention back to the station manager.

"Mother Featherlegs kin put you folks up for the night," he assured the travelers. "The Express Line will cover the cost of beans and a bed, seein's how you were inconvenienced out of your seats on the stage."

Inconvenienced wasn't quite the word Suzanne would have used to describe being held up and left stranded, but she merely tipped the man a polite nod.

"Thank you."

"I'll take your horses to the barn," he told them, obviously eager to make amends on behalf of the Express Line. "You folks go in and wet your whistle."

She glanced at Sloan. "Are you coming in, or should we say goodbye?"

Best to do it here in the street, quick and now. No sense dragging matters out. Jack acknowledged that fact even as he passed the roan's reins to the station manager.

"I'll stand you and the boy to a beer."

With a quick little nod, she gathered her skirts and mounted the single step onto the rickety porch. Jack eyed her trim backside and cursed himself for a fool.

He cursed again when Matt released his grip on

the pommel, took a single step and went so barrel-legged he almost landed in the dirt.

"Come on, kid." Hauling him upright, Jack walked the groaning youth up the step. "Let's put some vinegar back in your veins."

A few steps plunged them from new dusk outside to old gloom inside. A quick sweep told Jack that Mother Featherlegs Shephard's Saloon and Hurdy-Gurdy Parlor was no different from any of the hundreds of other similar establishments he'd strolled into over the years. The same odor of stale sweat and spilled whiskey soured the air. The same assortment of ranchers, wranglers and drifters hunched over their drinks, fingering the coins in their pockets as they waited their turn with one of the three hurdies working the sawdust-covered dance boards.

From the look of them, Jack guessed the women made more working the sod huts out back than they did on the boards. None of the three looked to be particularly light on her feet. Not that the men who paid for the privilege of pressing up against female flesh would mind. Women were as scarce as cow eggs on the frontier.

And women like Suzanne were even scarcer.

She paused just inside the door, a small, delicate thrush set down amid crows. The dancing slowed to a standstill. Every head in the windowless dance hall turned. Eyes popped. Jaws sagged. The wrangler cranking the hurdy-gurdy froze, and the last verse of "Sweet Betsy from Pike" died a wheezing death.

No one moved or spoke until a cigar-chewing hurdie gave her partner a shove that sent him stumbling halfway across the floor. Rolling the black stump of her cigar from one side of her mouth to the other, she ambled over to greet the newcomers.

Jack had no difficulty identifying Mother Featherlegs Shephard. The dingy gray pantalets billowing beneath her shortened skirts gave her the appearance of a fat, feathery hen on the strut. As she neared, she sent out waves of lavender scent. The oversweet odor fought a fearsome battle with the cigar smoke that wreathed her painted face and graying, corkscrew curls.

"If you folks are looking for the Express Office, you're at the right place."

With a nod, she indicated the Ticket Office sign nailed to the wall above the faro table. "Next stage won't be through for another couple of days, though."

"And that's only if it don't get holt up like the last one," a customer volunteered, elbowing his companion aside to get a better look at Suzanne.

"Actually, we were on the stage that was robbed," she explained to the gathering crowd.

"So you're the ones." Mother Featherlegs darted a quick look at Jack and the still weak-

kneed Matt before turning back to Suzanne.
"We'd heard some of the passengers got left behind. Word came up the line that you hightailed it
back to Ten Mile Station."

"We did. However, we decided not to wait there
for the next stage."

The saloon owner hooted, expelling a cloud of
blue smoke in the process. "I can't blame you
none for that. Nothing to do in that sorry hole but
scratch your fleabites. Well, come on in and sit a
spell, missus. I can't offer you wine or sarsaparilla,
but the beer don't pack too bad of a punch."

"A beer would be wonderful."

"You and your man will want a bed for the
night. I'll get the Chinee girl to put clean ticking
on mine. It's big enough to take you both. The boy
kin bed down out back."

"That's very kind of you, but this gentleman
isn't my, er, man."

"No?" Her gaze went to Matt. "Don't tell me
you're married to this great, beardless gawk."

"No, I'm not married to him, either. Forgive me,
I should have introduced myself. I'm Suzanne
Bonneaux."

"*Miss* Suzanne Bonneaux," Jack drawled.

She sent him a speaking glance over her shoulder, but the instant clamor that arose at the news
she was single precluded any comment. Like a

herd of love-starved buffalo, the saloon patrons snorted, stamped and pawed the earth.

"Here, miss!" A stooped, gray-bearded customer grabbed a chair. "Take yer weight off the feet and sit right down beside me."

A younger, randier buck whisked the chair from his hands. "She don't want to sit with a toothless old geezer like you." With a flourish, he thumped the chair down in the center of the room. "Sit here, miss."

"Kin I fetch you a beer, ma'am?"

The crush of male admirers carried Suzanne forward. The moment she was seated, a small forest of chair legs scraped the floor. Her smile faltered for a moment as twenty or more men surrounded her and avidly absorbed every detail of her hair, face and figure.

"I'm on my way to Fort Meade," Suzanne said, breaking the awkward silence. "Have any of you been there?"

"Yes, ma'am."

"I have."

"So have I!"

"Can you tell me how far it is from the fort to the Arapaho camp on the Cheyenne River?"

The three men immediately tried to impress her with their knowledge. Jack left Suzanne attempting to make sense of their conflicting estimates and Matt hovering at the edge of the circle.

Mother Featherlegs joined him at the scarred pine plank that served as a bar. The scent she'd doused herself with rolled from her in waves.

"What'll you have?"

"Whatever's wet."

"Pour him a whiskey," she told the attendant behind the bar. "Take the kid and the lady a beer, too, would you, Joe?"

"Sure thing, Bess."

Leaning her elbows on the rough-edged plank, the saloon owner puffed idly. "We don't get many unattached females passing through these parts."

"That right?"

"Don't get many men who keep their holster so well oiled, either."

Jack grunted and tossed back the shot. The raw-grained alcohol hit his throat with the kick of a half-broke mustang and bucked all the way down to his stomach.

"Are you carrying a name I should recognize, mister?"

"Sloan. Jack Sloan."

"Black Jack Sloan?"

He grunted again. It was the best he could manage with his gullet spitting fire.

A wary look came over the woman's face. With a jerk of her curls, she nodded to Suzanne. "You got a claim to the lady that she didn't want to tell me about?"

"You got some reason for wanting to know?"

"Look, I ain't prying into your business. I just don't want one of my customers layin' a hand on your woman and winding up with a bullet between the eyes."

The idea of one of these men putting his paws on Suzanne didn't go down any easier than the whiskey, but Jack forced a shrug.

"The lady can take care of herself."

"That little bit of a thing?"

"That little bit of a thing."

With a mental brace, Jack finished the rest of his drink. He'd done what he'd promised to do. He'd brought Suzanne and the kid into Rawhide Buttes. It was time, past time, to be shed of her. Digging into his vest pocket, he pulled out his roll.

"The whiskey's on me," Bess Shephard protested.

"This is for Miss Bonneaux and the kid." He peeled off a few bills, tossed them down on the pine plank. "Big Nose Parrott and his gang got her purse. 'Far as we know, they got the kid's stake, too. The Express Line will pick up the cost of feeding and bedding them down, but this should cover whatever else they might need."

The saloon-keep tucked the banknotes into the front of her sweat-stained bodice. "Short on cash, are they?" Puffing like a chimney, she let her gaze drift to Suzanne. "A woman like that one could make eight, ten dollars a night easy on the dance boards.''

The idea of Suzanne Bonneaux shuffling around the smoke-filled saloon was so absurd that Jack found himself fighting a grin. ''Thinking of offering her a job?''

''I lost one of my hurdies to a bleedin' lung a few months back. I could use another girl to replace her. It's honest money,'' she added. ''She wouldn't have to take no customers out back unless she had a mind to.''

''Why don't you talk to her about it?'' he suggested wickedly. ''See what she says.''

''I might just do that, long as you don't object.''

''What the lady does is no concern of mine.''

And yellow-eyed bats don't beat night air, Bess Shephard thought, inhaling deeply. She'd been around long enough to recognize a bad case of crotch itch when she saw it. Sloan might not have bedded that bit of fluff and lace, but he wanted to. Bad.

Smiling, she rolled her stogie to one corner of her mouth and bit down. Juice squirted onto her tongue and cut through the fuzz left by the young stallion she'd taken out to her sod hut a few hours back. He'd been so primed he could hardly wait till he got his pole between her gums before he let fly. But unless Bess missed her guess, even that young stud hadn't hurt for it the way Black Jack

Sloan was hurting for the woman he had brought into Rawhide Buttes.

She wanted him, too. Bess saw the eye games they'd played with each other, she all seemingly exasperated, he with a twist to his mouth that looked ugly but did funny things to a female's insides.

She hadn't missed, either, the size of the roll Sloan had pulled out of his pocket. A businesswoman first and foremost, she searched for a way to separate the gunman from a few more of those banknotes.

"You and the kid can bed down in Rosie's hut. I been renting it out to the stage line since we lost her." She rolled her cigar around. "If you're lookin' for company, I got a little Chinee girl who empties slops and scrubs the boards. She don't talk much, and lies stiff as a corpse under the men who climb on top of her, but there's some as prefer a woman who don't require a lot of fuss or botheration."

Unlike Miss Suzanne Bonneaux, Bess would bet.

"You want I should send Ying Li to you when you get ready to bed down?"

"No."

"You sure? You got the look of a man strung tighter than barbed wire."

Annoyed, Jack shoved away from the bar without bothering to answer. Four strides took him to the circle of men surrounding Suzanne. Her gaze met his over their heads. He saw the farewell forming in her eyes.

She'd make out all right. She had a whole passel of men panting to ride shotgun for her tomorrow. If she had any sense, though, she wouldn't choose the toothless old geezer as her escort. Despite his claim that he used to haul freight up from Cheyenne and knew every rut in the road from here to Fort Meade, he looked ready for the coffin-maker. The randy young buck didn't strike Jack as any more reliable. The fool made more noise than he did sense. In fact, none of the men clustered around her looked to be either safe or reliable.

Hell! One more day. He'd give her one more day.

"I'm going to see to the horses." Jack bit out the words so hard his teeth ached. "Can you be ready to ride at dawn?"

For the life of him, he couldn't tell whether her smile was one of relief or triumph.

"Yes, of course."

7

Mother Featherlegs Shephard herself escorted Suzanne and Matt through a yard littered with refuse to the four sod huts behind the saloon. Three were one-room shanties, no larger than the Ten Mile swing station. The fourth belonged to the saloon proprietor and boasted both a parlor and a bedroom, with a fancifully painted muslin curtain draped between the two.

Both rooms reeked of old cigar smoke and lavender-scented toilet water. The strong fumes made Suzanne's nose itch, while the corsets, stockings and other intimate apparel scattered carelessly in the parlor raised a blush in Matt's cheeks. He reddened even more when Mother Featherlegs whisked back the muslin curtain to reveal a massive four-poster bed.

Suzanne's jaw sagged. Not only was the bed the largest she'd ever seen, but each of its four posts was carved to represent a different mythical creature. A scaly dragon breathed fire in one bottom corner, a sea serpent writhed in the other. At the head, a thick-necked horse reared on its hind legs to paw at a fierce temple dog. Oriental symbols gilded with gold paint decorated the sideboards.

The saloon proprietor beamed at her stunned expression. "Something grand, ain't it?"

"It's incredible!"

"Bought it when I bought the Chinee girl. Her pa had it shipped clear across the Pacific and hauled up from the railhead at Cheyenne by freight wagon. Near broke the little bugger's heart to part with it, but I told him I wouldn't take the girl without the bed."

The casual remark considerably diminished Suzanne's delight in the artistry of the piece. She wasn't unaware of the custom practiced by some Chinese of selling unwanted daughters. Hundreds of thousands of Orientals had poured into the States to work the transcontinental railroad and the gold fields, with Chinatowns springing up at every railhead and mining camp of any size. In a land with so many lonely men and so few women to ease them, such transactions would occur despite attempts to stem them.

"I changed the straw in the mattress just last week," Mother Featherlegs told her. "You won't get bit to death by fleas."

"Thank you, but I don't wish to inconvenience you."

"You won't. I've done finished all the business I intend to do tonight." Her hostess hooked a thumb toward Matt. "I'll bed this one down next door with Sloan...unless you want Black Jack in here with you," she added, a sly look coming into her eyes. "You might sleep easier with him close to hand."

Suzanne suspected she wouldn't sleep at all with Jack close to hand. She'd barely slept last night, with him rolled up in a horse blanket just across the doused campfire.

"I appreciate your concern," she told Mother Featherlegs with a smile, "but I can take care of myself."

"That's what Sloan said. He also said you was short of cash."

"Yes, I lost my purse in the holdup."

"One of my hurdies died a month or so back. You could earn whatever cash you need on the boards. When I mentioned the idea to Sloan, he suggested I talk to you about it."

How like him! Suzanne thought, torn between exasperation and amusement. She could almost see the evil glint in his eyes.

Before she could decline the offer of employment, Matt choked out a shocked protest. "Miss Bonneaux went to school in Philadelphia! She kin recite lines from that Shakespeare fellow by rote. A lady like her wouldn't want to work the boards.''

Mother Featherlegs's ruff went up. "Even a lady's got to eat, boy."

Hastily, Suzanne intervened before Matt offended their hostess further. "The Express Line will pay for our food and a bed, but I'll write you a promissory note for any expenses we incur above that.''

"No need for any notes. Sloan passed me a wad of bills for you and the boy.''

"He did?"

"He did. Enough to cover a bath if you want me to get the Chinee girl to heating some water.''

Her surprise at Sloan's unexpected generosity became instant delight. "Oh, yes!''

The saloon owner turned a droll look on Matt. "Enough for you to get a few beers and a jiggle, too, boy, if you have a mind to.''

His blue eyes almost popped out of his head. Gulping, he cast a wild look at the bed, snatched his hat off his head and crushed it between his fists. "Thank you kindly, ma'am, but I don't... That is, I, uh...''

"Not with me, you big gawk. I've done finished my business for the night. One of the other girls might accommodate you, though, if you was to ask her nice.''

"I...I..."

He couldn't bring himself to look at Suzanne, but she could see that the idea had sparked his interest. Face burning, he turned and fled.

Disappointment and disapproval on the unknown Becky's behalf compressed Suzanne's lips. Toe tapping, she frowned as he disappeared back into the saloon.

"He's young and full of sap," the older woman commented. "Won't hurt him none to let some of it out."

"The girl he left back in Ohio might not agree."

Mother Featherlegs shrugged. "If she didn't want her man spurting his juice into another woman, she should have come with him and took care of him herself."

Suzanne had to concede the point. Even her mother would echo the saloon owner's sentiments, if not her exact phrasing. Like so many army wives, Julia Bonneaux Garrett had followed her husband from one frontier post to another, making a home for him and their family in tents, wagons and, at the larger posts, in spacious quarters.

Well, Matt would just have to decide for himself how he would take advantage of Sloan's surprising generosity. Suzanne had already made up her mind.

"You mentioned a bath. I should love one, if it's not too much trouble."

"No trouble at all." Rolling her cigar, she ambled to the open door and let loose with a bull-like bellow. "Ying Li! Haul yer skinny carcass over here, girl. Chop chop!"

The girl who tripped in on tiny, mincing steps some moments later could have been a younger sister to Bright Water. She looked almost Arapaho with her broad face, heavy-lidded eyes and long, black braid hanging over one shoulder.

But where Bright Water dressed with the style and grace of her people, this girl had obviously been handed the hurdies' discards. Her skirt of brown homespun was rolled at the waist and tied with a piece of rope, although a long tail still dragged the dirt. Her soiled calico blouse could have fit around her twice. Shoulders hunched, she kept her hands tucked into her sleeves and her eyes downcast.

"Mah-mah call Ying Li?"

"The lady's wanting a bath. Fetch some buckets of hot water."

Her dark eyes darted to Suzanne.

"Chop chop, girl. Chop chop."

Turning, she scurried out.

"Look at that." Mother Featherlegs shook her head in disgust. "I thought she might have the makin's of a hurdie when I bought her, but she skitters along like a field mouse. Can't keep up with the cowboys who like to go galloping around the boards.''

Rummaging around in her clothes press, she drew out a bloodred silk robe lavishly trimmed with long, dangling black fringe.

''Got this down to Denver some years back. It might hang a bit long on you, but you're welcome to it.''

''I shouldn't like to borrow something so fine,'' Suzanne protested. ''I might soil it.''

''Well, if it's plain muslin you're wanting, you won't find none of it in Rawhide Buttes. Besides, you wouldn't be borrowing this. Sloan said to give you what you needed.''

Somehow, Suzanne didn't think Jack had intended his largess to cover the cost of red silk dripping with black fringe.

Or perhaps he had.

She could imagine his mocking grin were he to see her decked out in the garment.

''Well, I'd better go see to my business. The privy's out back, and there's soap by the wash bowl. Help yourself to anything else you might need. I'll send Ying Li with some dinner after she gets your bath going.''

''Thank you.''

The tin hip bath the Chinese girl dragged in was almost as big as she was. Since the bed occupied every square inch of the back room, she positioned the tub in the center of the parlor. Tripping out, she returned some moments later with a bucket of steaming water. Grunting under its weight, she staggered toward the bath.

"Here, let me help you."

"No, no, missee. Mah-mah say Ying Li do."

The girl jerked away from Suzanne's outstretched hand. Hot water splashed onto her skirt. Wincing, she tottered to the tub and dumped the bucket. When she returned moments later with another, Suzanne had to bite the inside of her lip to keep from offering assistance once again.

Her lip was raw by the time the tin tub was filled with a mix of hot and cold water. Swirling a hand in to test the temperature, she smiled gratefully.

"I feel as though I'm wearing half of Wyoming Territory. I'll be glad to be rid of it."

The girl made no comment. Curious about her, Suzanne tried another smile.

"Mother Featherlegs said you don't work the boards."

"No, Missee. Ying Li only scrub floor and fuckee-fuck."

"I...see. Do you, er, like your work?"

"Sometime like, sometime no like." Beneath the soiled calico, the girl's shoulders lifted in a shrug. "All same, no matter."

Her attitude didn't invite pity. More curious than ever, Suzanne couldn't help probing.

"How long have you been with Mother Featherlegs?"

Her forehead crinkled. "Father sell worthless second daughter three, no, four winters ago."

Sweet heaven above! The girl must have been a mere child.

"How old are you?"

"Ying Li born the Year of the Dog."

No wiser than before, Suzanne tried to guess her age. They were about the same height, but that didn't mean anything. As Suzanne's younger brother liked to remind her regularly, she stood so short she'd have to borrow a ladder to spit in a grasshopper's eye. Well, whatever her age, the girl was obviously far older than Suzanne in experience, if not in actual years.

"Ying Li fetch missee's dinner now?"

"Yes, please."

While she waited for the girl's return, Suzanne removed the little derringer from her skirt pocket, then unhooked the waistband and let the navy serge pool around the tops of her borrowed boots. She'd seen enough of life on the frontier to know Ying Li could do worse than scrub floors and...and perform other tasks in Mother Featherlegs Shephard's Saloon and Hurdy-Gurdy Parlor. Much worse.

And better.

Frowning, she unlaced her boots. Inspection of her toes showed the blisters were still red but healing nicely. With fervent thanks to Bright Water for her remedies, she removed the rest of her clothing and stepped into the steaming water.

"Aah!"

With a fold of her arms and legs, she sank down and promptly forgot Ying Li, forgot her blisters, forgot everything but the pure, sybaritic joy of a good soak. Suzanne's head lolled back against the tin. Her legs dangled over the front edge of the tub. It was bliss. It was joy. It was heaven. Eyes closed, she remained motionless until the water cooled and her fingertips pruned.

Sighing, she pulled in her legs and wedged herself up on her knees to wash her hair. After rinsing the heavy mass with the bucket of clean water Ying Li had left, she climbed out of the tub, toweled dry with a length of coarse, unbleached linen and slipped into the red wrapper. Carefully, she rolled back the sleeves and knelt beside the tub to wash her drawers and chemise.

Determined not to be a burden on either her hostess or the Chinese girl, Suzanne scooped the water from the tub and made several trips to the door to dump the bucket. She was on her third trip when a broad-shouldered figure loomed out of the darkness.

"Oh! It's you."

Sloan strolled forward, declining to answer the obvious.

"I brought your bag," he said instead, passing her the burlap sack that contained the supplies and few necessities she'd gathered at Ten Mile Station.

"Thank you."

All too conscious of the way the wet silk clung to her skin, Suzanne put down both the bag and the bucket and fussed unobtrusively with the black fringe.

Not unobtrusively enough. Leaning a shoulder against the doorjamb, Jack let his gaze make its usual slow waltz down her front. The devil danced in his gray eyes when they locked with hers again.

"Mother Featherlegs said she was going to offer you a job."

"She's already made the offer."

"Let her get a glimpse of you in that get-out, and she'll up your starting wages for sure."

As much to divert his attention from the thin silk as to satisfy her own curiosity, Suzanne probed for the reason behind his change of heart.

"Why did you agree to escort me to Fort Meade?"

"I didn't say I'd take you all the way to Fort Meade."

"How far, then?"

"Let's just see where the road gets us tomorrow."

"Why did you change your mind?" she asked again, wanting to know. Needing to know, for reasons that got all mixed up in her head.

"You showed me you could keep up the pace."

"Keep up?"

"All right," he admitted with the beginning of a grin. "You can do more than keep up. I suspect you could throw dust in any man's eyes if you wanted to."

"I suspect I could," she replied smugly.

His grin slipped out. It was a real one this time, not the usual mocking twist of his lips. Suzanne responded to it as naturally as spring flowers opened to the sun after a shower. For a few moments, they shared an unaccustomed harmony.

Jack was the one to break it. Straightening, he tipped his hat to her. "I'll let you get back to your soaking."

"I'm done. You're welcome to use the tub," she added politely, too politely. "I'm sure Ying Li would heat more water."

His brow quirked. "Is that your way of saying I stink?"

"I wouldn't go *quite* as far as that."

"You wouldn't, huh?" The sardonic gleam she was coming to recognize slid back into his eyes.

"If I decide to take you up on the offer, would you scrub my back?"

She pursed her lips and pretended to be offended by the suggestion, although the idea of gliding her hands over Sloan's wet, slick muscles did queer things to her stomach.

"I'm sure Ying Li would do that for you, too."

"It's something how you can prune up that," he commented lazily, his gaze on her mouth.

"Indeed?"

"I expect you know damned well what it does to a man."

"Do, please, enlighten me."

She'd known before the words were out that she was playing with fire. She had no business standing here, bare as a skinned birch beneath the red silk. No business tossing barbs back and forth with Sloan, or cloaking dares in coy words and sissified looks.

She'd known, too, that he would take her up on the challenge. Her heart thumping, she watched him move a deliberate step forward.

"How about I show you instead?"

Reluctantly, Suzanne unpruned. Playing with fire was one thing. Letting this man burn her all to flinders was something else again.

"I don't think that would be wise."

"Stupid as hell," he agreed, taking another step. Always afterward, Suzanne would swear she meant to call a halt to matters then and there. If she hadn't tripped on her too-long wrapper as she hastily stepped back, she certainly would have.

But her foot trapped the hem. The gown gapped at the front and dragged at the back. Off balance, Suzanne made a grab for her neckline with one hand and for Jack's sleeve with the other. He caught her with a quick arm around her waist and hauled her against him. To her consternation, her legs slid between his, and the damned wrapper parted clear up to her hips.

She looked up, flushed and horribly embarrassed. Her eyes met his. She felt him stiffen beneath her hand. His arm cut like a tight leather cinch around her waist. She couldn't move, could barely breathe.

"Jack..."

She'd intended it as a protest. Even to her own ears it sounded more like a plea.

His mouth came down on hers. There was nothing gentle about the kiss, nothing tender in the way his muscles knotted and bunched under her fingers. The feelings of the past few days ripped free, and she heard the wild, primitive song of a full-blooded male.

Or maybe that was her own blood pounding in her ears. Suzanne didn't know. At that moment, she didn't care.

Her mouth opened under his. Wildly, wantonly,

she met the thrust of his tongue with hers. She'd never been kissed with such savage hunger, never answered with such unfettered delight. Wrapping her arms around his neck, she arched her body against his, wanting, *needing* to feel the rough contact of his belt and vest and shirt through the silk. When one of his hands went to her bottom and pressed her into his thigh, needles of pure sensation shot through her belly.

He held her tight against him, so tight they touched everywhere it was possible for a man and woman to touch. Her mouth, her breasts, her stomach, the aching, burning spot between her legs all felt the imprint of his hard flesh and roped muscles.

Suddenly, being held wasn't enough. Being kissed didn't satisfy the beast inside her. She wanted more. She wanted the panting, straining, sighing she'd heard from couples rolled up in buffalo skin the nights she'd spent with Bright Water in her father's teepee. Wanted whatever it was that put such a soft, dreamy expression on her mother's face when she came downstairs the morning after the colonel returned from a long patrol. Wanted what the Misses Merriweather had said no *real* lady ever wanted.

Prim, proper Suzanne Bonneaux—raised by a loving mother and devoted stepfather, petted by troopers at half a dozen different posts, sent back East for two years of polish and refinement,

courted by bankers' sons and fresh-faced West
Point graduates—wanted Jack Sloan naked. Or at
least naked enough for her to run her fingers over
his chest, his back, his arms. Naked enough for her
to wrap her hot little hands around the ridge of
hard flesh jutting against her belly.

She was so lost in the swirling, tumultuous sensations of his mouth and hands and thigh that the
sound of the door opening barely registered on her
consciousness.

It registered with Jack, however. He dropped her
like an anvil. Whipped out his Colt. Spun around.
Suzanne hit the floor at precisely the same second
a startled shriek split the air.

"Ai ya!"

Ying Li stood frozen in the doorway, Suzanne's
supper tray in her hands. The sight of a long-
barreled Colt pointed at her heart raised another
screech.

"Bu! Bu! Woo ni lai!"

She turned and fled, scattering tin plates and
cups as she went.

Sloan filled the air with a string of oaths. He
was strung tight as a roll of baling wire when he
turned back around. He went even tighter when he
looked down at Suzanne.

Belatedly, she realized she was sprawled at his
feet, legs wide, the red silk open from knee to

neck. Scuttling back like a frantic crab, she yanked the robe together.

With another curse, Sloan spun around and headed for the door.

"Jack! Wait!" She had no idea what she'd say to him, only that she couldn't let him walk out like this. "Where are you going?"

"To drink myself blind."

8

Shaking, Suzanne crawled into Mother Featherlegs's massive bed. The straw ticking rustled as she fanned her still-damp hair across the pillow and stretched out under the watchful stare of the carved wooden temple dog.

Now that the wild pounding in her blood had diminished to a stuttering throb, she couldn't believe how close she'd come to throwing all caution and common sense to the wind.

If Ying Li hadn't appeared when she did...

If Sloan had slammed the door shut instead of stalking out...

If Suzanne had shed the thin silk...

Her face flamed in the darkness. Sloan had seen her naked, or as close to it as didn't count. She should be writhing in shame, boiling in a stew of embarrassment. Instead, she felt the most absurd, the most *stinging* disappointment.

Flinging an arm across her eyes, she lectured herself sternly. He was a gunman, for pity's sake! A shootist! If half the stories written about him were true, he'd mowed down more men than Mr. Gatling's repeating gun, which was finally proving itself so effective within army ranks.

The lecture failed dismally to achieve its objective. As much as she tried to quell her riotous emotions, Suzanne couldn't block the searing wish that Jack had ripped off that gaudy dressing gown and tumbled her into a bed with sea serpents and dragons and Chinese characters picked out in gold.

Groaning, she rolled over and punched the pillow. With her next breath, she regretted the move. Odors rose in waves, lavender and straw and something she strongly suspected was a residue from Mother Featherlegs's customers.

She flopped onto her back once more and exchanged glares with the temple dog. It was, she decided, going to be a long night. A very long night, indeed.

Not thirty yards away, Matt unknowingly echoed her sentiments. The way his head whirled, he was sure he wouldn't live to see morning. The beer Jack had paid for sloshed in his belly as he squinted up at the sliver of new moon riding at a cockeyed angle. The stars fuzzed, sharpened, fuzzed again.

He had to relieve himself so bad he hurt, but the tilting moon made him almost too dizzy to stand. Propping a hand against the saloon wall to steady himself, he fumbled with the flap of his trousers.

"Aah."

Sagging with relief, he shot his stream into the night.

"Mah-mah no like customers piss on wall."

The voice came out of the darkness. Matt jerked around, spraying as he went.

"Cripes!"

A tiny creature glided out of the shadows. Mortified, he tried to cut off the stream, but he'd downed too much beer. He was forced to stand there, arcing full and long, while the girl observed the process. Face burning, he finally stuffed himself back into his trousers.

"You shouldn't watch a man attending to nature."

She lifted her shoulders. "All same, no matter."

All the same? Embarrassed as he was, Matt's masculine pride reared its head. He was a touch clumsy, sure, but he was big. Bigger than most, anyway. Not that he could argue the point with this slip of a girl.

"What are you doing out here in the dark?"

"Mah-mah send me. Say you want fuckee-fuck."

Matt's eyes bugged. "I want...what?"

Frowning, she made a circle with her thumb and forefinger and poked at it with the first finger of her other hand. The gesture was so graphic that his eyes bulged again.

"Mah-mah say I do dragon dance with you chop chop, pay for dishes and missee's supper, all broke."

His head whirling, Matt couldn't make sense of one word in three. He was still trying to interpret the singsong phrases when she stepped forward and reached for the trouser flap he'd buttoned all askew. The press of her palm against his pole sent him jumping back so hard and fast his shoulders slammed against the wall.

The girl's forehead creased. "You not want Ying Li?"

She looked worried, almost frightened. Hastily, Matt tried to reassure her. "Yes, sure I want you, but…"

"You want, I do."

Her determined little fingers went to work on his buttons.

"Not…not here!" he choked out, half embarrassed and wholly aroused.

"All right, come come." She heaved a long-suffering sigh. "All same, no matter."

Taking his hand, she led him like a bull with a ring through his nose toward one of the smaller sod huts.

* * *

It had turned out to be a real bitch of a night.

Jack rolled one of Mother Featherlegs's cigars around in his mouth, welcoming the bitter juice that spurted onto his tongue. He needed something, anything, to kill the taste of Suzanne.

The whiskey hadn't helped. He'd poured enough rotgut down his gullet to drop a fair-size mule. Between that and the cigar, every nerve in his mouth and tongue ought to be dead. Still he could taste her.

And see her. Nothing short of a shotgun blast between the eyes was going to blow away the image of Suzanne Bonneaux sprawled at his feet.

Jack stared blindly at the smoke swirling through the saloon. All he could see were long, curved legs, rounded hips and the tuft of curly brown hair between her thighs. His teeth ground together so hard the cigar shredded in his mouth.

"Hell!"

He spit the tobacco into a dented brass cuspidor crusted with brown leavings and reached for his glass. The whiskey burned a fresh scar inside his throat as he watched one of the hurdies swing her way through the crowd in his direction.

"Want to take a turn on the boards?"

Dark rings of sweat stained her dress at each armpit and her face paint had caked into the creases on her cheeks and forehead, but she didn't look bad. Not bad at all. In fact, Jack told himself savagely, she looked to be just the kind of woman he should take a turn with.

The kind who didn't tie a man up in knots. The kind whose lips didn't pucker up all prim and disapproving. Hell, this woman's mouth could probably pleasure a man in ways *Miss* Suzanne Bonneaux couldn't even begin to imagine.

Unless someone taught her.

The thought slammed into him, tightened his fist around the glass. He brought both down on the pine plank with a violence that widened the hurdie's eyes.

"Yeah," he growled, breathing hard through his nostrils, "I'll take a turn on the boards."

A series of loud thumps jerked Suzanne from sleep. She started up, blinking in the darkness, felt a small shriek rise up in her throat at the menacing figure bent over her. She fell back, gasping with relief when she realized it was the carved wooden temple dog.

"Miss Suzanne?" Another thump rattled the front door. "Miss Suzanne, you in there?"

"Matt? Is that you?"

"Yes, ma'am."

"Good heavens!" Shoving her hair out of her eyes, Suzanne jumped out of bed. Alarm laced through her as she yanked the red silk dressing gown together and ran for the door.

Had she overslept? Was it almost dawn? Had Sloan already ridden out? She supposed she shouldn't be surprised after last night, but that didn't make the possibility that he'd left her behind any easier to swallow.

She should be relieved she didn't have to face him again. Should be happy she wouldn't have to pretend she hadn't practically dragged him down to the floor. Instead, the mere idea that he might have deserted her made her so furious she yanked open the door.

"Is he gone?"

Matt looked at her stupidly.

"Sloan. Did he ride out already?"

"Don't think so." His forehead creased. "It's just an hour or two past midnight. Last I saw, he was pouring something wet down his throat."

He wasn't the only one, she realized. Matt's breath carried such a potent flavoring of yeast and hops that Suzanne's eyes watered. Resisting the urge to flap her hand in front of her face to dispel the pungent waves, she regarded him more closely.

"Are you drunk?"

"Yes, ma'am." Dragging his hat from his crop of marigold curls, he crushed it between his fists. "Drunk as two wheelbarrows."

She clutched the red silk together, fighting a giggle. He looked so solemn, so ridiculously pie-faced.

"So you availed yourself of Sloan's largesse, after all?"

"His what?"

"You used the money Jack left with Mother Featherlegs to treat yourself to a few rounds of beer?"

"Not just beer."

His expression swung from mortification to glee and back again so swiftly Suzanne could barely tell one from the other.

"The Chinee girl, Ying Li, she, er... We sorta, uh...became acquainted."

Suzanne lost all inclination to laugh. Damn Jack Sloan, anyway! This was his fault. He shouldn't have thrown out greenbacks like some gun-toting Midas. With a toss of her head, she dismissed as completely irrelevant the fact that Sloan's largesse had paid for her bath as well as Matt's debauchery.

"Did you wake me just to tell me you and Ying Li—" she couldn't quite hold back a sniff "—became acquainted?"

Matt blinked again, as if trying to remember just why he *had* hammered on the door. When his reasoning finally came back, it poured out in a rush.

"It ain't right, Miss Suzanne. She's no bigger than a kitten and near 'bout as helpless. Her pa done sold her and she can't leave till she pays back what Mother Featherlegs give for her. Her and the bed,'' he amended, shooting a fierce glare in the direction of the saloon owner's prized possession. "We can't leave her here."

Taken aback by his fervor, Suzanne blinked. "Does Ying Li want to leave?"

"She keeps muttering some gibberish about it all making no difference. But it ain't right,'' he said again.

"No, it isn't, but I don't exactly see what you wish me to do about it."

"Write one of them promissory notes for her, like you did for the supplies at Ten Mile Station."

"I, er..."

"I'll pay you back soon's I'm able." His jaw set. "I ain't leavin' without her."

"Oh, dear."

Suzanne could foresee all sorts of complications, not the least of which was explaining to Jack Sloan how their small party had suddenly expanded to include Ying Li.

"I'll write out a promise of payment if Mother Featherlegs will accept it. But do you think you should take Ying Li along with you?" She cleared her throat delicately. "Won't your Becky think it rather odd if she hears about it?"

The stubborn set to Matt's face became downright mulish.

"She'd probably just toss her head and say the

only way I could get a woman was to buy her. That may be so, but Ying Li didn't laugh at me. Not once, even when I, uh, near 'bout embarrassed myself the worst way a man can embarrass himself with a woman.''

"I understand," Suzanne said hastily. "Really, I do. It's just... Well..."

Well what? She'd felt the prick of her own conscience earlier, when the saloon owner had told her the conditions of Ying Li's purchase. And again, when the girl had described her duties.

Matt was right. They couldn't leave her here. Not if she truly wanted to leave.

Determining Ying Li's exact wishes in the matter turned out to be a laborious exercise. When questioned, the girl returned the same answer every time.

All same, no matter.

Once, only once, did Suzanne catch a gleam of hope, swiftly quenched, in her downcast eyes. Sighing, she swallowed her own doubts and sent the oddly mismatched pair out with a promise to see what she could do.

Since her blouse and undergarments were still damp from their washing, she wrapped the scarlet robe firmly around her waist and tucked it into her skirt. Without a corset or chemise to contain her silhouette, her breasts jutted all too prominently against the thin silk. Her little blue serge half jacket looked ridiculous over the robe, but at least it provided a modicum of modesty.

The best she could do with her hair was drag a comb through the damp tangles and tie it back with a bit of ribbon from her chemise. Thrusting her bare feet into the borrowed boots, she clumped out in search of Mother Featherlegs.

A raucous chorus of "My Darling Clementine" boomed from the saloon. The noise assaulted her as she picked her way across the yard. Once inside, the din rose up to roar in her ears like a jungle beast. Wheezing notes pumped out of the hand organ. Boots stomped puffs of sawdust from the floor. Hands slapped against tabletops. Skirts flying, curls bouncing, the hurdies whirled around the boards with their chosen partners.

One of whom, Suzanne noted, was Jack Sloan.

Like the others crowding the dance floor, Jack circled and swayed to the lively beat. Unlike the others, he moved with a grace that made even the sweat-stained woman in his arms appear as elegant as one of the ballerinas who performed at the Philadelphia Opera House.

Damn the man, anyway!

Her mouth drawn into a tight, firm line, Suzanne stepped into the saloon. As before, her presence produced a dramatic effect.

One by one, the patrons stopped their pounding,

stomping, and singing to gawk at her. The dancers slowed. The music died.

Suzanne wouldn't have been human if she hadn't experienced a fierce, feminine satisfaction at the stir she caused.

"Please, gentlemen," she said in her airiest manner. "Don't let me interrupt your entertainment."

Only after she was halfway across the room did her satisfaction take on a tinge of unease. She couldn't pinpoint exactly what caused her disquiet. Maybe the realization that the whiskey fumes rising on the smoke-filled air were heavier than they'd been when she'd walked into the saloon this afternoon. Or that men watching her every step did so with an unnerving intensity.

Including Sloan.

A muscle twitched in the side of his jaw. He looked anything but pleased to see her. Releasing his partner, he planted himself directly in Suzanne's path.

"Where the hell do you think you're going?"

The low growl brought her chin up.

"To speak to Mother Featherlegs. Not, I might add, that it's any of your business."

"It is if you want to ride out of here with me tomorrow. Look around you. Half the men in here are so liquored up they wouldn't know their own mothers. The other half probably never did. Sober, they wouldn't so much as spit in your presence. Drunk..."

"Drunk they might forget you're a lady," Mother Featherlegs finished, strolling over to join them. "You'd best hightail it out of here, missy."

"I will, as soon as I speak with you."

"What about?"

"Ying Li."

Exasperation put an edge to the older woman's voice. "I gave the girl a real chawin' on for dropping your supper and breakin' the dishes like she did. She was supposed to fetch you another plate. Don't tell me she dropped that, too?"

"This isn't about my supper."

"Well, what's it about, then?"

Suzanne drew in a deep breath. She would have preferred to conduct this business without a roomful of avid listeners and Sloan practically breathing down her neck.

"I should like to reimburse you whatever amount you paid for her."

"You want to buy her?"

"I want to pay off her debt to you," she corrected scrupulously. It wouldn't do to point out that the War Between the States, which had convulsed the entire country less than fifteen years ago, had made the abomination of dealing in human flesh illegal. "Actually, it's Matt who wants to see the debt paid, but I..."

She broke off, startled, as Mother Featherlegs gave a whoop of laughter. "Ying Li must have diddled him some good to make him want to buy her!"

Even Sloan snickered. When Suzanne turned a fulminating eye his way, he shrugged. "I didn't think the kid had it in him."

"Mathias Butts has a kind and generous heart," she said loftily. "He simply wishes to release the girl from her bondage."

"That's not all he wishes," the saloon owner said with a leer before the businesswoman in her took over. "How are you proposin' to pay for the girl? I thought Big Nose and his gang took your purse and left you hard up for cash."

"They did. If you would be so kind as to accept a written promise of payment, I guarantee it'll be honored."

The older woman hooted again. "Lord aw-mighty, I've collected so many worthless promises of payment, I use 'em in the outhouse to wipe my arse. No, I can't take nothing but cash or gold dust."

"How much cash or gold dust?"

"Two and a half ounces in dust, three hundred in cash."

"Good heavens!"

"It's what I paid for the girl."

"I seem to recall you mentioning that you also got the bed as part of the deal!"

"All right. Two hundred. But not a penny less."

Suzanne folded her arms. The toe of an oversize boot tapped the floor. Once. Twice. Lips pursed, she turned to Jack. The answer to her unspoken question was quick, flat and nonnegotiable.

"No."

"It would merely be a loan."

"No."

"Really, you must know Matt will repay you, and if he doesn't, I will."

"I don't know anything of the kind," he retorted. "Chances are, I won't see hide nor hair of either of you again after we part company."

"Jack, please." She forced a conciliatory smile. "Perhaps I've tried your patience a bit, but..."

His snort raised a flush in her cheeks.

"...but we should set aside our personal feelings for Ying Li's sake."

"No."

It was the whiskey talking. Jack was mean with it. Even meaner with the itch to grab this woman, sling her over his shoulder and haul her back to the sod hut to finish what they'd started. Jaw tight, he hooked his thumbs on his gun belt to keep from doing just that.

Her toe tapped again. She studied him in silence for a few moments.

"Are you a betting man, Mr. Sloan?"

"That depends on the stakes."

"I propose we settle this matter with a hand of five-card stud. You put up the two hundred dollars and I'll put up a note for the same amount."

"Not good enough."

It was the whiskey. It had to be the whiskey that made him rock back on his heels. "Seeing as how we don't know when, if ever, I'll collect on that IOU, I think you should tack on some interest."

A wary look came into her eyes. "How much interest?"

"Oh, I'd say the payment we talked about back at Ten Mile Station should about cover it."

She knew at once the payment he referred to. Her head jerked up. Her eyes flashed. Jack rocked back on his heels again, figuring Miss Suzanne Bonneaux was about to tell him to take himself and his salacious, audacious proposal straight to hell.

"One hand of five-card stud," she snapped. "We'll draw for the deal."

9

More of her real father's blood ran in Suzanne's veins than she'd realized. Only from the dashing, handsome riverboat gambler could she have inherited this simmering sense of excitement, this reckless willingness to stake so much on a turn of the cards.

She could almost hear Philip Bonneaux's teasing laughter as he held her in his lap and taught her how to fan the cards so only she could see what she held. Almost feel his fingers guiding hers along the side of a deck, showing her how to feel out cut or shaved cards. Almost see the flash of the sapphire ring he'd always worn on his left hand, until he had staked it on three kings and lost to an inside straight.

Philip Bonneaux had died just weeks after Suzanne turned seven, but she'd practiced the skills he'd taught her with a variety of partners over the years, including Bright Water and any of her step-father's troops she could talk into a game. They'd always played for pebbles, though. Or matchsticks. Never for money. The colonel made sure of that. And certainly never for stakes like this.

If she won, Jack would lend her the two hundred dollars, without interest. If he won, he'd not only charge her a very personal, private interest, he'd collect payment in advance. Tonight. In Mother Featherlegs's bed. Suzanne sensed it in the way he watched her, felt it in the mad fluttering of her pulse.

Every nerve in her body tingled with anticipation, with nervousness, with the exhilarating and altogether terrifying realization of how much she'd wagered on the turn of a card. Yet she refused to allow her wildly swinging emotions to show on her face. Chin high, spine every bit as straight as the Misses Merriweather could have wished, she seated herself at the drink-stained table hastily cleared for the game.

Sloan took the chair opposite hers. Leaning back, he stretched out his long legs and crossed his ankles. His comfortable slouch seemed to indicate a complete indifference to the outcome of the game. Only the glint in his gray eyes suggested otherwise.

"Here." Mother Featherlegs dropped a deck on

the table. "These are a bit greasy and worn, but they're the best the house has to offer."

Her customers crowded around. Caught up in the excitement, they called out side wagers that were met, doubled, snatched up eagerly. Their jostling and avid, intent stares didn't cause Suzanne any hint of unease now. Interest had shifted from her to the game.

Her interest was concentrated on the man seated across the table. With a polite lift of her brows, she reached for the cards.

"Shall I shuffle?"

"Be my guest."

To her relief, her hands were steady. She pushed the cards into a pile, gathered them up and divided them into two stacks. Mother Featherlegs was right. The pasteboard had worn thin. The surfaces felt greasy.

Calmly, Suzanne shuffled the two stacks into one. Sliding her fingers along the edges to straighten the cards, she divided the deck again and shuffled a second time, then a third. When she fanned the cards facedown on the table, she knew which one she would pick. Folding her hands, she waited for Sloan to make his choice.

He turned up a seven.

Suzanne flipped her card over. It was, as she'd suspected it would be, an ace. If someone went to the risk of shaving cards, he wouldn't mark the low ones.

"Looks like you've won the deal," Sloan drawled.

Her blood singing, she allowed herself a small, bland smile. "Looks like I have."

Her insipid smile stayed in place as she divided the deck again, shuffled and placed the stack in front of Sloan. His long, lean gunfighter's fingers meticulously straightened the edges. Too meticulously.

Her gaze flew up to meet his. Was he, too, getting a feel for the deck? Would he note the hair-thin differences? They were so imperceptible and the cards so well used that Suzanne had been forced to shuffle several times before she knew for sure their edges had been shaved.

Jack didn't alter his expression by so much as a flicker of an eyelid, damn him! One-handed, he cut the deck.

Her heart hammering, Suzanne gathered it into her left hand and prepared to deal. "First card down or up?"

"Let's keep it interesting. First card up, last card down."

"Whatever you wish."

Slowly, she dealt the cards. The audience crowded closer, cheering or groaning with the turn of each card. The ripe scents of tobacco, whiskey and old sweat battled fiercely with Mother Featherlegs's toilet water. Smoke from the sputtering oil lamps and the saloon owner's malodorous cigar stung Suzanne's eyes.

After the second card, her initial exhilaration was fraying at the edges. After the third, she began to suspect she didn't really have whatever it took to be a gambler. By the fourth, her nerves had rolled up into a tight ball.

Thank the Lord for her father and the Misses Merriweather! Philip Bonneaux had taught her to maintain a poker face, the sisters to keep a ladylike composure under all circumstances. Suzanne suspected her teachers had probably never envisioned circumstances quite like these, however.

"Last card down, *Miss* Bonneaux."

"I believe that's what we agreed to, *Mr.* Sloan."

Smoke curled around Jack's face, obscuring his gaze. Suzanne felt it, though. On her face. Her throat. Her hands.

"Think you can beat the pair of nines I have showing?"

His whisky-roughened drawl scratched her nerves.

"I certainly hope so."

The sleeves of the red silk robe fanned the table as she leaned forward to deal his last card face-down. Outwardly calm, inwardly a mass of quivering jelly, she dealt her own card and set the deck aside.

The silence grew as thick and heavy as the smoke. Suzanne thought she would choke on one or the other before Sloan reached out and flipped over his last card. Ironically, it was the jack of spades.

So all he had was a pair of nines! That's all she had to beat. A pair of nines. If she turned up another queen or ace to match those she already had showing, she'd win.

Her blood pulsed. Her breath stuck halfway down her throat. She fingered the corner of her last card, met Jack's heavy-lidded gaze across the table. If the feral light in his eyes was any indication, he was already anticipating victory.

Her belly clenching, she reached out to shield her last card with her palm and lifted its corner. Just an inch. Just high enough for her to see the markings. She stared at the yellowed bit of cardboard for what felt like two lifetimes before she looked across the table at Jack again.

Tonight. In Mother Featherlegs's huge bed.

The message was so loud he might have been shouting it for the whole saloon to hear. Slowly, so slowly, Suzanne let the corner of the card feather down.

"Your nines are high, Mr. Sloan."

Hoots, groans and curses filled the air around

her. Suzanne could barely hear the outburst over the buzzing in her ears. Stiffly, she gathered her cards and buried them in the middle of the deck. Pushing away from the table, she rose.

The crowd stumbled back. With a polite goodnight, she made her way to the door.

Jack sat unmoving, staring at the deck for some moments after Suzanne left the saloon. She'd folded a winning pair. He knew it as sure as he knew his own name. But why? What did she have to gain by offering herself as a stake in a poker game, then deliberately losing the hand? She had to have known that he intended to collect the debt she now owed him. He'd put it as plain as he could without saying the words outright. He wanted the payment they talked about back at Ten Mile Station. He wanted her.

What the devil was the woman up to?

The mere fact that he couldn't figure her out made him loco. And the fact that he'd been trying for three days now made him even crazier.

He'd boarded the Deadwood stage with one purpose, and one purpose only. To act as judge, jury and executioner for the man he'd been hunting the past three years. How in hell's name had he ended up as escort for a contrary female and an overgrown farm boy? What had come over him that he'd agree to fork over a good chunk of his roll to buy a Chinese whore, for God's sake?

He knew the answer to that one. Suzanne Bonneaux had come over him. All over him. He couldn't breathe without craving her so bad he hurt. Couldn't close his eyes without seeing her sprawled at his feet, her hair spilling down her back and her legs spread wide. Just thinking about the way she'd feel under him made sweat pop out on his palms.

She knew. She had to have known what she was wagering. She had to know what she'd just lost.

Abruptly, he shoved his chair back. He was done with trying to figure out the woman. Done with wondering just what crazy ideas were swirling around under that mass of silky brown hair. For whatever reason, she'd played her hand the way she'd wanted to, and Jack was going to claim his winnings.

He'd take it slow. Take *her* slow. He intended to savor every inch of her skin, every taste of her mouth and tongue, every nervous flutter of her pulse.

He didn't want her nervous, he decided. He wanted her eager. And hot. And panting.

Christ!

"Looks like you done bought you a whore, Sloan."

He jerked around, fists balling. A red haze rose

behind his eyes before he realized Mother Featherlegs was referring to the Chinese girl.

"Two hundred," she reminded him, her hand outstretched. "Cash."

Scowling, Jack dug into his pocket for his roll. It grew smaller each day he spent in Suzanne Bonneaux's company. He'd have to hire on somewhere to earn more cash after he tracked down Charlie Dawes.

Blowing out a blue cloud, Bess Shephard folded the bills and tucked them into her bodice. "You takin' the Chinee with you when you ride out in the morning?"

"I haven't got around to thinking as far as morning yet."

Hell, he couldn't think past walking out of the saloon, across the yard and stripping Suzanne down to her skin.

"Unless you put the girl up behind the kid, you're gonna need a horse and saddle for her."

His mouth twisted. "Maybe I should just buy a buckboard and haul the whole damn lot of you along to Fort Meade."

"Maybe you should," she agreed, grinning. "It looks to be an interesting trip."

With a grunt, Jack turned and wove his way through the crowd. Once outside, he paused beneath the stars to drag the clean night air into his lungs. Twenty yards away, an oil lamp flickered behind the curtains of Mother Featherlegs's sod hut. Jack caught the movement of a shadowy figure and went tight below the belt.

He started forward, only to freeze as the door opened and Matt Butts rushed out.

"Mr. Sloan! I want to talk to you."

"Do you?"

"Suzanne just told me you put up the money for Ying Li."

"Did she?"

Jack eyed him warily. Young and inexperienced though he was, Matt had set himself up as Suzanne's protector. But if he was thinking to get between Jack and the woman in that sod hut, he'd best think again.

"Suzanne said something about interest. Whatever it is, I'll pay it and gladly."

Jack didn't think so.

"You can work out any payments you want with Suzanne when you get your stake. In the meantime, she's covering the debt."

"I know." Matt grabbed his hand and pumped it. "Thank you! You won't regret this."

"Not for a few hours, anyway," he drawled, flicking a glance at the lighted window.

The kid pumped his hand again and hurried off, eager to make Ying Li understand that she was now free to decide her own future. Jack couldn't see that her future looked to be much different

from her past, but figured both Matt and the girl
would find that out soon enough. Right now, it was
his own immediate future that interested him.

Suzanne took her time answering his knock,
plenty long enough for Jack to wonder if she was
going to answer at all. He knocked again, and
didn't realize he was holding his breath until she
opened the door.

She wasn't wearing her Miss Prim look, the one
that got him all itchy and irritated, but neither did
she have on anything close to a smile. With the
red silk clinging to her skin beneath her little blue
jacket, just looking at her doubled the ache below
his belt. He'd take this slow, he reminded himself
savagely, almost desperately.

The flickering light of the oil lamp must have
reflected his thoughts. With a quick, hard swallow,
she stepped back to allow him entry. The fire in
his blood cooled a few degrees when he saw the
spots of color in her cheeks. Drawing rein on his
clamoring urge to tumble her down to the floor and
have her then and there, Jack curled a knuckle under her chin and tipped her face to his.

"Having second thoughts?"

"Second, third and fourth."

"You planning to renege on our bet?"

"Would you let me?"

He drew his thumb along her lower lip, testing
the slick wet flesh just inside.

"Not this time, sweetheart. You knew the stakes. You gambled. You folded your hand."

She trembled then, just the way he'd imagined she would. "Yes, I knew the stakes."

Every inch of him was coiled tight, ready to crush her against him. But this time he didn't plan on taking. This time he planned on getting.

"Time to settle up, *Miss* Bonneaux."

Jack didn't have any idea what he'd do if she balked. She'd nailed him the other night at Ten Mile Station. For all his hard talk and lethal skill with a Colt, he couldn't hurt her if he tried. But he wanted her. Lord, he wanted her. So bad he had to hold himself stiff and straight as a new oak when she cocked her head and regarded him warily with those cinnamon-brown eyes.

"I'd like to discuss the...the method of settling up with you."

His thumb stilled. "What's to discuss?"

"Well, I thought perhaps I might pay the interest out in installments."

"You want to trot that by me again?"

"You know. Like one of Mr. Greenleaf's watches. You pay for part of it now, pay the rest the next time he comes through. Then the watch is yours."

Alarm skittered down Jack's spine, dousing a bit of the fire heating his blood. He was talking one night, one hot, fast tumble to satisfy the craving she stirred in him. It sounded to him that she was talking something else altogether.

"You didn't say anything about installments when we set the stakes."

"I know."

She looked away. Pink feathered her cheeks. When she looked up at him, he saw her throat work, as if she had to force the words up and out.

"It's only a few hours to dawn. You said you wanted to ride out at first light. That doesn't give us time to, er, pay the interest in full."

Despite the tight kink in his belly, Jack felt a grin start. "I hate to be the one to tell you this, *Miss* Bonneaux, but what I have in mind doesn't usually take a few hours."

"How...how very unfortunate." Her chin still resting on his knuckle, she looked him square in the eye. "What I have in mind, Mr. Sloan, will take all night."

The grin fell right off his face. She was bluffing! She had to be bluffing. He'd bet every last cent in his pocket that demure, dainty Miss Bonneaux didn't have the foggiest notion how long it took a woman to service a man and vice versa.

Or did she?

She'd told Jack her stepfather was a cavalry officer. She couldn't have grown to womanhood without some understanding of what went on at the cribs and hurdy-gurdy houses that sprang up like weeds around army posts.

Or could she?

The uncertainty ate at him. Damn the woman! He couldn't figure her out to save his soul, and his was a soul that surely needed saving. Nor could he shake the suspicion that she'd been stringing him along since she dealt the first card.

To hell with it! He was done with being strung.

"All right. We'll do this your way." Scooping her into his arms, he started for the muslin curtain that divided the parlor from the back room. "I'll take the first installment now."

Startled by her abrupt shift from vertical to horizontal, she grabbed at his neck. "Don't you think we need to discuss the exact terms first?"

"We'll negotiate them out as we..." He stopped, his jaw dropping. "What is that?"

Disbelieving, he stared at the monstrous bed. Suzanne shifted in his arms and followed along as he took in the gaudy paint and four snarling creatures.

"Mother Featherlegs got it from Ying Li's father when she bought the girl."

"Good Lord!" A horrible thought occurred to Jack. "We didn't just buy it back along with the girl, did we?"

"No. At least, I don't think so. Although..." Her gaze went back to the massive piece. "It would make an excellent trousseau for Ying Li. Something for her to take with her into her new life.''

Jack kept his doubts about Ying Li's new life to himself. The girl hadn't looked to him as if she had the spine to make a new start, but she was the last of his concerns at the moment. Striding over to the bed, he opened his arms. Suzanne landed on the straw mattress in a whirl of blue serge and bare legs.

His heart jumped straight into his throat. She wasn't wearing her drawers! God help him, she wasn't wearing anything under her skirt at all.

His hands went straight for the buckle on his gun belt.

10

At the thump of Jack's gun against the bedpost, Suzanne's heart skipped a beat. The look in his eyes when he hooked the belt over the dog's outstretched paw killed any thought that she could negotiate the terms of her surrender.

Any thought that she *wanted* to negotiate flew right out of her head when he leaned over her. Bending a knee on the straw mattress, he slid a palm under her hair, pulled her forward and brought his mouth down on hers.

On a surprised reflex, Suzanne jerked away.

"I still feel you," she said breathlessly, feathering her fingers against her lips. "From before."

In that moment, everything changed for Jack. He wanted this woman so bad he ached all the way down to his boot heels. He'd come after her, fully intending to take what she'd staked on the turn of the cards, but he'd cut off his hand before he'd bruise her soft flesh.

"I'm sorry," he said gruffly. "I didn't mean to hurt you."

He started to straighten, intending to end matters, but she hooked a hand around his neck. Face flushed, eyes bright as stars, she brushed her lips along his.

"I was just surprised. It's all right. Truly."

"You sure?"

"I'm sure."

So sure, Suzanne thought she might die if he didn't claim the first installment. She stretched upward, curled both arms around his neck, took more, gave more.

He tasted of whiskey and tobacco, smelled of smoke and leather. Her mouth opened, and her tongue flicked against teeth and slick, smooth flesh. Arching her back, she dragged him down with her.

They landed in a tangle on the rustling mattress. He braced his weight on his arms to keep from crushing her into the straw, but Suzanne wasn't interested in such noble restraint. Not for the moment, anyway. She wanted crushing. Her whole body ached for the feel of his pressing hard on hers. She clutched at his shoulders, urging him down.

"I don't want to hurt you," he said again, resisting while he trailed kisses from her mouth to her chin to her throat.

"You're not. You are most definitely not hurting... Oh!"

With a little gasp, she bucked at the feel of his hand sliding under her jacket to close over a silk-covered breast.

"Easy, darlin'." His voice was low, his breath hot in her ear. "We'll take this slow and easy."

He might intend to take it slow and easy. Suzanne was about to crawl out of her skin. His palm felt hot through the thin silk; his fingers were skilled on her soft, mounded flesh. When the nipple drew up into a tight, hard bud, Jack teased it first with his hand, then, pushing apart the silk, with his mouth and teeth and tongue.

Suzanne's head went back against the heavily scented sheets. Eyes closed, she fought a moan as he peeled her jacket and the borrowed robe off her shoulders. With an arm under her waist, he lifted her up just enough to shove the bunched material down her arms, leaving both breasts bare and quivering.

The thought buzzed around in the back of her head that it was time to call a halt. Past time. She'd staked everything she had, everything she was desperately coming to want, on the turn of a card. Following her instincts, she'd played to Jack's pair of nines. He'd won that hand, but Suzanne fully intended to win the next.

Or that was her plan until Jack's rough whisper penetrated her whirling thoughts.

"You're so beautiful. Soft and smooth. Like thick, new-skimmed cream."

His weight lay heavy on her now, pinning her to the mattress. Somehow his knee had slipped between hers. With a flash of heat, Suzanne remembered the way she'd ridden his thigh earlier this evening. Her belly clenched in anticipation of the same hard pressure, the same rocking, dizzying, delicious sensation.

The stubble on his cheeks and chin scraped her skin as he trailed kisses to her throat, the hollow between her shoulder and neck, her breast.

When he found a tight, hard nipple, streaks of pleasure shot straight to her belly. Toes curling, Suzanne marveled at the extraordinary sensations.

So this was what caused women to shed their virtue like old cloaks! These sweet, shivery bursts of delight. They heated her skin, set fire to her senses. Instead of protesting when Jack shifted his attentions from one breast to the other, she arched her back and offered herself eagerly.

Deliberately, she closed her mind to the shrieks of her conscience. The Misses Merriweather would faint dead away if they could see their star pupil stripped to the waist, with Jack Sloan's stubbled cheeks dark against her pale breasts. She refused to even imagine her mother's reaction. Or the colonel's! All she could think about, all she cared about, was the feel of Jack's callused palm and the hot wash of his breath on her skin.

He was good at this, damn him! Too good. He knew just how to plump her tingling flesh, just when to stroke and when to suckle. With wicked deliberation, he alternated between slow, sensual tugs and sharp little nips. Suzanne thought she'd go mad, was sure she'd burst into a thousand pieces. The scrape of his teeth on her nipple caused a starburst of sensation that hovered between pleasure and pain.

She wanted more. Her body craved it. Squirming, she tried to work free of the twisted silk, wanting to touch him the way he was touching her. Wanting him to touch more than just her breasts.

It was then that she realized how close she'd come to total abandonment. Almost weeping with regret, she croaked out a plea.

"Enough." Her voice was so low and hoarse she scarcely recognized it. "Jack, please."

He raised his head and stared down at her. His gray eyes glittered behind his lashes.

"This..." She gulped in a shuddering breath. "This is enough for the first installment."

"Is it?"

His body felt rock hard every place it indented

hers. Red tinged his cheekbones above the dark stubble. Sudden doubts shivered through Suzanne. Would he heed her plea? Did she really want him to?

"Let me up."

He didn't move. Hampered by his weight, Suzanne couldn't move, either. She felt a flutter of panic, quickly come and just as quickly gone. He wouldn't force her. Not Jack. But the fact that she couldn't tell what he was thinking behind that intent look made her decidedly nervous.

"Let me up," she said again, more firmly.

"In a minute. First I want to know why you folded your hand."

"What?"

"You won that poker hand tonight, Suzanne. Why did you fold?"

Her head whirled. Here she was, sprawled under the man, as near to naked as didn't matter. Her skin still burned where his cheek had scraped it. Her nipples ached from his kisses. She'd had to fight with everything in her against the urge to give herself to him, and all the time he'd been thinking about the cards?

"What makes you think I won?" she asked, more than a little piqued.

"I've played a few hands of stud poker over the years. You dealt yourself a pair of aces, then changed your mind and tossed in your hand. Why, Suzanne?''

He was guessing. He had to be guessing. She could still brazen this out.

''Really!'' It was difficult to infuse both disdain and disbelief into her voice with her bare breasts still quivering, but Suzanne managed both. ''Are you implying that I cheated?''

''I'm not implying anything. I'm stating a fact.''

''I refuse to discuss the matter with you until you let me up.''

''Tell me.''

She put a huff in her voice. ''This is absurd! What in heaven's name makes you think I cheated?''

''A person doesn't ask for the shuffle unless they want a feel for the cards before the cut. You won the cut, and you dealt yourself the hand you wanted. Why did you throw it in?''

''What difference does it make what I threw in. You won, didn't you?''

''No, I didn't. You lost. On purpose. Why, Suzanne?''

''Oh, for pity's sake!'' Exasperated, irritated and rather embarrassed now, she tipped her chin. ''Let me up, Jack. I refuse to discuss this or any other matter in such an…an undignified position.''

''You didn't think it so undignified a few

minutes ago,'' he pointed out, quite unnecessarily, she thought.

Thankfully, he eased his weight to one side so she didn't have to respond to that particularly ill-bred comment. Disdaining his assistance, she scrambled off the bed and jerked her twisted garments into some semblance of order. When Jack rose as well, she eyed him with a mix of wariness and indignation.

"May I remind you, sir, you were the one who proposed the table stakes in the first place?"

"I don't need reminding. What I need to know is why you appeared so willing to pay them, or why you thought to do it with this crazy idea of installments."

Heat warmed Suzanne's cheeks. She wasn't sure she herself understood the insane impulse that had led her to agree to the outrageous stakes, much less throw in her hand. Her promise to help Matt and Ying Li was part of it, of course, but only part. The real reason, the overriding reason, stood before her.

She'd gambled on Jack. She was still gambling on Jack. Taking her courage in both hands, she tried to express her jumbled thoughts.

"We seem to…to strike sparks off each other. I've felt them, and so have you."

He didn't deny it. He couldn't, after what had just happened between them. Drawing in a long, tremulous breath, she reached out and laid a palm against his cheek.

"Those sparks could burn us...or ignite the kind of sure, steady flame that gives both warmth and light."

For a moment, a mere second or two, Suzanne thought she saw something that might have been understanding or agreement or hope in his eyes. It was gone before she could decide which, and a familiar look came over his face. She recognized that cold, flat expression now. It was the one he pulled on whenever she got too close.

Grabbing her wrist, he yanked it down. "Get this straight. All I was playing for was a roll between the sheets with a prime piece of woman-flesh."

Her cheeks burned at hearing him put it in such blunt terms, but she held her ground. "If that's all you wanted, why didn't you take your *roll* tonight?"

When he had her so hot and eager.

The words hung in the air between them, unspoken but as plain as if Suzanne had shouted them.

"I'll take it when I'm good and ready," he shot back, "but I want to make sure you understand a few things first."

"What things?"

His fingers tightened cruelly. "Don't be mistaking these sparks flying between us, sweetheart. You've raised a heat in me, I admit it. It's like a fiery itch just under my skin, one that needs a good scratching. But that's all it is.''

She wasn't letting him off the hook that easily. Her eyes flashing, she shook her head.

''It's more than that, Jack. You know it is. It is for me, anyway.''

He made a rude sound. His mouth curled downward in a way Suzanne had come to hate.

''Are you trying to say you've tumbled boots over bustle in love with me?''

''No, of course not. We hardly know each other. But they're there, Jack. Whatever caused them, the sparks are there. Who knows what they might lead to if we...''

''There's only one place they *can* lead. Don't try to dress this up in fine feathers, Suzanne. Women like you don't set up housekeeping with gunfighters. You're intrigued, maybe. Fascinated, even, by the aura of danger that comes with men like me. You want a taste of the danger, a little thrill on the side, but that's all you want.''

''Indeed?'' she said frigidly.

''Yes, *indeed*. You're not the first lady to send me sideways glances, and certainly not the first female to wonder if the piece I carry between my legs matches the size and firepower of the one strapped to my thigh.''

Suzanne pursed her lips, considered all possible replies and came up with only one.

"Hooah!"

His brows slashed down. "What did you say?"

"That, sir, is the biggest pile of hooah I've ever heard."

Silence descended. Forgetting that he still held her wrist in a brutal grip and that her heart was thundering like the twelve-pounders the artillery corps fired during practice session, she stared him down.

"Does that mean what I think it does?" he asked finally.

"Yes."

Cavalry troopers used the old army expression to refer to anything and everything, from a turn on guard mount, to a new commanding officer, to a steaming pile of horse droppings. Suzanne couldn't think of anything more appropriate to describe what Jack was trying to shovel her way. Angry now, she yanked her wrist free.

"You may choose to phrase what's happening between us in vulgar terms if you wish to. You may even deny that it's happening. But that doesn't alter the fact that we both *want* it to."

His answer came back just as hot, just as quick. "Wanting's not enough! Not for you, Suzanne. You deserve more. And I'm trying to tell you, as plain as I know how, you won't get it from me."

Just like that, he capped the head of steam she had building. He was serious, she saw. Dead serious.

"I'm good for exactly what we wagered," he said fiercely. "A nice, sweaty toss in the straw. That's all I can give you. All I can give any woman."

"Why?"

"Jesus!" He shoved his hand through his hair. "I told you! I'm living on borrowed time."

"Who isn't? I survived cholera as a child, Jack, and an attack by murdering mule drivers. I've seen what smallpox can do when it runs through a fort or an Indian village. We're all of us living on borrowed time."

"We're not all walking targets, dammit! Do you know how many drunken wranglers or swaggering bucks have come after me, thinking to prove themselves men by outdrawing Black Jack Sloan? Whoever's with me becomes a target, too, Suzanne. I wouldn't ask any woman to take that risk, even if I wanted to."

She had to know. "*Do* you want to?"

"I'm telling you that what I want doesn't matter two hoots in hell. That's just the way things are."

"Then change the way things are. Stop making yourself a target. Hang up your gun. Walk away from the next man who challenges you."

His jaw worked. "I can't."

"You can't, or you won't?"

"All right, I won't. I've got some unfinished business to take care of first."

"In Deadwood." Suzanne's breath caught. "You're going to Deadwood to shoot it out with someone, aren't you?"

He pulled inside himself, took himself to some place so distant he might have been a thousand miles away instead of just a few inches.

"Tell me," she insisted fiercely.

"His name's Charlie Dawes. I've been tracking him for three years. When I find him, I plan to put a bullet between his eyes."

"Why? Is there a bounty on him?"

"Not that I know of."

"Then why are you hunting him? What did Dawes do to you?"

"To me?" His eyes were as flinty as the granite hills of Dakota Territory. "Nothing."

Fists bunched, Jack kept his arms straight at his sides. He wouldn't reach for her. Wouldn't wipe that look of dawning dismay from her eyes.

He'd told her nothing but the truth. Charlie Dawes hadn't done a damned thing to Jack. He'd stood there, laughing, when one of his friends had laid the butt of his pistol to the head of the struggling, shouting twelve-year-old. Jack had dropped like a stone. He never knew which of the four men had pumped a bullet into his father's forehead, or how many of them had savaged his mother before she choked on her own vomit.

Jack didn't need to know. All four were dead men from the moment he'd piled the last shovelful of dirt on his parents' graves.

Charlie Dawes was the last.

For a moment, only a moment, he let himself think about what came after he left Dawes lying in the street, ready for the undertaker. Once more, his glance went to Suzanne.

No! It couldn't happen. He'd packed iron for so long, he wouldn't know how to walk straight without the Colt tied to his thigh. Even after Dawes, he'd still be Black Jack Sloan. Men would still come looking to test their skill against his, and no woman would want to live with someone who always sat with his back to the wall. No woman like Suzanne, anyway.

When she tipped her chin and pushed her lips together in that disapproving way of hers, he braced himself. He figured he was about to hear his character read back to him in Suzanne's own, ten-dollar words.

"I don't believe you."

He couldn't have been more surprised if that twisting sea snake on the bed behind him had jumped up and taken a bite out of his butt.

"What don't you believe? That I'm going to pump a bullet into Charlie Dawes's skull? I am."

She looked right into him, her eyes so brown and clear Jack had to fight to keep from flinching.

"I don't believe you've been hunting a man for three years for no particular reason. This man might not have hurt you personally, but obviously he did wrong by someone you care about."

Jack felt the hairs on the back of his neck rise straight up. In the space of a few days, this woman had come closer than anyone ever had to guessing at the spur that had dug so deep into his skin and driven him so relentlessly. The fact that she refused to believe he hunted Charlie Dawes in cold blood should have gratified him. Instead, it made him nervous and twitchy as an old dog dreaming new dreams.

"You believe whatever you want," he said roughly.

"I will."

He didn't know if it was her quiet reply, the look in her eyes or the whiskey he'd downed earlier that got to him. Suddenly, he felt so tired his bones wanted to curl up.

"I'm going to grab some sleep for what's left of the night. If you're riding out with me come first light, you'd better do the same."

Retrieving his hat and gun belt from the bedpost, he turned and strode toward the muslin curtain. A moment later, the door rattled shut behind him.

"I'm riding out with you," Suzanne said softly. "I am most definitely riding out with you."

11

Jack woke up feeling as friendly as a grizzly with a broken tooth. The back of his skull pounded as if a blacksmith was in there, going at his business with hammer and tongs. Eyes closed, he grimaced at the clanging and cursed himself for tossing back more than the one or two whiskies he ordinarily downed.

Fragments of the previous night sifted through the hammering in his head. A scarred, pine plank bar. Blue smoke snaking through the saloon. The snick of cards turning over, one by one. The kid rushing across the yard to pump his arm. Suzanne...

He grunted, and the smithy inside his head took another swing at the anvil. Gritting his teeth, Jack squeezed his eyes tight and let the image of Suzanne all tangled up in red silk dance on his lids.

She was still dancing when knuckles rapped

sharply against the door. Wincing, he pried his sandpapery lids open and stared up at the tattered playbill tacked to the wooden ceiling. The faded paper announced a special performance of *The Miner's Daughter,* a melodrama featuring Professor Jonathan Busbee and the sweetheart of the professor's traveling troop, Miss Kathleen Rose O'Bannyon. It took him a moment or two to associate Kathleen with the hurdie who'd died a few months back of a bleeding lung.

"Jack?"

Suzanne pushed the door open. Shards of blinding white light stabbed into his eyes. With another curse, he threw his left arm over his face.

"Mother Featherlegs said you'd bunked down in here. I came to see if you're still alive."

His lips pulled back in a snarl. "I'm not."

"Oh, dear. Feeling the whiskey, are you?"

The last thing he wanted at this moment was sympathy, particularly from the woman who'd landed him in hell and left him there to fry.

"You don't want to know what I'm feeling right now."

Her little *tch-tch* had him grinding his teeth.

"Well, I'm sorry you're not quite yourself, but it's after seven. You said you wanted to ride out at first light."

"I'll ride out when I'm ready. Go away."

"I had our horses saddled and brought around, but we need to talk about…"

"Go away."

"Oh, for pity's sake! Do stop snarling at me like that. It's most annoying."

Bringing down his arm, he shoved off the thin straw mattress. While he waited for the room to stop spinning, two thoughts speared into his brain. The first was that he needed to take a piss something fierce. The second was that the woman standing just inside the door looked a sight different from the fine, feathered miss he'd first run his eyes over aboard the stage.

Her hair hung halfway down her back in a thick braid, with soft, fine tendrils curling seductively about her face. The blue skirt and short blue jacket were the same, if considerably wrinkled, but her dainty shoes had given way to the oversize black boots she'd acquired at Ten Mile Station, and she now wore a sensible calico shirtwaist instead of the frilly, high-necked white blouse. The feathered hat had disappeared completely, replaced by a no-nonsense gray felt slouch with a broad brim and a rawhide thong at the throat. She carried what looked like a canvas duster over one arm, the kind cowboys wore on the range to keep the wind and rain at bay.

She must have borrowed the new items…or bought them with one of her damned promissory notes, Jack thought sourly. At the rate she was going, she'd leave a trail of paper from Ten Mile Station clear to the Cheyenne River.

"If you're done growling," she said with the patience a mother might show a fractious child, "we need to discuss a few matters."

"At this moment, all I care about is filling a slop bucket and then my belly."

She gave a long, fluttery sigh. "Very well. I'll leave you to take care of the first while I confer with Mother Featherlegs about the second. I'll wait for you in the saloon."

"You can wait until hell freezes over," Jack retorted, but the door had already closed.

It wasn't until he'd splashed water over his face, stomped into his boots and buckled on his gun belt that he admitted the truth. He wasn't ready to face Suzanne. Not with his head aching, his belly grumbling, and the memory of her soft, creamy breasts still burning like a brand into his palms.

He should have taken her, he thought savagely. Last night, when she was so hot and eager, he should have ignored all that nonsense about installments, ignored his suspicions that she'd thrown her hand, and taken her. Maybe that would have opened her eyes, or at least rid them of some of the crazy notions swirling around in her head.

He'd warned her, dammit. More than once. Last night, he'd told her flat out what he was, how he lived. She didn't want him. Not deep down. She couldn't.

He wouldn't let her.

Thoughtfully, Suzanne eyed the man who pushed through the door of the saloon. He wore the look of a sore-mouthed horse with the bit between his teeth. He was ready to bolt, and at the least provocation, he would.

"There's biscuits and cold beef," she said calmly, nodding to the plate waiting for him on one of the rickety tables. "Matt and I have already eaten. He's almost finished loading up, by the way."

A sourdough biscuit hovered in the air halfway to Sloan's mouth. "Loading what up?"

"Ying Li's belongings."

"Well, hell. Is she coming with us?"

"Yes, of course. Don't you remember? We talked about it last night?"

"We talked about a lot of things last night, most of them not worth repeating."

He was spoiling for a fight, she guessed. Still wound as tight as she was after their tussle in Mother Featherlegs's bed. He'd taken time to scrape off his bristles and had obtained a clean, button-over black shirt from someone—one of the saloon's customers, she supposed. His hair glistened wet and dark under his hat. With his reddened eyes and tight jaw, he looked lean and mean and too dangerous for anyone with half a brain in their head to cross.

Just the thought made Suzanne's pulse jump. Deliberately, she assumed her primmest manner, knowing it would set his teeth on edge. "Shall I see if Mother Featherlegs has any ammonia? The post surgeon used to mix fifteen grains of ammonia dissolved in water with two teaspoons of spirit of hartshorn to dose the troopers. It generally cured them of the after-effects of inebriation."

It made them sick as dogs first, of course, but after they finished puking up their guts, they were usually judged fit to return to duty.

Sloan must have experienced a similarly drastic remedy in the past. Shooting her a look of acute dislike, he declined the offer in what she considered particularly uncivil terms.

She left him slogging down a mug of black coffee and went outside. Behind the charred remains of the way station, the red rock buttes rose against a dull gray sky. The morning air carried a promise of rain and none of yesterday's sweltering heat, thank goodness. Enjoying the way the breeze lifted the tendrils escaping the fat braid hanging down her back, Suzanne turned her attention to her traveling companion.

Mathias, she decided, looked even worse after his night of debauchery than Jack. Red-eyed and green-gilled, he tugged at the ropes attaching the bundle containing Ying Li's few possessions to his saddle. Ying Li sat on the wooden steps, her hands tucked into her sleeves. Impassively, she watched his progress. Nothing in her expression indicated any particular excitement about the change in her situation.

"I'll go get another saddle blanket and fold it up for you to sit on," Matt told her. "So you kin hold on to me."

"All same…"

"I know, I know. No matter."

He walked away, muttering. Sensing that the young lovers were already experiencing some difficulties, Suzanne tucked her skirts under her and joined Ying Li on the step.

"I'm sorry I couldn't convince Mother Featherlegs to part with the bed she bought from your father."

She studied the girl's broad, flat face, fighting a tug of pity for a childhood lost and a future that seemed to hold so little promise.

"Are you sure you want to go with us? I could make arrangements to send you back to your family."

"Matt Butts say he go, I go, all same together."

"I see."

"You see?" She gave Suzanne a puzzled glance. "Ying Li no see. Matt Butts say Ying Li's cheeks make shame like lamp. If Ying Li make him shame, why he want we go, all same, together?''

''I'm sure I don't... Oh!''

Belatedly, Suzanne recalled her attempt to help Matt with his courting. Obviously, he'd tried out the lines from *Romeo and Juliet* on Ying Li.

Poor Becky.

''I believe he might have been quoting Shakespeare to you. Praising you. Telling you that you're beautiful.''

''Ying Li? Beautiful?'' She gave a delicate snort. ''Matt Butts drunk, only want fuckee-fuck.''

''Yes, well... He's not drunk this morning.''

''Matt Butts like fuckee-fuck,'' the girl said simply. ''Last night, this morning, all same.''

And that, Suzanne thought ruefully, summed up the situation with devastating accuracy. Not only did Matt appear to have discovered the pleasures of the flesh, his overdeveloped sense of chivalry could very well stretch his passionate encounter with Ying Li into a lifelong commitment.

For a moment, she felt almost envious. One tumble, just one, and the Chinese girl had made a conquest. Suzanne still couldn't get Jack to admit that she raised anything more on him than... How did he phrase it? An itch that needed scratching.

He'd certainly tried his best to reduce the hunger that gripped them both to crude, vulgar terms, she thought wryly. Last night, he'd infuriated her. This morning, she could freely admit that what she felt for Black Jack Sloan *was* crude. And vulgar. And so wildly, gloriously exciting that she was determined to see where it would take them.

Not just to a quick roll in the straw. The need was sharper than that, the hunger went deeper. With everything that was female in her, Suzanne needed more. Wanted more. Much more.

Jack Sloan didn't know it yet, but his days as a gunfighter were numbered.

She wasn't sure when she'd decided that. Sometime between their first, shattering kiss and the moment she'd picked up the deck of cards, she supposed. She'd known exactly what she was doing when she accepted the stakes, then proposed paying him the interest in installments.

An expression her family would have instantly recognized settled over her face. *Mulish,* her mother termed it. Her brother, Sam, called it something considerably less polite. Propping her chin on her hands, Suzanne contemplated the charred ruins of the way station across the street.

Jack would take some convincing to hang up his gun. He'd made his feelings plain last night. He'd also made it plain that he had business in Deadwood. Serious business, from the sound of it. Serious enough that someone was going to die. Either this Charlie Dawes he'd talked about or Jack himself.

A shiver rippled down Suzanne's spine. If her own business wasn't so urgent, she'd...she'd...

Do what? Go to Deadwood with him? Put herself between him and the quarry he'd been hunting for three years?

Suzanne wasn't naive. She knew that some men went so bad they deserved hanging or a firing squad. From the little Jack had let drop, she suspected this Charlie Dawes might be one of those men. It was the fact that she wasn't sure that bothered her, and made her realize how little she really knew about the hunter who stalked Dawes.

"Where's the kid?"

The bad-tempered growl brought her and Ying Li around. Jack towered over them, squinting in the gray morning light.

"Matt went to get a blanket for Ying Li to ride on," Suzanne replied. "He's taking her up behind him."

"Hell, he can hardly stay in the saddle himself!"

"Yes, I know, but..."

His bloodshot eyes went to Ying Li, then cut back to Suzanne. "I'm not riding easy. If either one of those two falls off their horse, they'll have to climb back on and catch up. They're not my responsibility."

"I know."

"You, either."

"I know."

There was nothing that tied them to each other except the fire they raised under each other's skin. Nothing!

"Damned fool."

He stomped past, leaving Suzanne to wonder if he was referring to her or Matt or himself.

Surprisingly, neither Matt nor Ying Li parted company with their horse. They even managed to keep up, although Jack was forced to slow the pace considerably, which didn't help his foul temper.

By late morning, the rolling, grassy plains had dropped behind. Ahead loomed the Black Hills of Dakota Territory. It was easy to see where the hills got their name. Blankets of blue spruce and dark, verdant pine covered the slopes, filling the air with the scent of sap and spongy, decaying vegetation.

The road split a few hours out of Rawhide Buttes. The left fork cut a zigzag path north through the wooded hills to Cold Springs, then on to Deadwood Gulch. The right fork wandered more easterly, through lush meadows shadowed by high granite peaks, toward Fort Meade and the Dakota Badlands beyond.

Jack didn't glance at the hand-scrawled sign pointing to Cold Springs, but a scowl settled like a thundercloud on his face. Wisely, Suzanne made no comment. The detour to Fort Meade would take him a good half day out of his way. He'd have to ride another half day back to pick up the road to Deadwood. Five more hours, she thought. Six at the most…if the weather cooperated.

Clouds had piled up in gray, cottony layers, but the wet held off and the going remained easy. Everywhere Suzanne looked, she saw splashes of color: spotted joe-pye weed with its cluster of pink flowers atop the tall purple stem; white and pink primroses fluttering like silk hankies amid the lush grasses; and wild indigo, so deep and true a blue that the flowers looked like lapis beads strung through the meadows.

Every so often they'd spot smoke curling in the distance or pass an isolated cabin. Twice, they exchanged greetings with travelers riding south. For the most part, though, they had the hills, meadows and small, perfect lakes to themselves.

Observing the peaks mirrored in the lakes' shimmering surfaces, Suzanne couldn't help but think the Black Hills beautiful. Of course, she was seeing them at their best. In winter, according to Bright Water, winds shrieked through the canyons, gathering fury with every twisting turn, then burst out onto the reservation at Cheyenne River like white-bearded hounds of hell, blowing snow almost to the tops of the teepees.

Those winds could strike at any time, Suzanne knew. Winter could descend with little or no warning. Bright Water's tribe might already be traveling west, hoping to beat the snows to the Shoshone Reservation. Or they might yet be using the last weeks of summer to hunt and smoke their kill before the long journey. She hoped so. Dear Lord, she hoped so.

A dozen different emotions pulled at her. The need to reach Bright Water, to make a last attempt to convince her friend to bridge the gap between their peoples, warred with concern over Jack and his showdown in Deadwood. Then there was Matt and Ying Li. Despite her fine talk about Matt being old enough to make his own decisions, Suzanne couldn't help wondering if he'd made the right one in this particular instance.

He looked so miserable, with his red eyes and pasty white face. He managed to stay in the saddle, although his legs wobbled like wet rope each time they dismounted to walk the horses. Manfully, he hid his grimaces as he lifted Ying Li down. For her part, the girl said little, replying with a shrug to whatever question or comment was put to her. Not until they stopped beside one of the small, sparkling lakes to graze the horses and prepare a noon meal of bacon and beans did she assert herself. Squatting down on her heels, she took over the frying pan.

"Ying Li cook. Missee, Mister Jack water horses. Matt Butts, you sit. Ground hard, saddle hard, all same."

"I'll help with the horses," he insisted.

"You sit." Suzanne echoed Ying Li's singsong order with a smile. "Ground hard, saddle hard, all same."

Her smile won the day. Biting back a groan, Matt lowered himself gingerly and propped his head in his hands. He'd hurt bad enough this morning, when he'd peeled back his eyelids and tried to swallow the fur fuzzing his throat. The past few hours had added a whole new set of aches to the ones he'd collected yesterday and last night.

Last night.

Another groan rose in his throat. Guilt beat at him with the rapaciousness of a buzzard pecking at his eyeballs. Guilt, and a swift, stomach-clenching hunger. As quick as that, he got hard.

He lifted his head and snuck a peek at Ying Li. He still couldn't quite believe that he...that she...that they...

Sweat popped out on his brow. He was a sinner. A fornicator. His mam would burn with shame if she knew what her youngest had done last night. She'd burn even more if she knew how much he wanted to do it again. And again. He hurt all over just thinking about it.

He'd have to find a preacher as soon as he could.

It wasn't right, him doing those kind of things with Ying Li, even if she was a hurdie. No, not even a hurdie. Just a whore.

He cringed a bit at the idea of taking her home and showing her off to his mam and pa. Even more at the idea of introducing her to Becky. Then he remembered that he wasn't going home. He was heading for San Francisco, or wherever his fancy took him once he struck it rich in the gold fields.

He'd take Ying Li with him. He'd find a preacher, have him say the words, then take her with him to the gold fields *and* to San Francisco. She could help with the sluicing and panning. Once they panned a bag full of gold, he'd buy her a new dress, one that didn't hang on her like that soiled calico blouse and tattered skirt. Some decent shoes, too, so she didn't teeter and stumble as if she was about to fall over all the time.

"Here," he mumbled, embarrassed by his sudden, rampaging lust for this woman. "Let me fry the bacon."

"Matt Butts sit. Ying Li cook."

"You gotta be as sore as me," he said gruffly. "You sit and I'll finish the cookin'."

She stared at him, as if astounded at the idea that she should take her ease while a man did women's work, then lifted her shoulders in a shrug.

12

"Looks like you've lost your beau."

The dry remark brought Suzanne's head up. She paused in the act of loosening the chestnut's girth and followed Jack's gaze to the couple sitting some yards away.

"Looks like I have," she agreed.

Ying Li perched on one of the boulders lining the shore of the tiny lake, her hands tucked into her sleeves. Matt crouched beside the cook fire. It hadn't taken him long to relieve Ying Li of cooking duties, Suzanne saw. He really was a kind soul. Too kind, perhaps.

They made such a contrast, she thought, as she reached up to scratch the chestnut's ears. Ying Li with her long, ink-black braid draped over one shoulder, Matt with his unruly gold curls. He was almost twice her size, as big and gawky as she was small and delicate. Their differences were more than physical, of course. They came from such disparate backgrounds, looked on the world with such different eyes.

As did she and Jack.

Her gaze drifted to the gunfighter. He was bent over, checking the shoe on the big roan he'd purchased from the Express company. His shoulders strained the seams of the black shirt. The sorrel leather vest molded his back and ribs. If she ignored the long-barreled Colt strapped to his thigh, she might have imagined him just another cowboy tending to his mount.

She gave the chestnut a final pat and picked her way through the boulders to the water's edge. The lake was as clear as glass, without a single ripple to disturb its surface. For a moment, Suzanne entertained the fancy that she was suspended in some nether region. Gray, scudding clouds and towering pines above, the same gray clouds and dark pines below.

Boot heels rattled on the stone behind her, and Jack's image joined hers in the mirrored surface. Like Suzanne, he appeared caught between earth and sky. She felt the most ridiculous wish they could remain suspended, just the two of them, alone with the quiet and primordial pines. Without Matt and Ying Li. Without her worries over Bright Water, or what would happen when Jack found the man he hunted. Only for a few days. A few hours, even.

Then Jack hunkered down on his heels to wash his hands, and their twin images washed away in a wave of ripples. Sighing, Suzanne knelt and plunged her hands in the cool water, as well. After patting them dry with a fold of her skirt, she claimed a boulder and watched Jack skim a flat rock across the lake's surface. It skipped three times before sinking. More ripples circled from each spot where it hit the water.

"I'm impressed," she said. "There's an art to skipping stones, or so my brother, Sam, informs me. I never could get one to fly."

"It's all in the wrist."

"That's what Sam says."

Jack sent another flat, flinty rock across the lake. This one bounced four times. "How old is this brother of yours?"

"He's just turned nine."

"That explains some things."

"What things?"

"I wondered about your menfolk. Seemed strange that they'd let you travel on your own through Indian and outlaw country."

"I expect my stepfather might have raised some objection," she admitted, "if he'd been home at the time. My mother tried to convince me to wait until he returned from patrol, but the situation is entirely too urgent.''

"Urgent how?''

"Are you aware that the Bureau of Indian Affairs has decided to move the Northern Arapaho from their reservation along the White River?''

"No.'' Propping a boot on the boulder next to hers, he hooked his wrists over his bent knee. "Where are they sending them?''

"The Powder River Reservation.''

"Powder River, over to Montana Territory? That's Shoshone country.''

"I know.''

"Why the devil would the bureau force old enemies onto the same reservation? They tried that once, back in '69, and it didn't work.''

"I don't completely understand the politics involved, only that the Dakota Territorial delegation convinced Congress and the president that the Arapaho had to be moved or they'll remain a threat to the miners and settlers.''

"The delegation heard reports of gold in the White River region, more like,'' Jack said cynically. "They want the Arapaho out of the way.''

"I suspect you may be right. All I know for sure is that many of the tribes have already begun their trek west. The few that remain plan to leave before the snows fall.''

"You still haven't told me why the Arapaho are any concern of yours."

"I tried to," she reminded him. "Back at Ten Mile Station. But you weren't in the mood to listen."

"I'm listening now."

"I have a friend at White River, a woman I've known since childhood. Her father was an army scout. We were as close as sisters once."

Her gaze drifted to the gray clouds painted on the surface of the lake. Memories of the hours she and Bright Water had spent together crowded in on her. They were such happy times...until drunken mule drivers had raped and murdered Bright Water's mother and Suzanne's own father had died saving his daughter from abduction.

"I knew her as Little Hen when we were children, before she took the woman-name of Bright Water. After her mother was killed, she went to live with her father's people. We visited each other often, and kept in touch by letter when I was at school back East. I can't just let her disappear into the Powder River Reservation."

"Sounds to me like that's her decision to make, not yours."

Suzanne's mother had made the same point. Rather forcefully, in fact.

"You don't understand. Bright Water is a healing woman. She's quite skilled with the remedies of her own people, and has spent countless hours working alongside the army surgeons assigned to treat the various tribes. I showed some of her letters to a physician in Philadelphia and he suggested she come East to study with him.''

''Ha! You hounded the hell out of the man until he agreed to your scheme, you mean.''

''What makes you think it was my idea?''

''I've been riding with you for three days, woman. I've learned a few of your ways.''

All right, Suzanne *had* hounded the man unmercifully, until he'd snarled at her to send the damned squaw back East. Jack Prendergast was rather a gruff sort, she reflected, not unlike Jack himself, with some sort of black cloud hanging over his past. The Misses Merriweather would never speak of it, but neither instructress could deny Prendergast was the finest physician in the city.

''The fact is,'' Jack said bluntly, ''you're as stubborn as that rock you're sitting on and too damned headstrong for your own or anyone else's good. I doubt you gave this doctor two minutes of peace until he fell in with this crazy plan.''

''Indeed?''

''Indeed,'' he mimicked. ''My guess is he's only one of a long string of tormented males who would dearly love to turn you over their knee.''

''I'm sure there were some who entertained such

thoughts,'' she conceded with a sugary smile, then patted her skirt pocket. "Perhaps my little Remington convinced them how unwise it would be to try.''

"How good are you with that thing?''

"Not as good as you are with the Colt, I would imagine, but I generally hit what I'm aiming at.''

"That time after the holdup, when you stuck the barrel between my ribs. Would you have pulled the trigger?''

"Yes.''

He studied her for long moments, then slowly shook his head.

"You don't believe me?''Suzanne asked.

"I believe you. But I'm damned if I can figure you out. One day, you're pursed up like a prune and all set to put a bullet through my lungs. The next, you're folding a winning poker hand and inviting me into your bed.''

Heat rose in her cheeks. "You don't know that I folded a winning hand.''

"Did you?''

She maintained a dignified silence.

"Did you, Suzanne?''

"You're like a hungry coyote with a chicken,'' she said, exasperated. "Tell me, Jack. Do you really intend to take me to Fort Meade and ride off without making any attempt to collect what I still owe you in interest?''

"Yes."

"Hooah!"

She left him skipping rocks, most of which, she noted with satisfaction, sank after the first bounce.

The skies opened in midafternoon.

Suzanne pulled on the canvas duster she'd purchased with a promissory note from one of Mother Featherlegs's customers, but the rain pelted her face and dripped from her hat brim down the back of her neck. Their small cavalcade was forced to huddle under a stand of trees until the drenching downpour finally let up. By that time the dirt track had turned to mud and the going was considerably slower.

A little more than an hour later, they caught the distant jingle of bridles, followed by the thud of horses' hooves on the road behind them. Suzanne's first thought was that it was a mounted troop, perhaps come in search of her. Her stepfather would have returned from patrol by now and heard about the holdup. He might have wired the post commander at Fort Meade, requesting he send a squad to provide her escort.

A patrol would have been coming down the road ahead, though, from the fort. Not from behind. A number of other possibilities flashed into her mind, not all of them reassuring. She didn't need Jack's urging to turn the chestnut off the road and head into a stand of pine. Matt followed, with Ying Li hunched against his back like a sodden kitten. Dismounting, Jack dragged fallen branches over the grass the horses had churned up. He barely made it to their hiding spot behind the thick stand of pines before a group of riders galloped around the bend in the road.

Jack identified them first. With a muttered curse, he reached down and twitched off the scrap of saddle blanket he'd used to keep the Colt dry.

"Who is it?"

Almost as soon as she'd whispered the question, Suzanne had her answer. Even if she hadn't recognized the leader's thick black mustaches and swarthy complexion, there was no mistaking his prominent beak.

"Big Nose Parrott," Matt exclaimed.

"In the flesh," Jack confirmed grimly.

"Why is he riding for Fort Meade? He must know the soldiers will shoot him on sight."

"He's probably going to cut east and head for the Badlands. Word is he holes up there."

Suzanne knew that the bandit could hide forever among the twisting canyons and dry gulches that formed the Badlands of the Dakota Territory. Her pulse tripping, she watched the stage robbers gallop toward them.

"They're certainly in a hurry to get back to their hideout," she murmured.

"Too much of a hurry," Jack said, his eyes narrowed.

"Do you think someone's chasing them? A posse, perhaps?"

"Could be. We'd best stay where we are for a while until we know for sure."

The outlaws were bent low in their saddles. Mud flew from their horses' hooves as they thundered past. Suzanne had just let out a ragged sigh of relief when the lead rider suddenly reined in. She recognized him from the holdup. It was the one with the crossed bandoliers and wide-brimmed hat banded with silver conchos.

The others pulled up, milling about in a loose circle while he dismounted and walked a few yards farther down the road. Kneeling, he examined the muddy track. After a moment or two, he rose and shook his head.

Jack cursed, low and long. "They're not being chased. They're tracking someone or something."

"Us?" Matt asked with a gulp.

"Your guess is as good as mine, kid."

The dismounted outlaw gestured as he gazed back along the road. Big Nose twisted in his saddle, searching behind him. He said something to his men and brought his mount's head around. Slowly, the gang began to retrace its way.

Suzanne's stomach constricted. It wouldn't take the robbers long to find where they'd left the road.

Their horses' hooves had sunk too deep into the rain-softened earth for Jack to completely cover them.

"Should we make a run for it?" she asked softly.

He flicked a glance over his shoulder at the wooded slope behind them, then at the young couple on the dappled gray.

Suzanne guessed what he was thinking even before he shook his head. Neither Matt nor Ying Li was a good enough rider to make it up that steep slope without tumbling right out of the saddle. For the same reason, they couldn't risk breaking cover and trying to outrun the outlaws.

That left only two options. Let Big Nose find them, or retreat deeper behind the trees and shoot it out. With her double-barreled derringer and Jack's six-shooter against eight or nine heavily armed men, the options narrowed down to one.

"What do you propose?" she asked quietly. "Should we wait for them to spot the tracks, or ride out of the trees now?"

"I propose you three stay right where you are, keep your mouths shut and let me handle things." His glance went from her to Ying Li, hardening when it lit on Matt. "You got that, kid? Let me handle things."

Matt nodded, but his glance was worried. Big Nose and his men hadn't shown any indication they intended to molest Suzanne during the bungled holdup attempt, but then, they'd hardly had time to show their true colors before the bullets started flying and the stage horses bolted. Who knew what the robbers might do to her this time? Or to a young Chinese girl? More to the point, what dangerous risks would Matt take if he felt compelled to shield her and Ying Li?

And what risks would Jack take? He'd thrown her down in the dirt and covered her body with his the last time they'd encountered Big Nose and his gang. What did he plan this time?

A sick feeling curled in Suzanne's belly. "You're not going to do something foolish, are you? Like try to take them all down yourself? Jack, you won't...?"

"Quiet!"

Swallowing her sudden, gut-twisting fear for the man beside her, she peered through the pine boughs. Big Nose and his men had backtracked almost to where the three horses had plunged into the woods. Suzanne held her breath, praying they'd miss the churned-up grass and leaves, knowing they wouldn't.

When the bandoliered outlaw swung out of his saddle and kicked aside the branches Jack had dragged over their tracks, the sick feeling in her stomach congealed into a hard, tight ball.

"Here!" he called to the others. "They took to the woods here!"

Through the screen of branches, Suzanne saw the men whip out rifles and pistols. Her own hand slid into her skirt pocket.

"Stay here," Jack ordered fiercely. "Don't come out unless I tell you."

"All right, boys," Big Nose was ordering. "Let's go in after 'em. Alejandro, you 'n Pete swing left. Me 'n Curly here will...."

He broke off, whipping around at the sound of a branch cracking. When the big roan picked its way out of the trees, every outlaw had his gun aimed at Jack's chest.

"Well, hell, Sloan! You near 'bout got yerself punched full of holes."

Calmly, Jack rested one hand on the pommel, the other held the Colt steady. "So did you, Big Nose. Care to explain why you're tracking me?"

"Well, now, we are and we aren't. It's the girl we're after. We heared she's riding with you."

"How'd you hear that?"

"Curly here was hanging around Custer City after the holdup," Big Nose explained. "Word came down the telegraph line 'bout you and Miss Bonneaux walkin' back to Ten Mile Station. So Curly come to find me, and we come for her."

"Why? You got her purse and her luggage. What do you want with her?"

"Well, it's like this. There weren't no more 'n five hundred dollars in the strongbox, a good sight less 'n that in the bags we picked through. The girl's worth at least that much. More. The way I figure it, Colonel Garrett will pay real sweet to get her back."

"Garrett? Andrew Garrett?"

"Hell, man, didn't you know you done took up with the daughter of the meanest horse soldier that ever rode?"

Enjoying the fact that he had one up on Sloan, Big Nose elaborated with some glee.

"It was Garrett who hunted down Spotted Tail years back. Brung him 'n a whole passel of his braves to Fort Laramie in chains. Took all the fight right out of the Ogalalla Sioux with that one raid, he did."

Suzanne could have told him that wasn't the way it had happened at all. But it *was* true that her stepfather had convinced Chief Spotted Tail to make peace against all odds. As a result, the colonel had caught the fancy of the Eastern press and his reputation as an Indian fighter and frontiersman had grown to gargantuan proportions.

Parrott obviously placed great faith in the written word. "If you've messed with Garrett's girl," he predicted cheerfully, "he'll string you up by your heels, carve out yer liver and eat it raw, with you watchin' the whole time."

"He'll do the same to anyone who kidnaps her and holds her against her will," Jack pointed out.

"Hell, we ain't gonna hurt her none, less'n we have to. We'll just take her to the Badlands with us 'n keep her fer a while, till her pa comes up with the cash."

The affability faded from his voice.

"Tell her to come outta the trees, Sloan, or we'll go in 'n get her."

13

Suzanne didn't wait for Jack to call for her.

She didn't dare.

So far, Parrott hadn't mentioned Matt or Ying Li. Maybe the outlaw didn't know about the other two. Maybe he didn't care. She couldn't take the chance.

"Stay here," she hissed. "If you get away and make it to Fort Meade, go straight to the commander and tell him what happened."

"Jack said to let him handle things," Matt reminded her in an agonized whisper.

"I'm the one they want. They'll shoot him to get to me."

"But...!"

He made a grab for her reins but Suzanne jerked them out of his reach. Digging her heels into the chestnut's sides, she shouted a warning.

"I'm coming out!"

Bending, she dodged the low-hanging branches and cleared the trees. When she took the gelding down the grassy slope and drew up beside Jack, ice had formed in his eyes. The look he gave Suzanne sliced right through her skin, flaying her to the bone.

She'd hear about this, she guessed. Later. Right now, her main concern was leading Big Nose and his gang away from Matt and Ying Li.

"I heard what you said," she told the outlaw.

"'Bout holding you for ransom?"

She dipped her head in a regal nod. "You know, of course, that if you persist in this foolish scheme, the colonel will cut you into bite-size pieces and feed you to the crows."

Big Nose grinned. "He'll have to catch me first, missy. Every lawman and blue-belly in three territories been searchin' for George Parrott for a good ten years. No one's caught up with me yet."

"You haven't had Andrew Garrett on your trail."

"Well, I have 'n I haven't. He sent a patrol after me once, when we hit a train down south of Fort Laramie. We got away, but me 'n the boys run four good horses into the ground while we was doin' it." Still grinning, he gave her a once-over. "You look a sight different from the last time we seed you."

"Indeed?"

Her frigid accent and tightly pursed lips had considerably more impact on the outlaw than they did on Jack. Hastily, he assured her he meant no disrespect.

"It's not that you ain't pretty as any picture. It's just that hat..." He waved a hand at the floppy gray felt. "And them boots..."

"If you've quite finished discussing my raiment, Mr. Parrott, may we please proceed? I should like to get this unpleasant matter done with as quickly as possible and continue my journey."

"Lordy, how you do talk! All right, we'll proceed. Alejandro, grab aholt of the lady's reins. We don't want her deciding to make a run for it, now, do we?"

Deliberately, Jack kneed the roan and put it between Suzanne and the Mexican.

"She's not going anywhere I don't go, Parrott."

"Now, hold on, Sloan! This here ransom was my idea. Why should I cut you in?"

"Because she's riding with me. I've got first claim on her." Casually, Jack thumbed back the hammer on the Colt. "And I'll put a bullet in anyone who thinks different."

Parrott's eyes narrowed above his bushy black mustache. "You can't take us all. One of my men will surely to goodness get you."

"One of them surely will, but when I go down, you go with me, George."

Suzanne's heart banged against her ribs. Every bit of air squeezed out of her lungs as the seconds stretched interminably. Slowly, so slowly, she let the reins slip through her fingers and inched her hand into her skirt pocket, already planning her shot.

When Big Nose let out a booming laugh and tipped up his pistol barrel, she could have wept with relief.

"I ain't ready to eat lead yet, Sloan. Not as ready as you are, anyway. Tell you what. You and the little lady come along friendly-like, and I'll give you a share of the takin's. That way, no one gets hurt."

The click when Jack released the hammer and let it down was as loud as a rifle shot. When the rest of the outlaws followed Parrott's gruff order and holstered their weapons, Suzanne felt every ounce of starch go out of her. Boneless with relief, she had to clutch the pommel to keep from sliding right out of the saddle.

"Well, missy, how much do you think we should ask for you?"

"I beg your pardon?"

"I have to send a couple of men back to collect yer ransom. I'm thinking maybe five thousand."

"Five thousand dollars!" Recovering, Suzanne tossed her head. "Obviously you don't have any idea how much army officers receive in pay each month.''

"I got drunk 'n signed up once. Could only take it a month or so afore I went over the hill, but I know officers make a damn sight more 'n privates.''

"Not five thousand dollars more!''

"All right then, a thousand.''

"My parents don't have that kind of ready cash,'' Suzanne lied.

"Then they kin go to the bank 'n borrow some.''

The absurdity of the fact that she was sitting here bargaining with a stage robber over the amount of her own ransom raised a bubble of near hysteria in her throat. With some difficulty, she countered Parrott's argument.

"One has to offer surety for a loan of that amount. Land or cattle or a business of some sort. My stepfather's a military man. He doesn't run cattle or hold title to any land.''

Her mother did, however. After a lifetime of following the drum, Julia Bonneaux Garrett had insisted on purchasing a sizable tract of land outside Cheyenne, which she held in her own name.

Big Nose Parrott didn't need to know that, however. Nor, as it turned out, did he particularly care about such small, annoying details. His jaw jutting, he set her ransom at a thousand dollars and dispatched two men with instructions to obtain the money from Garrett without getting their necks stretched in the process.

"All right, boys, let's ride."

"Wait a minute," the one called Curly protested. "What about the kid they said was riding with Sloan? He's probably still up in them trees."

Suzanne's heart thumped. Tipping her chin, she forced a cool, haughty tone.

"If you're referring to Mr. Butts, we parted company some miles back, where the road forked. He was anxious to get to the gold fields."

"We'd better go have a look-see," Curly insisted.

Suzanne was fumbling for a more convincing lie when Big Nose made it unnecessary.

"Hell, if it's that overgrowed farm boy from the stage you're talkin' about, I ain't got no interest in him. 'Sides, we'll be lucky to make the Badlands before nightfall. I don't fancy tryin' to find my way through them gulches in the dark. Let's ride."

Anxious to reach his hideout, Big Nose set a brutal pace.

For the first hour, Suzanne felt only relief that Matt and Ying Li hadn't been forced to come along. Neither of them could have stayed in the saddle. For most of the second, third and fourth hour, she concentrated all her energy on staying in hers.

Veering southeast, the fast-moving riders soon left the wooded Black Hills and reentered the vast, treeless plains. Gradually, what seemed like a distant hump on the horizon gained size and definition. It was The Wall, a barrier of striated rock that ran from north to south for a hundred miles. Originally a flat escarpment cut by the White River as it meandered across the prairie, The Wall had been eroded by wind and rain, gradually losing layer upon layer of topsoil. The same wind and rain had then sculpted the uncovered rock into an endless maze of knife-creased slopes, turreted pinnacles and tortuous gullies.

Settlers traversing the Great Plains cut north or south to go around The Wall. Homesteaders avoided its barren, windswept slopes. Even the Sioux claimed only a small portion of the Badlands at its southern end, near Wounded Knee Creek. Outlaws such as George Parrott and his gang, however, could lose themselves indefinitely among its twisting ravines.

Up close, Suzanne found the endless stretch of cliffs and spires even more formidable than when viewed from a distance. She had no idea why Big Nose chose to head for a particular ravine. There was nothing to mark it as the entrance to his hideout. No tree branch stuck in the rock, no symbol painted on the cliff face, nothing.

With Parrott in the lead and Jack right behind him, they passed single file through the narrow opening. As quickly as that, the prairie behind them disappeared. Ahead loomed an unending maze of rock, crowding so close in spots that Suzanne couldn't imagine how they'd get through. When her right stirrup scraped the side of the narrow gully, she heeled in as tight as possible and reached down to yank the canvas duster around her calves and ankles for added protection. Only then did she notice that her stirrup had gouged a long scar on the soft rock surface.

Suddenly, her breath hitched. She slid a quick glance over her shoulder, saw that the man directly behind her was scanning the upper ridges. Searching for familiar landmarks, she guessed.

Surreptitiously, she gave the long coat another twitch. The canvas settled over the top of her borrowed boot. At the next branch in the ravine, she guided the chestnut close to the wall and used the cover provided by the duster to mark the rock wall with her heel. She had no idea if she and Jack could escape, but if they did, they'd never find their way out of the maze without something to guide them.

She repeated the dangerous maneuver whenever the gully narrowed enough to allow it. With each scrape of her heel against rock, she expected to hear an outraged bellow from the rider behind her. She could only thank God for the rapidly descending dusk that bathed everything below the very tips of the rock spires in deep shadows.

She was a quivering mass of nerves by the time they rounded yet another sheer outcropping and faced a ravine so narrow and arched with overhanging ledges that it looked like a tunnel. Big Nose drew up at the entrance, pulled his rifle from its scabbard and fired twice into the air.

Instantly, a monstrous cloud of birds swarmed up from the surrounding crevices. No, not birds, Suzanne saw with a gasp. Bats. Thousands of them. Squeaking and beating their wings, they made such an ear-shattering din she had to jerk hard on the reins to check the frightened chestnut.

The horrific noise had barely died down when an unseen sentry boomed down from above, "That you, Big Nose?"

"It's me."

"We wondered if you 'n the boys was going to make it back tonight."

"Took us a while longer than we expected to find Miss Bonneaux here. Let the others know we're comin' in."

The sentry fired three shots in quick succession. Bending low over his pommel, Parrott entered the tunnel. Even Suzanne had to duck to keep from hitting her head on the overhanging rock. She'd never particularly enjoyed exploring caves or narrow spaces. This one stretched her already screaming nerves as taut as new rope.

After what seemed like miles, the tunnel debouched into a small box canyon. With night falling swiftly now, she couldn't make out its exact size, but the darker shapes along one side of the canyon indicated the presence of a few scraggly cottonwoods. And where there were trees, there had to be a creek or underground spring of some sort.

Wondering how in the world Big Nose had ever managed to find water in this arid maze, Suzanne followed him and Jack across the canyon to the cluster of buildings set against one sheer wall. She counted a cabin, a barn of sorts, a corral and what she sincerely hoped was a privy. She didn't particularly care for the idea of attending to life's basic necessities with an audience of outlaws looking on.

Light spilled through the open door of the cabin. Two men waited in the dirt yard.

"Did you git her?" one called out eagerly.

"We got her."

"Whooee! I ain't had no woman under me since that half-breed whore down to Durango. Is she as young and ripe as we heared?"

"She's young 'n ripe enough, but we done talked about this. We ain't gonna hurt her none less'n we have to. Besides, Sloan's already laid claim to her.''

"Sloan? Black Jack Sloan? Well, shee-it! You brung him, too?''

Chuckling, Big Nose swung out of the saddle. "He brung himself. Now, don't get yer balls in a twist, O'Reilly. With the money we get fer this little filly, you kin buy yerself a dozen half-breed whores.''

Ambling over to where Suzanne sat stiff-spined and thin-lipped, he gave her a wide grin.

"Don't fret, missy. None o' my men is crazy enough to draw down on Black Jack Sloan. Long as he's claimin' you, you don't have to worry.''

Not particularly reassured, Suzanne dismounted.

"The cabin ain't got but one room 'n a sort of woodshed,'' Big Nose warned, escorting her inside. "We've cleaned out the shed so's you kin have a bit of privacy.''

The rank odors of stale sweat and unwashed long johns assailed Suzanne the moment she stepped into the cabin. Drawing in shallow breaths, she surveyed the litter of discarded clothing, old horse blankets and dirty dishes with distaste.

"You and your men don't appear to have benefited significantly from your chosen occupation, Mr. Parrott.''

"Well, we have and we haven't, missy. We rob us a train or a stagecoach, live happy as hogs in slop for a spell, and afore we hardly know it, the money's done gone.''

''Indeed.''

Grinning beneath his bushy mustache, he looked to Jack. ''She talk like that all the time?''

''Near about.''

''Kin she cook as fancy as she talks?'' one of the outlaws asked hopefully.

Suzanne was damned if she was going to fry up so much as a single johnnycake for this sorry lot of murderers and robbers. Sending Jack a warning look, she answered for herself.

''I'm afraid cooking isn't one of my particular skills. But I should be happy to sketch your portrait if you'll supply paper and a pencil.''

Big Nose hooted. ''I expect you should! And make a copy to be printed up in every newspaper in the territory, I'm guessin'. Hobbs here wouldn't be able to walk down a street without someone tryin' to shoot him in the back for the reward money.''

''I would think that is a natural hazard of your profession,'' Suzanne said coolly.

''Well now, it is and it isn't. Most of these boys could stroll into a saloon and no one would recognize them, 'cepting maybe Alejandro here, on account of those silver conchos of his. 'N me, of course.'' He tapped his beak with a forefinger. ''None of them Wanted posters show this jest

right, though. You kin draw me if you have a hankerin' to, 'n pass the picture to the newspapers with
my welcome. Show the world what a handsome
fellow George Parrott really is.''

Wishing in no way to pander to the man's van-
ity, Suzanne returned a noncommittal answer and
asked to see her living quarters.

The small, cramped storage room was little more
than a cupboard cut into the wall. A row of shelves
contained sacks of dried beans and flour, as well
as tins of fruit and boiled beef. Stacked against the
walls were cans of lamp oil, sacks of potatoes
sprouting long roots through the burlap and a
wooden box with Union Pacific Railroad stenciled
on its sides. A thin straw mattress covered most of
the floor, and a three-legged wooden stool had
been pressed into duty to serve as both chair and
table.

At least the small room had a door. With a latch
on the outside.

''I shall need some rope or other means of securing the door on the inside,'' Suzanne said
firmly, tossing her hat and canvas coat onto one of
the potato sacks.

Parrott rubbed his nose. ''Well, I guess a bit of
rope won't do no harm. We kin shoot through it
quick enough if we had to.''

His glance slid to Jack. The outlaw looked as if

he intended to say more, but shrugged and sent one of his men out to cut the rope.

A short time later, Suzanne sincerely regretted her decision to refuse cooking duties.

She was offered a plate of watery, grayish-brown soup with what looked like chunks of innards floating in it. Jack spooned down his stew without comment, but the best Suzanne could manage was to soak a rock-hard biscuit in the juice and nibble on the softened edge. At least the coffee was palatable. Thick and hot, it packed a mule-size kick.

It also kept her nerves jumping like Nebraska grasshoppers. She made a visit to the primitive latrine facilities, then performed a quick wash with water hauled from the stream in a bucket and placed on a stump outside the cabin for her use. Since she was escorted to the privy and remained an object of considerable interest while bent over the bucket, Suzanne finished quickly.

Jack flicked her an unreadable glance when she returned and indicated the lean-to with a little jerk of his head. Suzanne took that as a signal she should retire. She was only too happy to comply.

"Good night, gentlemen."

A half dozen pairs of avid eyes followed her across the dirt floor. Appropriating one of the oil lamps hanging from nails pounded into the overhead beams, Jack escorted her to her cramped quarters.

The lamp cast the small, windowless addition in a dismal light. Someone—Jack, she guessed—had brought in her bedroll and spread a blanket atop the straw mattress. The sack containing her few possessions rested beside her hat and canvas duster.

Wrinkling her nose at the moldy smell of sprouting potatoes and old burlap, Suzanne turned to face the man standing ominously silent beside her. It was the first moment they'd had alone together since Big Nose Parrott had caught up with them. She guessed he'd have some words to say to her, and fully expected him to unleash the fury she'd glimpsed in his eyes when she'd broken cover and ridden out of the pines.

He didn't disappoint her. Shouldering the door shut behind him, he took hold of her braid and wrapped it once around his fist, pulling her face to within inches of his.

"When we get out of here, you'll be lucky if I don't use my belt on you."

"When we get out of here, you're certainly welcome to try."

The tart reply locked his jaw. "I told you to stay hidden and let me handle things, dammit."

"They would have killed you to get to me, Jack."

"I still had some talking to do. You forced my hand."

"Yes, well..."

"That's the last time, Suzanne. Do you hear me? The last time."

"I hear you. Have you finished?"

"Not quite." He gave her hair a sharp tug. "Why didn't you tell me you're Andrew Garrett's daughter?"

"I did!"

"No, *Miss* Bonneaux, you didn't. All you said was that your stepfather is a cavalry officer."

"If you'd displayed the least bit of curiosity about me or my background, I'm sure it would have come out in conversation. What's the matter?" she asked nastily. "Are you worried about the colonel's reputation?"

"I'd be a fool if I wasn't. From all I've heard of him, Andrew Garrett's not a man to cross lightly."

"Well, you needn't be concerned. You haven't done anything that would cause him to string you up and gut you, as Big Nose suggested."

"Not yet, I haven't. That's about to change."

"I beg your pardon?"

Releasing her, he reached for the length of rope Big Nose had supplied at Suzanne's request and secured the door on the inside with a few quick loops. His expression was unreadable when he turned back to her.

"Jack..."

"You heard what Parrott told his men. As long as I'm claiming you, you don't have to worry."

Her heart stopped dead, then started again with a painful kick. "Are you claiming me?"

He tossed his hat down to join hers atop the burlap sacks. "For the time being."

"I...see."

His hands went to his gun belt. Deliberately, he unhooked the buckle and laid the heavy belt beside his hat, positioning the Colt's grip within easy reach.

The most ridiculous nervousness attacked Suzanne. They'd played this game of cat and mouse before, she reminded herself sternly. After the holdup, when she'd shoved her Remington between his ribs. At Rawhide Buttes, when they'd faced each other across a poker table. Later, in Mother Featherlegs's carved bed. Each time, the stakes had risen higher and higher.

They couldn't go any higher, she admitted with a sudden, searing rush of heat. All the irritation, all the arguing, all the sparks they'd struck off each other had led to this moment, in this small, musty storeroom.

14

He didn't touch her.

Suzanne's pulse pounded. Every muscle in her body quivered. She stood locked in a cage of raw, screaming nerves, and the damned fool didn't so much as touch her.

When he lifted the glass on the oil lamp and blew it out, plunging them both into darkness, she fully expected him to reach for her. Then she heard the rustle of straw and braced herself for a brusque order to take off her clothes and join him.

None came. She had no idea how long she stood in the darkness, fists clenched at her side, heart hammering. Only gradually did her singing, searing anticipation give way to doubt, then to indignation, until she had to exercise considerable restraint to keep from delivering a swift, hard kick in the general direction of the mattress.

"You do know, don't you, that you're quite the most irritating man I've ever met?"

When he didn't respond, she gave a little huff and put the matter square before him.

"Do you really intend to just...just lie there?"

The answer came out of the darkness, dry as the desert. "I don't intend to put on a sideshow for Big Nose and his men, if that's what you're asking."

She didn't harbor any particular desire to put on a sideshow for the road agents, either. They were probably listening avidly for any sounds of activity, their tongues hanging out. The fact that her own tongue had been doing the same thing a few moments ago made her decidedly snappish.

"You might have said as much, instead of making me think you were going to...to..."

"Take what you've been offering me these past days?" he drawled. "That'll come, Suzanne."

"Indeed?" she said icily. "May I inquire when?"

"Feeling the heat, are you?"

"Damn you!"

Giving in to her frustration, she drew back her foot. Before her boot could connect, Jack whipped out a hand, caught her ankle and gave it a hard tug. Off balance, she tumbled down.

He rolled over, pinning her under him. His face

was a pale blur above her, his body hard and un-
yielding atop hers.

"It'll come, Suzanne. I'm promising you that."

"If I don't shoot you between the eyes first!"

She heaved upward, trying to dislodge him. He
wouldn't be moved.

"I'm not going to share you with Big Nose and
his men, which is what could happen if we roll
around in here, grunting and groaning, and get
them all pokered up."

He was right. She knew he was right. But that
didn't ease the sharp bite of her hunger.

"It'll happen," he promised again, his face a
mask of shadows. "I've given up telling myself it
won't. But not until I get you out of here and I
don't have to keep one ear cocked or my Colt
within easy reach."

"Jack…"

He stopped her protest with a swift, punishing
kiss. At least she had the satisfaction of knowing
that he wanted her as much as she wanted him
before he roughly shifted positions. She lay in his
arms, her face turned to the wall, and felt him hard
against her hip.

"We'll take a look around tomorrow, get the lay
of the land. Now, for God's sake, Suzanne, go to
sleep."

* * *

They couldn't escape.

That much became clear the next day. Although Big Nose acted the genial host, he made sure Suzanne and Jack stayed in sight at all times. He also kept a guard at the narrow entrance to the canyon night and day. Even if they had been able to make a break for it, Jack didn't place a lot of confidence in Suzanne's revelation that she'd traced their route through the maze with her boot heel.

"Chances are the wind's already eroding the marks," he said during a moment together in the barn.

Working a currycomb through the roan's mane, he flicked a quick look at Alejandro. Hat tipped back, swarthy face raised to the sun, the Mexican sat on an upturned barrel just outside the barn.

"Even if the marks are still visible," Jack muttered, working the comb, "we'd have to go slow, search each one out. We couldn't do that with Big Nose riding hard on our tail."

"I've considered that. We'd have to create a diversion of some sort."

"A diversion. Right." His sardonic glance met Suzanne's over the roan's back. "You have something in mind?"

"Not at the moment. I'm sure we'll think of something."

"What I'm thinking is that it's safest for you to sit right where you are until your stepfather pays your ransom."

"He won't do it," she stated without hesitation. "If the colonel gets his hands on the men Big Nose sent with the ransom demand, he might smoke them over a slow fire until they agree to lead him through The Wall, but he won't pay blood money to a murdering stage robber."

The sour look on Jack's face suggested he was remembering Parrott's prediction that Garrett would do the same to anyone who messed with his daughter.

"We'll think of something," she said again, with a good deal more confidence than she felt at the moment.

She was still thinking a few days later when two rifle shots cracked through the air.

She was at the stream, wringing out her just-washed petticoat, trying not to think about the un-appetizing midday meal waiting for her back at the cabin. Jack leaned against a cottonwood a few yards away. The short, scraggly bearded outlaw named O'Reilly loitered nearby.

The first shot sent Suzanne's heart into her throat. The three that followed a few moments later plunged it back down to her boots. Whoever had arrived at the tunnel entrance was a friend, or the sentry wouldn't have signaled safe passage.

Jack had reached the same conclusion. His face tight, he shoved away from the cottonwood and watched while Parrott and his men spilled out of the cabin. The outlaws were waiting when a lone rider broke clear of the rocks.

Spurring his horse into a gallop, the newcomer raced across the canyon. He pulled up mere yards from Big Nose, vaulted out of the saddle and left the panting animal with its sides heaving and the reins dragging dirt.

"Do you recognize him?" Suzanne asked Jack. "Is it one of the men Big Nose sent to deliver the ransom demand?"

"No."

"What do you think all the excitement's about, then?"

He shushed her with a quick slice of one hand and joined the group clustered around the new arrival.

"...full shipment of gold dust," the man was saying excitedly.

"You sure it's a full shipment?" Parrott wanted to know.

"That's what Dawes heared."

"Dawes!"

Jack's exclamation knifed through the air. Startled, the outlaws spun around. He shouldered his way through their ranks and confronted the sweating rider.

"Are you talking about Charlie Dawes?"

"What business is it of yours if I am? For that matter, who the hell *are* you?"

"Sloan, Jack Sloan."

The man's eyes popped. "Black Jack Sloan?"

He dropped his gaze to the Colt holstered low on Jack's hip, then darted to Big Nose. "What's he doin' here?"

Parrott hooked a thumb toward Suzanne. "He come along when we took her."

"So you got her, did you?"

"Yeah, we got her. Now we're jest waitin' for Garrett to pay up. But maybe we kin get us a little bonus while we're waitin'." Gleefully, he rubbed the side of his nose. "When did you say that stage is leavin' Deadwood?"

"Tomorrow morning. Dawes done bought himself a ticket, thinking we might need an inside man for this one."

"Good. All right, boys, get saddled up. Alejandro, you 'n O'Reilly stay here with Miss Bonneaux and Sloan. You kin trade off keepin' watch at the tunnel with Jacobs. Unless..."

He cocked his head, studying Jack through shrewd black eyes. "You seemed powerful interested in Charlie Dawes."

"I am. I didn't know that he's riding with you these days, Big Nose."

"Well, he is 'n he isn't. Since he drifted down to Deadwood he's mostly jest been markin' coaches for us, like he done this one. What's between you 'n him?''

"We have some unfinished business to settle."

"It's like that, is it?"

"It's like that."

Parrott chuckled. "You want to ride along with us and finish it?"

He wanted to go, Suzanne saw with a lurch. Desperately. The fierce, primal gleam of a hunter closing in on his prey flared in his eyes. His right hand fisted, flexed, then fisted again, as if he was already mentally preparing to draw down on Charlie Dawes.

Suzanne stood rooted to the dirt. She couldn't force even a squeak through her tight-closed throat, had no idea what would come out if she did, but inside she was screaming.

No, Jack! No!

The idea that he'd ride off and leave her with O'Reilly and Alejandro didn't frighten her nearly as much as the distinct possibility that he might not ride back again. If one of Parrott's men decided to side with Dawes and took aim at Jack from behind... If Big Nose himself decided to eliminate the added risk Sloan represented in the matter of collecting Suzanne's ransom...

"I'm staying."

The reply came out so hard and flat it might have been chipped from solid granite.

"But you can tell Dawes that I'm coming after him as soon as I leave here."

"I'll pass along the message," Parrott promised. His amiable grin intact, he swung up his rifle and aimed it square at Jack's chest. "You know I gotta have yer gun, Sloan. I can't leave you here with jest two men between you 'n that Colt."

"This gun has ridden my thigh for close on to eighteen years."

"You'll git it back. Pull it out easy-like. Use yer left hand."

Slowly, Jack reached down and drew the revolver from its leather nest. Suzanne's heart hammered so hard her chest ached. She'd have to be blind as a tree stump not to see that parting with the Colt was the hardest thing Sloan had ever done.

Keeping his rifle trained on Jack, Parrott motioned for Alejandro to take the revolver.

"If we do this one right, we'll be back tomorrow night," he said with unimpaired good humor. "The day after at the latest. Meantime, I'm thinkin' things will be easier on Alejandro and O'Reilly here if we lock you 'n the little lady up. It's a tad small in that lean-to, but you might as well cuddle up close to her while you kin. Once Garrett pays up 'n has his girl back, he ain't gonna let a gunslinger like you within a long, lonesome mile of her."

* * *

Jack's mood was so savage, Suzanne didn't volunteer a word during the first half hour or so they spent locked in the small storage room. She sat on the mattress with her legs folded under her while he stood, arms crossed and jaw set, listening to the activity outside.

When at last he swung around to face her, she could see he wasn't happy…and very much wanted her to know it.

"It doesn't serve the least purpose for you to glare at me like that," she said calmly. "It was your decision not to go after Dawes."

"I should have left you at Rawhide Buttes, you and the kid."

"Well, you didn't."

"You'd better give me your Remington."

Obediently, she handed over the weapon she'd kept hidden in the folds of her skirt. Jack hefted the small piece in his palm. With its pearl-handled grip and decoratively engraved double barrel, the weapon looked like a child's toy against his callused hand.

"It shoots a few inches to the left," she said coolly.

He grunted in acknowledgement. "I don't suppose you tucked a few spare rounds in your other pocket?"

"No, unfortunately. The box of bullets was in my bag aboard the stage."

''That's what I figured.''

Sliding the derringer into his vest pocket, Jack eyed the door. A hard kick would shatter the wooden latch on the other side. If he was the only one locked up in here, he'd bust open the door, dive through and take aim while still twisting in midair.

He could hear Alejandro and O'Reilly in the other room. They'd go out sooner or later, either singly or together, to feed the horses or get water. Or relieve the guard Big Nose had left posted in the rocks above the tunnel. Jack hadn't forgotten him.

The third outlaw wouldn't be a problem once he got his hands on a rifle or pistol. The problem was Suzanne.

His fists bunched. Dammit it all to hell! He couldn't remember now a time when worry for the blasted woman didn't hang like a millstone around his neck. Adding to his frustration was the fact that he couldn't trust her to crouch behind the potato sacks and stay out of harm's way.

If he'd had any doubts at all on that matter, she resolved them when she politely asked what he wanted her to do when they made their break.

''We're not making a break.''

''Of course we are. We'll never have a better chance than now, when Parrott's away.''

"It's too dangerous, Suzanne. You could get hurt."

She didn't dismiss the risk. "I know. So could you. But the alternative is to just sit here and do nothing while Big Nose holds up another stage. He killed our driver, Jack. He might kill another, or perhaps an innocent passenger. We have to get out of here, have to make it to Fort Meade. The commander can telegraph the Express Office in Deadwood and tell them Dawes marked tomorrow's stage."

Dawes! With a silent curse, Jack consigned the man's murdering soul to the hottest reaches of hell.

"We've got to try," she said quietly. "You know we do."

She could tell from his face that he'd already weighed the odds, decided how he would handle matters.

"Tell me what you want me to do."

"I don't want you to do anything."

"Hooah!"

He bent down and took her upper arms in a brutal grip. "Listen to me, woman. I can't take aim on those two out there if I'm looking over my shoulder to make sure you're not in their line of fire. I'll get us out of here when the chance comes," he said fiercely, "but only if you promise to stay where I put you this time."

* * *

The chance came sooner rather than later.

And when Jack smashed his boot against the door, Suzanne stayed flattened against the wall, right where he'd put her.

Bursting into the other room, he fired before he hit the dirt floor. She heard a howl, the sound of a heavy object slamming against the wall, a string of curses in Spanish.

Rolling to his feet, Jack raced to the writhing, cursing Alejandro and snatched up his pistol. With the gun trained on the wounded man, he grabbed the rifle propped against the wall and yelled to Suzanne.

"Here!"

She caught the rifle he tossed and pumped the lever to feed a shell into the chamber.

"Stay back," he barked.

She slammed up against the cabin wall. Her shoulder blades had no sooner made contact than heavy footsteps pounded toward the cabin.

"Hey!" O'Reilly shouted. "Mexican! That you doin' the shootin' in there?"

Alejandro's hoarse warning sounded only a second before Jack dived out the window. The wavy glass shattered. O'Reilly spun around.

Two pistols spit smoke.

"You sorry bastard!" Screeching, the outlaw danced from one foot to the other and clutched frantically at his fingers. "You done shot away half my hand!"

Jack didn't waste either time or sympathy on the man. Rolling to his feet once again, he shook off a shower of glass shards and gestured toward the cabin door.

"Inside."

Cursing and holding his injured hand tight against his chest, the robber stumbled in. Jack followed, swung up his arm, and smashed Alejandro's pistol down butt first. O'Reilly crumpled with a small, gobbled squawk.

"Keep them covered while I find some rope," Jack instructed Suzanne tersely.

Jack made quick work of binding and gagging the two outlaws. He yanked the still-unconscious O'Reilly upright and tied him back-to-back to the protesting, groaning Alejandro. Only after he was satisfied they posed no immediate threat did he tear one of the men's shirts into a rough bandage for the Mexican's wound, rip another strip for the Irishman's bloody finger stumps and join Suzanne at the door.

"I haven't seen anything moving," she told him.

"The sentry must have heard the shots."

Squinting through the afternoon sunlight, Jack scanned the rocks on the far side of the box canyon for a glint of steel, a moving shadow, anything that might pinpoint the guard Big Nose had left at the entrance. All he saw were the swirls of dust tossed up by the wind as it soughed through the tall rock spires and narrow creases.

Well, they couldn't wait for the man to work his way around the upper reaches of the canyon. Once in position to cover the cabin, he could keep them pinned down indefinitely.

"I'll make a run for the barn. Stay here until I bring the horses."

"Jack, wait!"

"Dammit, you promised you'd do what I told you to."

"I will! I just couldn't let you go without this."

Grabbing a handful of vest and shirt, she yanked him down and herself up. The kiss was hard and fierce. Suzanne held nothing back. Nothing.

When she pulled away, he shook his head. "You are one bodacious female, *Miss* Bonneaux."

"Why, thank you, Mr. Sloan. I do believe that's the first compliment you've paid me in the entire course of our acquaintance."

Praying it wouldn't be the last, she curled her hands into tight fists as Jack made another quick scan of the canyon, then exploded through the doorway. With every step he cut across to the barn, Suzanne expected to hear a shot and see him spin around. Her nails had dug deep gouges in her palms before the shadows inside the barn swallowed him whole.

After another search of the canyon walls, she made a quick dash to the storage room to retrieve her hat and canvas duster. Spinning around, she started out, then whirled back and stuffed tins grabbed at random from the shelves into the duster's deep pockets. She was back at the door long, agonizing moments before Jack reappeared.

He came out of the barn riding low and fast on the big roan, tugging the chestnut's reins. At his call, Suzanne dashed out, tossed him the rifle and scrambled into the saddle. They took off at a dead run for the narrow tunnel.

Halfway across the canyon, a puff of dust flew up only yards to their right. The crack of rifle fire followed a second later. She heard a grunt, then whipped her head around just in time to see Jack yank on the reins.

Her heart stopped dead in her chest, then started again with a painful kick when he cut right and brought the roan up between her and the shooter. Shielding her with his body, he cocked the rifle and returned fire while they raced side by side for the narrow opening in the rocks.

15

They made it!

With a joyous prayer of thanks, Suzanne flattened herself against the chestnut's neck and plunged into the tunnel. Jack and the big roan pounded in behind her. Pulling frantically on the reins, she twisted around as much as the crowding rock walls would allow.

"Jack! Are you all right?"

"Yes."

"I heard you grunt. Were you hit?"

"Just ride!"

The tunnel had seemed endless when Suzanne had first traveled through it days ago. Now it stretched into infinity. Bending so low that the chestnut's mane flayed her face, she rode almost blind. Rock closed in on her from all sides. The echo of iron-shod hooves thundered in her ears. One narrow, twisting turn followed another. Finally—*finally!*—she caught a slice of open sky up ahead.

The chestnut burst out of the tunnel and into a wide, winding ravine. She kicked him into a gallop and charged straight for the first bend. She had no idea whether Jack had disabled the sentry, no notion of whether the man could scramble to cover both the entrance to and exit from the tunnel, but she wasn't taking any chances.

Only after she'd rounded the bend and ridden almost into a series of tall, wind-sculpted spires did she draw rein. Her breath knifing into her lungs, she twisted around and waited for Jack to pull up beside her. When she saw the blood tracing a bright red path down his chin and neck, her stomach lurched.

"You're hit!"

"It was just a sliver of rock."

A swipe with his forearm smeared the red across his cheek. The cut looked deep, but the blood had already slowed to a sluggish trickle. Jack ignored it as he scanned the forest of spires ahead. His glance cut sharply back to Suzanne.

"Guess this is where we learn whether you're as good a pathfinder as you are rider. Which heel did you use to make those marks, right or left?"

"My right mostly."

"We would've been coming from the opposite direction, so look to your left."

Three different trails cut through the towering stone pinnacles. They found the small white scar some thirty or so yards down the second path. Suzanne sidled the chestnut next to the rock to measure her heel against the mark.

"This is it!"

"Looks like."

She couldn't resist a triumphant grin.

"I wouldn't be feeling too smug," Jack advised, eyeing the winding gully beyond. "We've got a good-size chunk of Badlands ahead, and two stage robbers likely to come charging out of that tunnel behind us at any minute with guns blazing."

"Three, counting the guard."

"Two," he said flatly. "Let's move."

Despite Jack's grim prediction, neither Alejandro nor O'Reilly came after them. Jack must have done a good job with the knots. Tied back-to-back as they were, they'd be ready to eat nails by the time they finally worked loose or Big Nose returned.

The possibility of meeting Parrott and his gang riding in while they were on their way out kept Suzanne and Jack straining to find the heel marks. It was slow work, far slower than Suzanne had anticipated. They had to explore each side turn, then backtrack after a mile or more passed with no small, white scar to guide them. Any hope of clear-

ing The Wall before nightfall and reaching Fort
Meade in time to telegraph a warning to the stage
line soon faded.

They stayed in the saddle until huge black
clouds of bats began their exodus from the caves
hidden among the rocks. By then shadows had
grown too deep to see the path ahead, much less a
faint scrape in the rock. Dust coated Suzanne's
face and thirst scratched at her throat, but those
mild irritations faded in comparison to her fierce
satisfaction at having escaped.

"We'll hole up in here."

The gully Jack selected looked identical to dozens of others they'd passed. Spires of rock guarded
its entrance, so fat and round the horses could
barely squeeze by. Once past, the columns formed
a perfect screen.

Suzanne cast a glance at the rock that surrounded her on all sides. By day, the Badlands appeared both formidable and desolate. By the light
of the rising moon, the striated cliffs and wind-
carved turrets took on a luminous sort of beauty
all their own. Dismounting, she loosened the chestnut's cinch and left him ground-tied to graze on
the sparse clumps of grass poking through the dirt.
They'd have to find water tomorrow. The horses
could go some miles yet without solid feed, but
they needed water.

So did Suzanne. Water, or any other liquid to

wash the dust down her throat. Claiming a flat rock, she emptied her pockets.

"When did you think to grab those?" Jack asked in surprise.

"While you were saddling the horses. I wasn't sure how long it would take us to find our way through The Wall."

Admiration flickered across his face. "You keep your head about you, I'll say that for you, Miss Bonneaux."

"My goodness! Two compliments in one day." She fluttered her lashes, simpering coyly. "Do have a care, Mr. Sloan. You'll turn my head."

His laughter rolled down the small ravine, rich and deep. As near as Suzanne could recall, that was the first time she'd heard it.

How odd. How very odd! They'd shared so much this past week, yet she'd never heard him laugh until this moment. A little ache started just under her breastbone. She made a silent vow to give him many, many more opportunities to laugh with her.

"Let's see what we have here." She squinted to read the labels in the fast-descending darkness. "One tin of bully beef, one of pickled pigs knuckles and—" she tilted the cans to catch the light of the moon just climbing above the rocks "—two of stewed pears."

"The beef and pig's knuckles will be swimming

in brine," Jack said. "We'd better leave them until
we find water."

"We can make do nicely with the pears. How
shall we open them?"

"A sharp-pointed rock should do the trick."

He hunted around until he found one that suited
him. Drawing up her legs, Suzanne rested her chin
on her knees while he attacked the tins. The rising
moon cast enough light for him to work and her
to note the concentration that furrowed his brow
and squared his jaw.

The ache that had begun with his laughter suddenly intensified into a needle-sharp longing. Her
fingers tingled with the need to trace the line of
that set jaw, to brush the new bristles on his chin,
and feel the firm, smooth line of his lips.

He looked up at that moment and caught the
longing on her face. "Hungry?"

"Yes," Suzanne murmured. "I am."

Peeling back the jagged tin, he offered her the
first bite. "Careful. Don't cut your fingers on the
edge."

She picked out a juicy morsel and brought it to
her mouth. Glancing up, she caught an odd look
on Jack's face. Half amused, half something she
couldn't quite decipher.

"You should see yourself," he said, joining her
on the flat rock. "You're almost lost in that hat
and dust catcher. Your face carries at least an inch

of red dirt, and yet you're holding your pinky up as dainty as you please.''

"To quote my instructors at the Misses Merriweather's Academy for Select Young Ladies, 'One should maintain one's dignity in all circumstances.'"

Which was hard to do, she discovered, with pear juice dribbling down one's fingers. She popped another morsel into her mouth and then promptly abandoned her dignity and licked the juice from her fingers.

They finished the first tin in short order but decided to save the second for tomorrow. Judging by their difficulty in locating the marks Suzanne had made this afternoon, it would take some hours yet to find their way out of the red rock maze. The rest of the pears would have to serve as breakfast and possibly lunch. Ignoring her belly's rumbling protest, Suzanne swiped her hands on her skirt.

"You've got juice on your chin," Jack told her with a crooked smile.

When she missed the glistening spot, he reached over. "No, right here."

Without thinking, she turned her head and licked the drop of juice from his finger. "Mmm. You taste good."

He would have pulled away then, but she caught his wrist. Her tongue made another swipe, slower this time. Across the rough, callused pad. Up one side. Down the other.

"*Very* good."

"Suzanne..."

The need she'd felt earlier stabbed into her again, swift and sharp. Ignoring his low growl, she brushed her lower lip from side to side against his fingertip. His rough skin scraped the slick, satiny inner lining.

He had such strong hands. She couldn't help remembering the sensations their touch had raised on her throat, her breasts, the quivering skin of her belly. Her lids drifted down, shutting out the deep shadows, the crowding rocks, the man standing taut before her. Her tongue explored the hard ridges and leathery creases, stroking softly.

When she took his forefinger in her mouth and sucked slowly, he made a strangled sound and took control. Catching her chin, he angled her face to his.

"Do you know what the hell you're doing?"

Her lids flew up. Head back, she stared into the gray eyes boring down into hers.

"Yes."

The soft, sure reply hit Jack square in the gut. He was already hard. Now he hurt.

He couldn't take her here, in the open, up against a rock, for God's sake! He had to consider Alejandro and O'Reilly. If the outlaws had wrestled free of their ropes, they could be searching even now. Night would slow them, just as it had Jack and Suzanne, but...

"Kiss me, Jack."

"Christ!"

"Kiss me. Please."

The soft entreaty destroyed what little was left of his control. He wanted her, had wanted her almost from the moment he'd tumbled her into his arms after the stage holdup. He'd tried his damnedest to keep his hands off her, but he was done fighting the desire she'd teased and tormented into a raging need. Sliding his hand to the back of her head, he brought his mouth down on hers.

She opened for him joyfully. Her tongue danced with his, so clever, so quick. So damned busy. He tasted dust. Syrupy sweetness. Warm, willing woman. Looping her arms around his neck, she took greedily.

Her eagerness pushed Jack right over the edge. He had to have her, had to finish what they'd started in Mother Featherlegs's bed. Finish it now. Here. With half an ear cocked to the sounds around them and the rest of him twisted tight as baling wire.

Cupping her bottom, he dragged her against him. The canvas coat flapped open. Her skirt tangled around her knees. With an impatient yank, she got it out of the way and scooted forward another inch or two, until their bodies were fused at hip and chest and mouth. Her breasts pressed his chest, but she'd passed the point of needing Jack to stroke and suckle her into readiness.

She was hot and wet. He could feel the damp heat between her legs, where they were separated only by the barrier of her drawers and his trouser flap. He lifted her, canting her hips into his, letting her feel his hardness. It was a warning, the last warning he'd give her.

She tore her mouth away. Wide-eyed, she stared up at him. He saw a flash of uncertainty, and every muscle in his body screamed a protest.

"Jack, I don't...I don't..."

"It's all right," he ground out, forcing a space between them.

"No!" She clutched at his arms and dragged him back. "I...I don't know what to do. You'll have to show me."

Reeling, he felt as though she'd reached into his chest and wrapped both small, dainty hands around his heart.

"Look?"

"You don't do anything, sweetheart." Sliding his palm down her belly, he found the slit in her drawers. "Not a single thing."

"Then what...? Oh! Oh, my!"

Her head went back. In the light of the glowing moon, her eyes were wide and startled. Gently, he stroked her wet, slick flesh. She squirmed at his touch, half embarrassed, more than a little nervous, yet still so eager her breath came in swift, painful pants.

Blood rushed to his shaft, swelling it against his trousers. Beads of sweat popped out on his brow. Deliberately, he pushed a finger inside her.

"Jack!"

He claimed her mouth again. One hand tangled in her hair, the other probed gently. She was so tight. So damned small and tight.

He'd never bedded a virgin before. Never particularly wanted to. Now he knew why. The idea of breaching her shield, of thrusting into Suzanne's quivering flesh and causing her pain almost unmanned him.

Almost.

Another part of him, a dark, primitive side, raged with the savage need to claim this woman, to mark her in the most elemental way a male can mark a female. The primal need swept through him, so fierce and urgent he didn't even try to beat it back.

He deepened the kiss, slanting his mouth over hers. Began a slow, steady rhythm that soon had her squirming frantically. He was sweating now, and so hard he hurt all over.

Still, he made himself wait until he was sure she could take him. Until she cried his name. Until the first, convulsive spasms gripped her. Then, and only then, did he tear at the buttons on his trousers, take hold of her hips and steady her. With a swift thrust, he breached her.

She cried out again. Jack heard the surprise, the shock, but no note of pain or fear. Relief pounded through him, and gave way almost instantly to roaring, rushing need.

The haze in Suzanne's mind slowly lifted.

Gradually, she became aware of a dozen different sensations, each one strange and unfamiliar. A faint throbbing at the juncture of her thighs. A sticky wetness between her legs. The remnants of the most incredible pleasure.

And Jack.

Jack, cradling her against his chest. Jack, stroking her hair. Jack, alternating muttered curses with gruff endearments.

"...such a damned fool!"

She took a deep breath and pulled away. "Are you referring to me or to yourself?"

"Me." His jaw tight, he straightened her skirts. "You deserved better than this your first time."

She thought back to the moment her entire universe had dwindled to a single point of bright, white-hot pleasure.

"I must defer to your judgment, of course, but I hardly see how it could have been much better."

"No, you wouldn't."

With a little cluck, she patted his cheek. "Really, Jack, do stop fretting. What we just did was quite...satisfactory."

That caught his attention. He stared at her for long moments, his face bathed in moonlight.

"Satisfactory, huh?"

"Yes. Quite."

To Suzanne's intense relief, a gleam of laughter started in his eyes and worked its way down to a slow, heart-stopping grin.

"Well, as long as you're *satisfied.*"

Still grinning, he dropped a kiss on her mouth. "Unless you plan to curl up and spend the rest of the night on this slab of rock, I'd better clear a spot for us to get comfortable."

He chose a hollow depression against the gully wall and set about kicking aside brush, fallen bits of shale and any unwanted residents. Suzanne slipped off her perch, intending to help him, but the stickiness between her legs drew a grimace. She threw a quick glance Jack's way, then ducked behind the rock, tore a strip from her already ragged petticoats and tended to herself as best she could.

By the time she joined him, their spot was cleared. She slipped out of her duster.

"Better keep it on," Jack advised. "There'll be a bite in the air before morning."

"It's big enough to wrap around us both."

"I don't need it. The rocks still hold some of the sun's heat. I'll sit here, with my back to the wall, and you can warm my front."

Since he refused to consider any other arrangement, Suzanne pulled the duster on again and joined him on the ground. He held her loosely, providing a convenient pillow. She found a comfortable spot between muscle and bone and let his warmth surround her.

Above the narrow gully walls, the moon rode high in a jet-black sky. A thousand stars seemed to hang suspended over her. The night had taken on its different voices. The ever-present wind sighed through the rock spires. She heard a whir of wings. Bats, she supposed, or a night owl searching for prey. In the distance, a lone coyote howled mournfully.

Behind her, Jack's chest rose and fell. His breath stirred the fine hairs at her temple, calm and steady. For all his seeming ease, she knew he wouldn't sleep. He'd close his eyes, relax his body, just as he had when they'd lain side by side in that small, musty storeroom. But the faintest sound, the vaguest hint of danger would bring him awake and on his feet, Alejandro's pistol in his hand. She couldn't imagine how he'd existed so long with so little sleep.

Or what had brought him to the state where he didn't dare let down his guard.

"Why are you hunting Dawes?"

His sure, steady breathing stilled.

"Why, Jack?"

The question went unanswered for so long Suzanne almost repeated it yet again.

"Dawes murdered my folks. Him and his three friends."

"Dear Lord!"

She tried to sit upright, but he tightened his hold, keeping her in place.

"They rode up to our place just as it was coming on to noon. Said all they wanted was a hot meal and feed for their horses. My father didn't like the looks of them and sent me running to fetch his rifle, but..."

"But?" she whispered.

"But they left him lying gut-shot in the hay field and cut me off before I reached the house."

She could feel him against her back, tight, taut. Hear the emptiness in his voice.

"They laid open my head with a rifle stock, then took turns with my mother. I learned later she fought so hard they had to tie her down and stuffed her shirt in her mouth to stop her curses. She choked to death on her own vomit. I found her there, tied to the table, when I came to. I buried her and my pa, strapped on his Colt and rode out the next day.''

The stars that had glittered so brilliantly a moment ago lost their sparkle. Suzanne shut her eyes to block the horrific image.

"I sold the homestead, took whatever jobs came my way...punching cows, riding guard for the railroad, putting out drunks at saloons. Once I even hired on with Wells Fargo. But all those years I was hunting."

She didn't speak. There was nothing she could say.

"I tracked three of them. Dawes is the last. He's a dead man, Suzanne. As soon as I get you safe, I'm going after him."

16

They found a line of scraggly cottonwoods just before noon the next day. Suzanne didn't remember passing them on their way in. Nor did Jack. Twisting in his saddle, he scanned the narrow ravine behind.

"We must have missed a mark."

The fact they might have lost their way didn't worry Suzanne at that moment half as much as the prospect of wetting her throat thrilled her. Where there were trees, there had to be water. Quivering in anticipation, she guided the chestnut toward the stunted growth.

The cottonwoods clung to the base of a tall cliff, obviously sucking life-giving moisture from an underground stream. With Jack close behind, she followed the curve of the cliff.

"Look! Look at that!"

Not ten yards away, the stream bubbled to the surface in a small, clear pool. With a glad cry, Suzanne dismounted and sank to her knees at its edge. The water was clear, cold and so wonderful she barely noticed the bitter tang of minerals that leached from the porous rock. With Jack hunkered down beside her, she scooped up the precious liquid with both hands and drank her fill.

When she was done, she heaved a huge, contented sigh and flopped back on her elbows. Tipping her face to the sun, she closed her eyes and gave herself up to the sheer pleasure of the moment.

"We'll stop here awhile," Jack said. "Give the horses time to rest and graze."

"Mmm."

"Give us time to rest and clean up some, too."

She opened her eyes then, and found him regarding her with a familiar glint in his gray eyes.

"Don't say it!" she warned.

With her hat hanging by its rawhide strings, frowsy strands of her hair blown loose from her braid and her face streaked with muddy dust, she knew she looked like some creature from the wilds...and didn't particularly care.

"Now you've seen me at my best and my worst," she told him wryly.

The glint in his eyes deepened. "Which is this?"

"Why don't you tell me?"

"All right." He traced the tip of his forefinger along the line of her wet chin. "This, sweetheart, is your second best."

"Indeed?"

"Indeed. Your best was last night," he said slowly. "With your head thrown back and moonlight on your face. I'll carry that picture with me wherever I go."

She died a little at that moment, but somehow managed a bright smile.

"Well, neither one of us is going anywhere right now. Let's tend to the horses, then decide between the pig's knuckles or bully beef."

Despite her determined cheerfulness, Jack's words echoed in Suzanne's head while they wiped down the horses and left them to graze. She was still thinking about them when he went back on foot to try to find their missed turn, leaving her to mull over their choices for the midday meal.

Since neither particularly appealed to her, Suzanne put off the decision in favor of soaking her toes. Her blisters had completely healed, she saw when she dumped her boots on the grass at the water's edge. Wiggling her toes, she stuck them in the pool.

The water had a bite to it and raised goose bumps up and down her legs, but it felt so wonderful Suzanne swiftly altered her plans. The chance to wash away a few layers of dust was worth a few shivers. Her canvas duster, shirt and skirt floated to the ground, followed by her ragged petticoats. As she waded into the pool wearing just her camisole and drawers, the rusty stains on the inner legs of her drawers caught her eye.

She sank down, scrubbing at the evidence of her lost maidenhood. Only then did the enormity of what she'd done finally begin to seep in. Falling asleep in Jack's arms had kept all doubts at bay last night. Thirst and the sheer effort of searching out their trail had occupied her mind this morning. Now, with her scratchy throat eased and cold, bracing water lapping at her hips, Suzanne had time to reflect on her recklessness.

She waited for shame, for fear, for a stinging rush of regret over the realization she wouldn't bring her most precious gift to her marriage bed. All that emerged from her chaotic thoughts was a fierce joy.

Last night belonged to her. Like Jack, she'd carry the memory of that stolen hour wherever she went. Unlike him, however, she refused to believe last night was the only memory she'd take away with her. They'd come too far together, crossed too many miles.

She wouldn't let him ride out of her life. She couldn't. He was burned into her heart now. He'd left his mark on her, like a hot iron on rawhide.

Setting her jaw in a way her parents and brother would have recognized instantly, Suzanne raised her hands and let water trickle down her neck and bosom while she debated various ways to make Jack see they belonged together. The most obvious one didn't occur to her until she heard a strangled sound just over her shoulder.

She whipped her head around, feeling a bit foolish to be caught sitting in little more than a puddle of water. Her embarrassment fled when she noted the raw, unguarded hunger on Jack's face.

A hammering started just under her ribs. Slowly, she scooped up another handful of water. Just as slowly, she let it flow through her palms.

Her wet camisole clung to her body. Her drawers lay plastered against her hips. She watched Jack's gaze take in every inch of her body and thrilled to the red that rose in his cheeks.

"Why don't you come in and join me?" she murmured. "The water's cold but not icy."

She thought he'd refuse. Was so sure of it, in fact, that a sharp pang of disappointment pierced her when he turned away. His protective streak had reared its head, no doubt. He wouldn't unbuckle his gun belt, strip down and cavort in a few inches of water while they still had to find their way out of the Badlands.

Or would he?

When his hat hit the grass, Suzanne's lungs squeezed. By the time he'd shed every piece of his clothing, she could hardly breathe.

She'd never seen him naked before. Had never seen any grown man naked, for that matter, although she and Bright Water had once stumbled across several troopers scrubbing themselves down in the river. She'd viewed a goodly number of Greek statues in books and museums, however, and decided on the spot that Jack Sloan compared favorably to any Greek. *Quite* favorably. The afternoon sun bronzed his skin everywhere it hadn't tanned to dark mahogany. Swirls of dark hair gleamed on his chest and stomach and...and lower.

Heat rushed into Suzanne's cheeks. She tried to look away. She honestly tried. But a need had sprung to life low in her belly, and she'd passed beyond the point of maidenly embarrassment.

Jack waded in, his eyes on the woman who drew him like the sirens he'd once heard about who lured sailors to their doom. He was a fool to give in to the hunger clawing at him, worse than a fool.

He deserved to be shot for what he'd done last night. Yet he could no more resist the curves displayed so provocatively in wet linen than he could stop the wind from whistling through the canyons.

Just once more, he swore. He had to hold her just once more before they followed the mark he'd found and rode out of the Badlands. He'd do it right this time. Bring her slow and sweet to her pleasure. Show her how it could be. How it *should* be.

He'd bare her to the sun and let his hungry gaze take in what he'd glimpsed only by moonlight last night. Her eyes ablaze with passion. Her silky skin flushed. Her breasts firm and high, their red-brown nipples peaked.

A tiny vein throbbed in her throat as she tucked her legs under her and sat back on her heels. Jack joined her, his hands curling into fists as his hungry gaze took in the ribs beneath the wet linen, the curve of her stomach, even the tiny hollow of her belly button.

"You're so small," he said, his voice rough with need. "So delicate."

"I believe you've mentioned something of that sort before," she reminded him on a shaky laugh. "Right before you remarked that I carried more weight on me than appearances would lead one to believe."

"I want to see you, Suzanne. All of you."

She took her lower lip between her teeth but didn't shy away when he reached for the hem of her camisole. Trembling, she raised her arms while he drew the wet shift up and over her head. Her belly quivered under his touch as he untied the strings on her drawers.

The wet linen parted. She knelt before him, young and proud and so perfect Jack couldn't believe she'd let him touch her, much less lift her face to his and return his kiss with a hunger that matched his.

This time, he loved her exactly as he'd vowed to. Stretching her out on the grass beside the small, glistening pool, he brought her slow to pleasure. Showed her exactly how sweet the joining could be with the discomfort of her breaching behind her.

And this time, Suzanne learned the unexpected and completely intoxicating joy of giving as well as receiving. Her mouth and tongue and hands eager, she explored Jack's body, took him into her own, cried out in wonder, in delight, in aching, panting, need.

They remained at the water hole long enough for the horses to graze their fill and the wind to snap most of the dampness from Suzanne's wet undergarments.

Big Nose had said he and his men might be back as early as tonight if they managed this holdup right. Suzanne had no desire to meet up with the outlaws on the way out of the Badlands. Still, her feet dragged as she went to saddle and bridle the chestnut.

Everything in her cried for one more day, just a few more hours. Jack would leave her once they reached Fort Meade. The need to avenge his parents burned too deep to give up now that he'd closed in on his last quarry.

Time was running with him...and against Suzanne. She couldn't linger at Fort Meade, waiting while he hunted down Charlie Dawes. If she still had any chance at catching Bright Water, she'd have to leave immediately for the Arapaho camp. Maybe afterward, she thought as she grabbed the saddle horn and levered up enough to get a boot in the stirrup. Maybe Jack would come hunting for her after he finished with Dawes.

She nursed that silent, secret hope throughout the rest of their tortuous journey through The Wall. The going was slow, too slow for Jack's liking. With each passing hour, he ranged farther and farther ahead of Suzanne, searching for her marks, determined to draw fire and give her time to escape down one of the endless gullies if necessary. By the time they found the last gouge, shadows crawled across the canyon walls and Suzanne's own nerves had all but shredded.

"We're close to the entrance," Jack said, nodding to a rock turret sculpted by the wind into the shape of a camel's head. "I remember that formation."

"So do I."

"We've still got an hour or more of daylight. If the moon's as full tonight as it was last night and we make it to the main road, I'm thinking we should push on to Fort Meade. It'll be a hard ride, but…"

"I can make it."

"I know you can." Despite the tension that knotted his shoulders, he flashed her a grin. "I'm just worried about keeping up with you."

Suzanne was carrying that grin in her mind when they rounded a massive formation and broke through The Wall. After the narrow, crowding rocks, the sight of the sun flaming bright and low over rolling prairie gave her spirits a much needed jolt.

The plume of dust that appeared to the north less than twenty minutes later gave them another jolt. It was too far away to see who or what raised it, but it was coming their way, and fast. Her heart in her throat, Suzanne drew in close to Jack.

"Do you see that?"

"I see it."

"Big Nose?"

"That's my guess."

Swallowing, Suzanne threw a look over her shoulder. The Wall bared its jagged teeth to the sky, waiting to consume them once more.

"Should we go back?"

"Too late," Jack said grimly. "If we can see their dust, they can see ours. We turn tail and run back, they'll follow our tracks easy enough."

"So we cut south, away from them, and hope they're so dead set on reaching their hideout they don't follow?"

"You have a better plan?"

Suzanne sent a nervous glance toward the rising cloud of dust. "Not one I can think of at the moment."

"Then head south, sweetheart, and fast."

Always after, Suzanne believed they would have made it if their horses hadn't gone two days with only minimal grazing and one watering.

The animals made a valiant effort. Their sides heaving, they flew across the prairie. Wincing at the effort she demanded of the chestnut, Suzanne kept him in a reckless, headlong gallop. All the while, she prayed the riders bearing down on them from the north would turn and disappear into the rocks.

She thought they slowed, was sure they turned toward the entrance to The Wall for a few, heart-stopping seconds. A wild hope rose in her chest, only to shatter into a thousand pieces when the half dozen or so riders aimed their mounts straight south.

Bent low over their mounts, she and Jack raced across the prairie. The drum of hooves pounding dirt matched the hammering of her heart. Foam bubbled around her mouth's bit and flew back, splattering in Suzanne's face.

From the corner of one eye, she saw the roan hit a prairie-dog hole, stumble, go down. Jack went with him, yet somehow managed to keep his seat as the panting, white-eyed gelding pawed its way back to its feet.

Frantic, Suzanne sawed on the reins and brought the chestnut around. The roan hadn't come up lame, she saw with a sob of relief, but the poor beast took several precious seconds to regain its stride.

"Keep riding," Jack shouted. "I'll drop back and draw their fire."

"No!"

"Dammit, Suzanne, ride!"

For a heartbeat, maybe two, she considered

yanking on the reins, whirling the chestnut around and racing back to give herself up. She was the one they wanted, the one they intended to collect the ransom for.

But Jack would follow...and pay dearly for both their escape and the men he'd taken down in the process. Her throat tight, she slashed the reins down on the chestnut's sweat-soaked shoulders.

The first crack of rifle fire jackknifed her almost double in the saddle. Fear slamming through her, she craned her head and saw Jack drop back to widen the distance between them before he returned fire. With the pop of gunfire filling the air, Suzanne raced toward a rise some half mile or so distant, intending to put at least that much cover between them and their pursuers.

That was when she heard the tinny call of a bugle—or thought she did. Her breath rattled like sabers in her ears and her heart slammed so hard and fast against her ribs she was sure at first that she'd imagined the faint signal.

Seconds later, the trumpet sounded again, clearer this time. With a wild whoop, Suzanne twisted in her saddle and screamed at the man now almost a hundred yards behind her.

"Jack! Did you hear that? Those are cavalry bugles!"

"Keep riding!" he shouted. "I don't hear any—"

He broke off, his startled gaze fixed on a point beyond Suzanne. She whipped around and gave another joyous shriek. Digging her heels into the chestnut's sides, she sent him careening headlong for the troop of soldiers who'd topped the distant rise.

As she neared the small detachment, she recognized the red-and-white pennant snapping in the wind. It was the standard for B Company, Second Cavalry regiment! One of her stepfather's companies!

Wild with excitement, Suzanne charged straight for the blue column. The canvas duster flapped open. Her skirts whipped around her ankles. Yanking off her hat, she waved it madly as she raced toward the troopers.

"Toujours pret!" she screamed, knowing the officer in command of the column would recognize the Second Cavalry's regimental motto of Always Ready. *"Toujours pret!"*

She heard a shouted order, thought she caught a glimpse of gold glinting on the shoulder epaulets of the officer leading the troop. In a well-practiced maneuver, the front elements of the detachment split to allow her to gallop through, then closed ranks behind her.

Suzanne sawed on the reins, brought the chestnut to a plunging, pawing stop and spun him around. Glad cries bubbled up, only to get caught in her throat. Instead of breaking to allow Jack through, the front ranks of troopers had shouldered their rifles.

Shock slammed into her. Too late she realized that they thought Jack was chasing her! That he'd been firing at her! Him, and the half-dozen outlaws now frantically wheeling their horses and scrambling to get away.

"No!"

Her scream ripped through the air at the same instant the front rank of troopers opened fire. Frozen in horror, Suzanne watched Jack jerk to one side, yanking the reins with him. The roan reared, lost its footing and went down.

17

"Miss Bonneaux!"

The dust-covered lieutenant in charge of the troop made a grab for the chestnut's reins as Suzanne tried to cut through the front ranks. She recognized him then, but had no thought to spare for the dashing young lieutenant who'd waltzed her around a dance floor the very night before she'd set out on her journey in search of Bright Water.

Her only thought, her every thought, concentrated on the man lying in a heap on the grassy plain.

"Let go of my reins!"

Busy shouting commands to his troops, Lieutenant Carruthers either didn't hear or chose to ignore her frantic demand.

"Corporal Stanislaw, remain here with Privates Dubois and Patterson to guard Miss Bonneaux. Bugler, sound the charge."

In a swirl of choking dust, creaking saddles and rattling sabers, the troop swept past Suzanne. Before the last man had cleared, she sent the chestnut's muscled shoulder into the corporal's mount, shoving both horse and rider aside, and took off as well. With a shout of alarm, the corporal scrambled to follow.

As she drew closer to the figure sprawled facedown on the prairie, terror squeezed her lungs in so tight a vise she couldn't breathe. Blood had already spread under Jack, staining the earth. His leather vest had darkened to a wet, glistening black.

"Oh, dear God, please!" she sobbed, almost incoherent with fear. "Please!"

Terror choked her as she flung herself down beside Jack and reached for him with frantic hands. It took her several precious seconds to determine he was still alive, but the bloody bubbles that frothed the corner of his mouth left her sick with terror.

Even before she screamed at the trooper to help her turn him over, she knew Jack was lung-shot. She'd aided her mother during too many hours of volunteer work in post hospitals not to recognize the signs.

"Gently!" she cried. "Gently!"

They rolled him onto his back, then saw he'd taken a bullet in the thigh as well as his chest. The corporal kneeling beside her gave a grunt of satisfaction.

"This one's a goner. Good thing, too. One less of Big Nose Parrott's murderin' gang for us to haul back to Cheyenne for a necktie party."

"He's not part of Parrott's gang!" Suzanne said fiercely, tearing at her ragged petticoat.

"Then why was he chasin' after you?"

"He wasn't! Now move aside and let me tend to him!"

The next hour was the most terrifying of Suzanne's life.

She knelt beside Jack, calling to him hoarsely, applying pressure to the torn linen she'd placed over his wounds, refusing to relinquish her place at his side until the corporal produced his field kit.

Instructing him to keep pressure on the chest wound, she snatched at the kit with bloodied hands and dug through it for the meager medicinal supplies every trooper carried into the field.

"'Two layers of lint, an inch-and-a-half square,'" Stanislaw recited by rote, "'saturated with cold water and placed on each orifice of the wound.'"

"I know," Suzanne snapped, as familiar as any trooper with General Order No. 77.

Old Seven-Seven, as it was known throughout the West, provided a compendium of useful tips for service in Indian country, detailing everything from care of animals on the march to guidance for commanders concerning the employment of Indian scouts. One section dealt specifically with the treatment of gunshot wounds.

"I need your canteen. Now!"

"Yes, ma'am!"

While Stanislaw scrambled to obey, Suzanne folded the clean lint into a rough square. After soaking it with canteen water, she substituted it for the blood-soaked strip of petticoat.

"I don't know if the bullet went through," she told the corporal worriedly. "We'll have to check his back. I'll keep this bandage in place while you tip him on his side. Gently, for pity's sake!"

She hoped the slight movement would wrench Jack into consciousness, ached desperately for a groan or even a curse. All that came was a fresh gush of blood.

"Don't see no hole in his vest, ma'am."

The fact that the bullet hadn't gone through gave her a glimmer of hope. Maybe his ribs had deflected the bullet. Maybe it hadn't shredded his lung, just nicked it.

Praying she was right, she instructed Stanislaw to lay Jack down. "I need another square of lint, then oiled silk to cover this wound before I can attend the one in his thigh."

They bound the bandage on Jack's leg in place

with the corporal's yellow cavalry neckerchief, the
bandage on his chest with another long strip torn
from Suzanne's petticoat. Her ragged underskirt
rode well above her knees now. She didn't care.
She'd strip down and walk naked across the prairie
if it would save Jack. Sinking down on her heels,
she dipped another bit of lint in water and began
to wash away the blood that had crusted on his
lips.

The sound of pounding hooves broke into her
fierce concentration some time later, but she didn't
bother to look up until the patrol had come to a
halt and a well-loved voice shouted her name.

"Suzanne!"

Wrenching around, she saw the man who'd
raised her leap from his saddle. Tears stung her
eyes as she pushed to her feet and threw herself
into his arms.

"Colonel!"

She'd never called him Papa. That was reserved
for the laughing, handsome riverboat gambler
she'd so adored as a child. But over the years this
tall, lean officer had won her love and become her
father in every sense of the word.

He'd worn major's leaves when Suzanne and her
mother had found themselves stranded at Fort Laramie all those years ago. Short weeks after Andrew
Garrett and Julia Bonneaux had sorted through

their tangled past and forged a future together, he'd received a promotion to lieutenant colonel. Someday soon, he might very well wear general's stars.

He'd always be Colonel to her, though, the horse soldier who'd bought a pony for a fussy, fretting six-year-old. Taught her to ride. Held her close when she was deathly ill, and healed the ache in her heart over her papa's death.

He gathered her against his chest now, as he had so many times in the past, and stroked her hair with a big hand encased in buff leather.

"Shh, poppet. Shh. You're safe now."

Suzanne's short, furious storm of tears passed almost as quickly as it had come. Pulling away, she scrubbed at her eyes with her sleeves and demanded an accounting.

"Did you get them? Big Nose and his men?"

"We captured four of them. Three others escaped into The Wall. Lieutenant Carruthers is searching for them now."

He wouldn't find them, she guessed, but was too consumed by a volatile combination of worry and relief to care at the moment. With a shaky hand, she shoved her windblown hair from her forehead.

"I didn't know you were here. I didn't see you at the head of the column when I charged past."

"I wasn't with the column. I've been tailing Parrott since he robbed the stage this morning."

Only then did she notice her stepfather's dress.

Instead of regulation blues, he wore a fringed buckskin jacket. That in itself wasn't unusual. Both officers and enlisted troops on the frontier often adopted the eminently practical, waterproof garment. Her stepfather displayed no sign of his rank on the jacket, however. Even his dark pants lacked the yellow cavalry stripe down the outside of each leg. The only item with any connection to the military were his buff-colored gauntlets.

"I don't understand. Why aren't you in uniform? And how did you pick up Parrott's trail?"

"I was on the stage when he robbed it this morning," the colonel said with a small, tight smile. "Me and two of my best scouts. He hasn't been out of our sight since."

"And Lieutenant Carruthers and his troop?"

"I positioned them away from the stage road, well out of sight. We've been communicating with mirror signals at regular intervals since the holdup. I didn't want him coming in too soon, before Parrott led us to you."

"But however did you know Big Nose would hold up that particular stage? Oh!" A smile darted into her eyes. "How clever of you! You baited a trap with rumors of a gold shipment, didn't you?"

"Yes."

"I *told* Jack you wouldn't pay ransom to a murdering thief like Big Nose Parrott!"

"Jack?" Her stepfather's glance went to the wounded man. "I take it that's Sloan?"

"Yes." She swallowed a hard lump. "Lieutenant Carruthers and his men fired on him. He's lung-shot, Colonel."

The planes of her stepfather's wind-honed face hardened. "Good. It'll save me lashing the bastard to two horses and sending them off in opposite directions."

"What?"

"I won't tell you how worried I was when I heard you were riding with Sloan. I'm sure you've figured out by now he marked your coach."

Conveniently ignoring the doubts that had crept into her own mind right after the holdup, Suzanne shook her head. "He certainly did not."

"Did we get the story wrong? We heard Sloan disarmed one of the passengers who tried to take aim on Parrott during the robbery."

"He did, but the man was drunk and dangerous."

"I also received a telegraph from Fort Meade. The commander reported that someone called Butts rode in with a young woman soon after you were kidnapped."

Relief made Suzanne light-headed. "His name's Mathias Butts. The girl is Ying Li."

"Yes, well, this Butts reported that George Parrott offered to cut Sloan in on your ransom."

"But Jack didn't take him up on the offer! Well, he might have let Big Nose think he would, but... Oh, this is all too confusing to sort out right now. Will you send the medical orderly to look at Jack, please? Corporal Stanislaw and I followed Seven-Seven and covered his wounds with lint and oiled silk, and..."

"The rest of the troop's coming in, sir!"

The shout brought both Suzanne and the colonel around. Promising to send the orderly to see to the injured man, her stepfather went to take Lieutenant Carruther's report.

Suzanne sank down on her knees beside Jack once more, her heart wrenching. The black stubble on his cheeks and chin stood out in stark, grainy shadows on his leathery skin. White lines bracketed his mouth. Cold sweat beaded his temples.

"Jack? Can you hear me? Jack?"

He opened his eyes and seemed to focus on her for the merest moment. Before she could speak or call his name again, his lids fluttered down.

Helpless, she stayed beside him while the sergeant who acted as the troop medic during field deployments checked the bandages, complimented her on their neatness and told her there wasn't anything more he could do.

"Miss Bonneaux?"

Aching, Suzanne pulled her gaze from Jack's

still form. Lieutenant Carruthers leaned over her, his handsome face caked with dust. She couldn't believe only a little more than a week had passed since this dashing young cavalry officer had walked her home from the company ball and begged a kiss in the moonlight.

Jack hadn't begged, she thought with a sharp, piercing hurt. On the contrary, he'd flatly refused what she'd ached to give him until she all but forced herself on him.

"The colonel would like you to identify the four men we've taken into custody," Carruthers said, offering a hand to help her up. "Unfortunately, we lost the rest of them in The Wall."

"I'm not surprised."

His glance slid to the wounded man. "Colonel Garrett informs me that's Black Jack Sloan."

"Yes, it is."

His sun-bleached brows drew together. "We were told he was working with Parrott."

"You were misinformed."

He looked as though he might argue the point. Suzanne flashed an unmistakable warning.

"At all times in our short acquaintance, Mr. Sloan has acted with great courage and consideration for my person."

"At all times" stretched matters considerably, but Richard Carruthers didn't need to know that.

It was obvious in any case that he'd already formed his own opinion of the notorious gunfighter.

His jaw squared in a way that added years to his clean, sharp West Point image. "If Sloan is such a gentleman, perhaps you'll explain why he forced you into a poker game, with a Chinese hurdy-gurdy girl as the stakes?"

Dear heavens! Had Matt spilled that tale, too? Tilting her chin, Suzanne offered the lieutenant a frigidly polite smile.

"You'll excuse me, I'm sure, if I fail to see how that particular incident is of the least importance at the moment. Now, shall we do as the colonel requests and take a look at the prisoners?"

It required only one glance at the four scowling men held under close guard to see that Big Nose had escaped. Suzanne gave the captured outlaws' names as best she recalled them, then the colonel instructed his men to remount.

"We have little chance of finding his hideout in that maze, but I'm damned if I'm going to leave without one more try. Lieutenant, you'll select a detail of eight men and escort my daughter and the prisoners on to Fort Meade. Have the men fashion a travois from tent poles and a horse blanket for Sloan."

"While they're doing that," Suzanne interjected, "I'll tell you how to find Parrott's hideout."

Surprise etched sharp grooves in her stepfather's weathered face. "You remember the way?"

"No, but I marked a trail."

His surprise gave way to a slow grin. Hooking an arm around her shoulders, he dropped a kiss on her temple.

"You're just like your mother."

Taking that as the high compliment it was intended to be, she returned his hug. It wasn't until she'd finished describing the few landmarks she could recall and the marks she'd left on the rock wall that she remembered to ask her stepfather about the other passengers on the stage this morning.

"There were only three," he told her, "in addition to me and my two scouts."

"Was one of them named Charlie Dawes?"

"A thin, pockmarked drifter? About my age or older?"

"I don't know what he looks like. The man who rode in to tell Big Nose about the gold shipment said Dawes had bought a ticket on that run. He was going to act as inside man if necessary."

The fact that he had sat right across from one of Parrott's cohorts without knowing it curled the colonel's mouth into a tight line of disgust.

"Well, Parrott didn't need an insider on that run. We *wanted* him to take the strongbox. The driver reined in and handed it over with hardly a curse or a spit. We'd filled it with gold-painted lead ingots, by the way.''

"I should hope so," Suzanne murmured, nibbling on her lower lip. The gold held less interest for her at the moment than Charlie Dawes's whereabouts. "So this pockmarked drifter stayed on the coach after you left it?"

"As far as I know. Why does he interest you in particular?"

"Dawes is the reason Jack was headed for Deadwood."

"Sloan's hunting him?"

"He has a score to settle with the man."

"From what the medical orderly tells me," the colonel said, his blue eyes keen and piercing, "it's even money whether Sloan will live long enough to settle much of anything."

"He's hung on this long," Suzanne said desperately. "He'll make it to Fort Meade. He's got to make it."

The journey that should have taken four or five hours stretched late into the night. The troop kept their mounts at a slow walk so as not to unnecessarily jar the wounded man being dragged on the makeshift travois. Suzanne slowed the pace even more by insisting on regular stops to check his condition.

She was sagging with fatigue and constant,

crawling fear by the time the small detachment spotted the pinpricks of light that constituted Fort Meade. Constructed just last year near a natural gap in the outer rim of the Black Hills, the fort was the home of the Seventh Cavalry, only recently re-formed after their disastrous defeat at the Battle of the Little Big Horn.

A chorus of yips and barks shattered the night as the weary patrol rode past the outlying buildings, tents and teepees toward the main post. Two off-duty and obviously drunk troopers staggered out of a tent saloon, blinking in surprise as the small detachment rode past. Several squads of sentries challenged the arrivals before they reached the grounds of the fort itself.

Like so many other frontier army posts Suzanne had lived on, Fort Meade consisted of long, double-story barracks, various administrative buildings and rows of officers' quarters clustered around a central parade field. Although defensive redoubts of adobe or sharpened stakes were still necessary at some of the more remote outposts, no perimeter walls enclosed these moonlit grounds. The army relied on massed troop strength and firepower to defend its larger, more settled frontier forts.

Lieutenant Carruthers led the detachment across the parade ground to Officers Row and halted before a two-story house lavished with white trim and decorated with dozens of pointed eaves and gables. Swinging out of the saddle, Suzanne went immediately to Jack's side while Carruthers sent a man to rouse the commanding officer's aide and ask him to inform the colonel of their arrival.

"The acting post commander is Lieutenant Colonel McCormack," the lieutenant told Suzanne. "He telegraphed Colonel Garrett word of your disappearance and sent out several patrols to search for you. He and his wife have been most anxious for your safe return…as have so many of us."

His cool tone drew a quick glance from Suzanne. A week ago, she would have laughed and flirted and teased him out of his stiffness. Tonight, she had no energy to spare, no thought for anything or anyone but Jack.

"I appreciate your concern, Richard. Truly I do."

"Miss Bonneaux… Suzanne…"

He took a step toward her, but whatever he intended to say was lost when Fort Meade's commanding officer and his wife rushed through the door. Clutching the shawl hastily thrown over her billowing nightdress, the stout matron bustled down the front steps.

"Miss Bonneaux! How happy we are to know you're safe! Do come inside and…" Dismay filled her plump, round face as she caught sight of the travois. "Oh, dear, was one of the troopers wounded?"

"No, this is Mr. Sloan. He was on the stage with me when it was held up."

Her husband stepped forward. "Black Jack Sloan? Good work bringing him in, Lieutenant. We'll keep him under close confinement in the guardhouse until the territorial authorities decide where to hang him."

Suzanne fought down a sigh. "The story's become somewhat garbled. I assure you, Mr. Sloan had nothing to do with either the holdup or my kidnapping."

"What's that you say?"

"Please, may I beg a bed for him and the attendance of the post surgeon? He's been shot."

Seeing the officer was still doubtful, Lieutenant Carruthers stepped forward. "Colonel Garrett's compliments, sir. He requests you provide Miss Bonneaux and Mr. Sloan all possible assistance while he pursues the outlaws who kidnapped her."

Her stepfather's name worked magic.

"Yes, yes, of course. Carry him in, men. Elizabeth, show them which room you wish them to take Sloan to."

Suzanne watched anxiously while her escort detail unhitched the travois and grasped the four ends of the tent poles. With the commander's wife issuing crisp instructions, the troopers carried Jack

up the front steps. Suzanne followed the stretcher
into the house for a few steps, then whirled and
rushed back to the porch.

"Richard?"

Lieutenant Carruthers paused in the midst of
making his formal report to McCormack and
joined her on the front steps. She felt a twinge of
guilt at his eager expression.

"May I ask a favor of you?"

"Of course."

"Send a detail to the Arapaho camp beside the
Cheyenne River. Ask them to escort a healing
woman named Bright Water to Fort Meade as
quickly as possible. If you'll wait here a moment,
I'll pen a note for them to take to her."

Richard Carruthers himself rode out the next
morning. He returned to Fort Meade the same afternoon with the woman known as Bright Water.
Her heart bursting with relief and joy at seeing the
friend of her youth, an exhausted Suzanne clung
to her.

The following day, another small detachment
rode onto the post, this one escorting Colonel Andrew Garrett's wife and son. A flustered Mrs. Mc-
Cormack hastily rearranged her large family so the
commander's residence would accommodate not
only the invalid and his two nurses, but Suzanne's
mother and brother as well.

Colonel Garrett's arrival that same evening with three additional prisoners, Big Nose George Parrott among them, set the whole post to buzzing.

The stir didn't penetrate the drawn curtains shielding the windows of the McCormacks' upstairs second bedroom, however. The inside of the room was dim, the air heavy with the scent of poultices, sweat and gritty determination, as three women fought to keep the man known as Black Jack Sloan from standing in judgment before his Maker.

18

Jack lay trapped at the bottom of a deep, dark hole. Every time he tried to crawl up toward the light rimming the top, the crushing weight on his chest proved too heavy to shift and he sank back down into the darkness.

Once he heard Suzanne murmuring to him in a soft, soothing voice. She sounded strange coming to him through the endless, echoing tunnel, but just knowing she was close made the ache in his chest a little easier to bear. He heard other voices as well, seeming as if they were raised in argument at one point. He couldn't summon the strength to sort them out.

The hurt in his chest was strange, too. At first it felt as though someone had stabbed icy needles straight through him. He was so cold, so damned cold down there at the bottom of that black well. The next thing he knew, a raging fire consumed him. Every hair, every inch of his skin burned with vicious, unrelenting heat.

The voices dimmed, went away completely. For endless hours, the only sound he could distinguish, the only sound that came to him through the roaring flames was a low, repetitive hum. Almost a chant. Drowning in sweat, his blood on fire, Jack narrowed his concentration and drew a tight bead on that murmur, like a sharpshooter would sight a distant target. It was all that kept him from the flames. All that he could remember when he pushed up on an elbow, grunting as a red-hot lance speared into his chest, and croaked out Suzanne's name.

"She is near," a voice murmured.

Blinking, he tried to clear the haze of pain and sweat filming his eyes. Swirling images slowed, unblurred. He saw the glow of an oil lamp. A water pitcher and wash bowl painted with yellow roses. A pair of luminous black eyes.

"I am Bright Water," the owner of those fathomless eyes said quietly. "A healing woman in my tribe and friend to Suzanne."

"How…? Where…?"

"That does not matter at this moment. You must rest, Jack Sloan."

"Too hot…"

Nodding, she slipped a hand around his neck.

"Drink this, all of it, and the fires will not burn so fierce."

She tipped a bitter liquid down his throat. Jack gagged at its vile taste but didn't have the strength to turn his head away.

He woke the second time to the peculiar scent of burnt oranges and a narrow slice of gold knifing through a murky dimness. He lay still for long moments, frowning at the contrast of bright against dark, until the gilt slowly resolved into a sunbeam. Dust motes danced on its slanting bars. He followed one particular swirl all the way down to the floor.

His frown deepened. Was that a carpet? He was sure he'd never seen floorboards covered with snaking green vines and pink cabbage roses before.

"Mama, he's awake!"

"So I see. Run downstairs and fetch your sister, Samuel."

Gritting his teeth, Jack turned his head in the direction of scurrying footsteps. Scratchy linen rustled under his ear. The scent of starch and the lingering odor of burnt oranges almost drowned the stench of his own sweat.

A stranger leaned over him. An exquisite stranger, with a crown of braided, blue-black hair and violet eyes marked by a tracery of fine lines at the corners.

"Shall I bathe your face and make you a little more comfortable while we wait for Suzanne?"

Her voice was cool, with a curious lilt Jack couldn't quite place. Taking his silence for assent, she drew a straight-backed chair close to the bed, dipped a cloth in the porcelain washbasin and wrung it out with slender, capable hands.

"You've given us quite a scare. Even Bright Water despaired of you a time or two."

"Who...?" Swiping his tongue along dry, cracked lips, he tried again. "Who are...?"

"I'm Julia Garrett. Julia Bonneaux Garrett. Suzanne's mother."

"Where...?"

"Where are you?" She drew the damp cloth down his cheek. "At Fort Meade, in the home of Lieutenant Colonel and Mrs. McCormack."

Fort Meade. Julia Garrett. Suzanne. With a fierce effort, Jack grabbed hold of those basic facts.

"You've been here five days. No, this morning makes the sixth." Dipping the cloth again, she carefully moistened his lips. "You've been very ill. You still are. One bullet pierced your lung, another went through your thigh. Just when you began to breathe a little easier, the wound in your leg grew inflamed. We feared it would turn gangrenous, but Bright Water brewed a poultice that drew the infection out."

A faint smile edged her lips.

"I'm afraid the post surgeon became somewhat indignant at that point. He's just out from the States, you see, and too new to frontier service to put any trust in Indian remedies. But Suzanne declared herself in charge of matters and she can be, well, quite adamant when she wishes to."

"Damned...stubborn, you mean."

Her coal-black brows lifted. "You've discovered that about my daughter, have you?"

Before Jack could croak out an answer, footsteps thudded on the floorboards.

"Mama?" With a swish of skirts, Suzanne rushed into the room. "He's awake?"

"Yes, *ma petite*." Gracefully, Julia relinquished her seat beside the bed.

Still groggy and weaker than a new-whelped pup, Jack almost didn't recognize the woman who dropped into the chair and groped for his hand. Her floppy hat and long, fat braid had disappeared, as had her borrowed boots and calico shirtwaist. She was all corseted up and bustled into an apple-green striped skirt, black stomacher and high-necked blouse. Her honey-colored hair was piled high on her head and anchored with tortoiseshell combs. Her eyes were the same, though. Clear and cinnamon brown and sparkling bright.

"It's about time," she said on a husky note, carrying the back of his hand to her cheek. The smooth, cool touch drew some of the heat from his skin. "We've been waiting for you to regain consciousness since your fever broke two days ago, but...but..."

"But he needed to find his own way through the smoke and darkness," another voice finished calmly.

A second arrival appeared at Suzanne's shoulder. The healer from Jack's dreams. Bright Water. She glided toward the bed, a tall, statuesque figure in beaded buckskins tanned to a pale, supple frost.

"The spirits summoned you, Jack Sloan. Your medicine is very strong."

"Yours is...stronger, I think."

He was still trying to get a hold on himself when more visitors crowded into the room.

The inquisitive, bright-eyed boy with a cowlick must be Suzanne's brother. He possessed the same fine features, although his were cast in a more youthful mold. Dragging another youngster in by the sleeve, he pointed to Jack.

"See. I told you he doesn't look anything like the pictures in your magazine. Pay me the penny you owe me and make it quick, so's the others kin come upstairs."

"Samuel!" his exasperated mother admonished. "This is neither the time nor the place to put Mr. Sloan on exhibition."

"But, Mama..."

"Not now, Sam."

Only moderately abashed, the boy dragged his friend toward the door and dodged around two other arrivals on the way in. Hands tucked in her sleeves, Ying Li joined a beaming Matt at the bedside.

"We all thought you was a goner for sure," Matt exclaimed. "Glad you decided not to cock up your toes, after all."

"From what I hear," Jack croaked, "the decision wasn't entirely mine to make."

"That's right enough. Near 'bout everyone in this room was makin' promises in your name to your Maker. Even Ying Li hunted down some hoss sticks and lit them for you."

"Joss," the girl corrected. "Ying Li burn joss."

That explained the burnt oranges. Jack knew little enough about the ways of Orientals, but the Chinese immigrants he'd come across at various mining camps and railroad towns were always burning scented incense sticks to some god or ancestor or another.

"It's a heathenish sort of thing," Matt said, apology in his blue eyes. "I'm hopin' she'll stop such things when we're married."

"Married?"

Jack's croak raised a flush on the younger man's face. He tried to look proud as he wrapped an arm around Ying Li's thin shoulders.

"The post chaplain is going to say the words over us soon as he gets back from his furlough."

Jack's glance went to the girl. She stood docile in Matt's loose hold, her face impassive. Like Suzanne, she'd cleaned up some since he'd last seen her. Prettied up, too. Someone had found her Chinese clothing, probably purchased from the throngs who camped outside every western fort. The black pajama trousers and high-necked blouse in silky turquoise made her look exotic, like a small, delicate flower.

When she caught Jack's narrow glance, she shrugged. "Matt Butts like fuckee-fuck, but I say all same, no matter."

"Ying Li!" Red-faced, the kid squeezed her shoulders. "It does, too, matter, and haven't I told you that you shouldn't be talkin' like that?"

"Matt Butts tell Ying Li many things," she said with another, somewhat more defiant shrug.

Abandoning the argument, Matt turned back to the patient. "I got a job loadin' and unloadin' freight for the quartermaster. I'll earn enough to get Ying Li 'n me through the winter quick enough, and start payin' you back what you gave for her."

"I'm not..." Jack struggled for breath. "I'm not calling in your markers."

With so many people crowded into the room, the orangey scent seemed twice as powerful. So did the heat. A bead of sweat trickled down Jack's temple. He didn't realize that his grip had locked bone-tight on Suzanne's hand until she wriggled her fingers and looked to her mother. An unspoken message passed between the two women.

"I think Mr. Sloan has had enough company for the moment," Julia said calmly. "Let's leave him to rest and regain his strength, shall we? Suzanne, I'll send up fresh water and perhaps a bowl of broth."

With Bright Water's assistance, she cleared the room and closed the door firmly behind her. Jack's eyes felt as though they were packed in sand when he brought his gaze back to Suzanne.

Once more the difference struck him. He'd grown so used to seeing her nose tipped pink from the sun and her hair flying in fine, loose tendrils around her face. This starched and frilled Suzanne added a layer of unease to the bone-deep weakness that seemed to grip him. Disliking both sensations intensely, he shifted and tested his strength.

Suzanne noted the movement. Her brown eyes flooded with worry. "Are you hurting?"

In every muscle and bone in his body, Jack discovered. Setting his jaw, he flexed his gun hand. The mere effort of making a fist started the room spinning. Without warning, the blackness reached out to swallow him once more.

* * *

Suzanne sat with him until the lamps were lit and Bright Water came upstairs to check her patient.

"It is good he sleeps," the Arapaho told her worried friend. "The spirits battle fiercely within one such as he."

She looked so calm, sounded so wise. The laughing, merry child Suzanne had shared her secrets and sorrows with had grown into a woman of silent strength. Her braids hung thick and glossy almost to her waist, and the eyes that looked out from her wide-cheeked face reflected an acceptance of the world as it was.

An acceptance Suzanne had yet to achieve. Aching at the thought she could still lose both Jack and the friend of her heart, she took Bright Water's hand and led her to the chairs grouped beside a round, gate-legged table. Her voice low but determined, she renewed the battle she'd been waging without notable success since Bright Water's arrival at Fort Meade.

"I'm so glad Lieutenant Carruthers caught you before your band had traveled too far."

"I shall have to ride hard to catch up with them."

"Why must you catch up with them? Why must you go to Wind River at all? With your father gone, his brother's son is the only one left to watch over you until you take a husband, and you still haven't found one to your liking.''

"I will, when the time is right.''

"You have as much family here, with us, as you do with your own people.''

"Your parents have good hearts, my friend. I am honored they call me daughter. But they are not of the People. My way lies with them.''

Stubbornly, Suzanne refused to give up. "You can choose another way. If Jack survives, it will be because of you.''

"It will be because he's not yet ready to go to his next life.''

"Hooah!''

Bright Water smiled, as familiar with the cavalry's favorite expression as her friend.

"The poultice you brewed drew the gangrene from his leg,'' Suzanne argued. "The post surgeon would have cut it right off. You must see how much you and other healers have to teach the white world. Please, please, think again of going to Philadelphia!''

"I thought you wished me to study with this physician to learn his medicine,'' Bright Water said dryly, "not teach him mine.''

"You can learn from each other, and bring the best of both worlds back to your people.''

"I have seen what happens to those of our people who try to follow the white man's ways. Do you remember what the soldiers called the Sioux and Cheyenne who lived at Fort Laramie?''

"Yes." Suzanne dragged out the answer reluctantly. "The Laramie Loafers."

Every military post attracted a whole population of hangers-on. In the East, brothels, rum parlors and tobacco shops sprang up like weeds around citadels. In the West, the tent cities adjacent to every frontier post included teepees and lean-tos inhabited by the families of the troopers and Arapaho scouts. Members of other tribes made homes with the whites as well, supplementing the rations provided them under treaty by running errands or grooming horses, or simply loafing in the sun.

Bright Water squeezed her friend's hand. "It is always the same when the red man tries to walk with the whites. I do not know how long we can keep to the ways we hold dear at Wind River. I know only that I cannot wear two skins simply because you wish it, Little Soldier Girl."

"But…"

"You cannot order how the winds will blow, my friend. Sometimes you must simply listen to what they tell you."

Julia Garrett voiced somewhat the same opinion when she insisted Suzanne leave Jack to Bright Water's care for a while and take some air.

"I've brought your shawl," she told her daughter. "Let's walk outside."

With a last look at the sleeping patient, Suzanne followed her mother along the upstairs hall. Sounds of boyish laughter came from behind one door, low murmurs from another. They were all here, crowded but comfortably housed by the accommodating McCormacks.

All except Matt and Ying Li. Colonel McCormack had found the couple temporary shelter with the widow of a trooper in the tent city outside the fort. There, Suzanne had learned, rumors were already starting to circulate about Ying Li's previous occupation.

Rumors Julia had heard as well. That became evident soon after she and her daughter listened in companionable silence to the bugles announcing first call for evening retreat. Both women took comfort in the familiar notes, which they'd heard so many times at so many different posts over the years.

"I'm afraid Matt and Ying Li face some difficult times ahead," Julia commented when the bugle's call had faded away.

"I'm afraid so, too."

"He seems an honest, hard-working young man."

"He is. He'll honor his debts. So will I," Suzanne added, thinking of the trail of promissory notes she'd strung along the Cheyenne-to-Deadwood road.

Her mother hesitated, then probed gently. "Is that what you feel for Mr. Sloan? An obligation you must repay?"

"No! At least..."

Suzanne drew in a slow, fluttering breath. She'd had plenty of time to dissect her feelings for Jack during the long, desperate hours by his bedside, many opportunities to relive their brief time together. She knew so little about his past, only the tales spun about him by the penny presses and the sparse, horrific details he'd shared with her about his parents' deaths.

Not that she needed to know more. He called to something in her no one else had ever touched. Something deeply, wildly, gloriously female.

"I suppose I do feel some measure of obligation," she admitted. "I certainly imposed my wishes on him from the moment we were left stranded in the road. To aid Matt and me, Jack changed his plans. Not very graciously, but he did change them."

"From what you've told us, you left the man little choice in the matter."

"It was the oddest sensation, Mama. As if I knew deep inside that I couldn't let him ride away. The feeling grew stronger each hour we were together. I wouldn't have given myself to him otherwise.''

Behind her calm facade, Julia's heart pinched. Suzanne had told her what had happened between her and Sloan, but repetition didn't make the hearing easier. Her baby, her child, the dainty, delightful daughter who'd been the center of her life for so many years, had all but seduced a hard-eyed stranger. A gunfighter, no less.

And he'd let her, the bastard!

Just the thought roused the passion of Julia's Creole heritage. Swift, hot rage coursed through her, made all the more potent because she couldn't give it vent. She'd learned long ago that recriminations would change nothing when it came to dealing with her strong-willed daughter.

Although usually polite and well-behaved, Suzanne had earned her share of scolds. In each instance, she would look up at her mother with the most sincere regret in her brown eyes and apologize prettily for having worried or annoyed or angered her. In a small, solemn voice she'd promise to *try* to be good, but both mother and child knew the vast distance between trying and actually doing.

For that reason, Julia had gone against the urgings of her own heart and sent her daughter back East for schooling. Suzanne needed to appreciate the dictates of polite society as well as the army rules and regulations governing all aspects of life at frontier posts. Not that those two years in Philadelphia appeared to have altered her daughter's basic disposition.

Nor, Julia admitted wryly, had she really expected it to. Only two weeks home and Suzanne had insisted on taking the stage to Deadwood. In the course of her short journey, she'd managed to become entangled in the lives of an overgrown farm boy, a Chinese saloon girl and a shootist, not to mention a band of scruffy road agents.

Now here they all were, descended on Fort Meade like a flock of long-necked, nip-tempered geese. How long they would stay was anyone's guess, although Andrew would have to depart soon to deliver his prisoners and resume his duties at Fort Russell.

Thinking of her husband, Julia smothered a sigh. Andrew's jaw had clamped shut when Suzanne revealed what had happened between her and Sloan, and had yet to unclamp. It would be a miracle if he didn't carve out Sloan's liver before he rode south. He, or Lieutenant Carruthers.

How like Suzanne to lose her heart to a man like Jack Sloan instead of Richard Carruthers! The handsome young cavalry officer would have made a perfect husband for a girl who could recite the rhyming rules of horsemanship before she'd learned her ABCs. In the two short weeks since

Suzanne's return from Philadelphia, the lieutenant had been smitten. His ardor had cooled in the past few days, but it was still there, carefully banked.

Why was it that the heart rarely followed where the mind led? If Julia had wanted proof of that inescapable fact, she needed only to look to her own tumultuous past. Suddenly, she felt every one of her thirty-four years.

"You say you couldn't let Sloan walk away," she said to her daughter. "Are you so sure you can hold him even after all you've been through together?"

"No, Mama." Clutching her shawl, Suzanne met her mother's troubled gaze. "I'm not sure at all."

"Then perhaps you shouldn't try."

19

"I will leave Fort Meade today."

Bright Water made the announcement in the kitchen, where the McCormacks and their guests had congregated for breakfast. It was a noisy gathering, with the children giggling and squabbling at their end of the scrubbed oak table, the men discussing Colonel Garrett's departure later that morning and the women dishing up bowls of honey-sweetened mush. Bright Water's calm pronouncement cut through two of the three lively conversations.

Dismay clouded Suzanne's face. Setting a bowl of mush on a wooden tray, she swiped her hands on the towel wrapped around her waist.

"It is time," her friend said firmly, preempting all arguments. "I will leave when the colonel does, so I may ride with his troop until we find my people's trail."

"You'll ride with me until we find your *people,*" Andrew Garrett corrected her. "Lieutenant Carruthers and his men can escort the prisoners south while we make a slight detour."

"More than slight, I think. The band will have traveled many miles now."

"We'll catch them."

A smile fluttered in Bright Water's heart. He was a good man, this stern-faced long knife. He'd held the respect of her mother's uncle, Chief Spotted Tail, and had risked his career to help her father avenge Walks in Moonlight's brutal death. Despite the sorrows he'd endured during the war the whites had fought with each other so many years ago, he'd found peace in the vast, untamed land of the Sioux and Arapaho. And great joy since he'd taken Suzanne's mother to his bed.

Bright Water could only hope that Suzanne would find the same joy with the man she'd taken into her heart…and her bed. That her friend would yield the precious gift of her maidenhood to such a one as Jack Sloan didn't surprise Bright Water. Suzanne would ever reach out and snatch at what others might walk away from.

Just to look at her now, her lips pressed tight, her eyes stubborn, softened the smile in Bright Water's heart.

"Do not frown so," she said. "We do not lose

each other, Suzanne. We merely walk different paths.''

"But this one takes you so far away!''

From the children's end of the table, Sam piped up. ''Didn't you study your maps at that fancy school you went to? Wind River's a lot closer than Philadelphia.''

''I don't recall asking your opinion in the matter,'' his sister snapped. Unfazed, the boy dug his spoon into the sweet, steaming mush.

''It would be best if we all left today,'' the colonel said. ''I don't like leaving you and Sam and your mother here, Suzanne. We've burdened our host and hostess enough.''

''You mustn't think such delightful company could ever be a burden,'' Mrs. McCormack hastened to assure him. ''We hardly know Suzanne's here, she's spent so much time caring for her... Ah, her...''

''Her patient,'' Julia finished calmly, ignoring the red that crept into the woman's cheeks. She couldn't, however, ignore the way her husband's eyes narrowed. The mere mention of the gunman in the colonel's presence was enough to kill all conversation on the spot.

As it did now. An ominous silence fell, broken after an awkward moment by the scrape of Andrew's chair. Pushing to his feet, he nodded to the tray.

"Is that for Sloan?"

"Yes." Suzanne eyed him cautiously. "I was just getting ready to carry it upstairs."

"I'll take it."

"He's weak as a spring lamb, Colonel."

"I'll take it."

She threw an agonized look at her mother. Julia shook her head. Both women knew the confrontation had to come sooner or later, but Suzanne had hoped for later. Much later. When Jack could at least defend himself.

Chewing on her lower lip, she surrendered the tray.

When the door behind him opened, Jack had one arm hooked around the bedpost and one leg in his pants. Bright pinpricks of light danced before his eyes. Fire streaked down his leg. The mere effort of rolling to the edge of the mattress, grabbing hold of the post and hauling himself out of bed had drenched his nightshirt in sweat.

Damn fool inventions, nightshirts, he thought irritably while he waited for the room to stop spinning. The shirttails flapped about his knees. Cold air speared up under the hem and raised goose bumps on his butt. He didn't know where his long johns were and wouldn't have the strength to fetch them if he did. Just crawling into his pants made his chest hurt like a son of a bitch.

The sound of the door opening brought his head up. Clenching his teeth against the pain that speared into his lung, he studied the man filling the door frame.

So this was Garrett. Cold-eyed, stiff-spined and more intimidating than Jack would admit in his blue uniform with its gold-braided epaulets and brass buttons. Beneath all the braid and brass, he showed the weathered skin of an experienced plainsman…and the friendliness of a Comanche all set to lift a scalp.

"Going somewhere, Sloan?"

Cursing silently at being caught bare-assed, Jack hung on to the bedpost, shoved his other leg into his pants and dragged them up. Sweat stung his eyes by the time he got the tails tucked in.

"Suzanne said you're taking your prisoners south today. I have a little business with Parrott before you go."

"What kind of business?"

"He took something that belongs to me."

The cavalry officer moved into the room and deposited the tray on the bed. Beside a napkin-covered plate lay a long-barreled pistol.

"This what you're talking about?"

Relief shimmied down Jack's spine. He'd felt naked without the Colt, lost, like a man with no name, no past.

"That's it."

"I heard your father carried that gun in the War Between the States."

Jack lifted his gaze. Gray eyes met blue, held.

"Suzanne tell you that?"

"Among other things."

The hair on the back of his neck prickled. He'd been anticipating this interview since he'd regained his senses yesterday. So, apparently, had Garrett. His voice low and dangerous, the officer made his feelings plain.

"The bullets you took trying to save Suzanne are the only reason I don't skin you whole." He let that sink in before adding, "I might do it yet, if you've got any fool notions of marrying my stepdaughter floating around in your head."

A muscle flexed in the side of Jack's jaw. He knew damned well he wasn't fit husband material. He didn't need this starched-up horse soldier driving the point home with all the finesse of a dull-edged sword.

"I'm not a man to run from his responsibilities, but I'm letting you know straight out that I don't look to make Suzanne a widow before she's a wife."

"Good. I suggest you tell her that."

"I have."

"Tell her again."

"I will, but in case you haven't noticed, she doesn't listen real well."

Garrett didn't bother to answer. Turning on his heel, he marched to the door.

Suzanne was waiting at the bottom of the stairs. "Did you leave him in one piece?"

"I did. This time."

Making no effort to disguise her relief, she hooked her arm in his and dragged him into the parlor.

"Tell me what you said to him."

She drew him to the horsehair sofa and perched beside him. Andrew stretched out his leg, stiff from old war wounds.

"I told him he'd better not think about laying another hand on you. Not if he wanted to keep it attached to the rest of his arm."

"Indeed? And what, may I ask, did he say?"

"He agreed as how it was best all around for you both to go your separate ways."

"I see." Her toe tapped the carpet. "Have you thought about the possibility I may be breeding?"

Andrew winced. "I've thought about it. So has Sloan, judging from our conversation a few minutes ago. He claims he won't walk away from his responsibilities, but..."

Anger built, hot and swift. Jack wasn't going to walk away at all. Not if Suzanne had any say in the matter.

"But?" she echoed dangerously.

"Do you want your child to carry the name of a killer, poppet?"

As fast as it had built, the steam went out of Suzanne. "Oh, Colonel, he isn't the man the penny presses have painted him. I couldn't...I couldn't ache for him so if he was."

Andrew looked down into her brown eyes and felt a knife twist in his gut. He'd held this girl's small, cholera-ravaged body in his arms, lifted her onto her first pony, taught her how to handle a Sharps carbine with the same deadly accuracy as her derringer. He'd walk through fire for her, and the idea that she'd given herself to a man like Black Jack Sloan punched a hole right through his heart.

"I'm not saying Sloan didn't have good cause to strap on that Colt," he conceded, "but he's a shootist by choice and by profession."

They'd had this discussion several times in recent days. Suzanne argued Sloan's cause as fiercely now as she had each time before.

"If it's by choice as you say, Jack can choose another profession after he settles matters with Charlie Dawes."

"It doesn't work that way. A man like Sloan doesn't just put his reputation on the shelf and forget about it, even if it's more legend than fact. You saw what happened to Bill Hickok."

She bit her lip. Like Black Jack Sloan, Wild Bill

Hickok had been a favorite of the Eastern press. Was still a favorite, two years after his death. The frontier dandy had scouted with Custer, served as sheriff of Ellis County and toured with Bill Cody's Wild West Circus. Suzanne had met the flamboyant frontiersman any number of times when Andrew was posted to Fort Riley, Kansas, and Hickok served as marshal of Abilene. She'd been in Philadelphia when papers across the country had trumpeted the news that he'd been shot in the back of the head while sitting at a poker table, holding pairs of aces and eights. Already folks were calling it the Dead Man's Hand.

"Hickok turned in his badge and went up to Deadwood to try his hand at gold prospecting," Andrew reminded her. "But his reputation with a gun so worried the swindlers who preyed on the miners that they hired McCall to gun him down."

"I know that."

She met his gaze head-on, her chin set in a way he recognized all too well.

"I also know that you risk taking a bullet or an arrow or a spear every time you lead out a column of troops. Violence is as much a part of your life as it is Jack's. You can't get away from it, any more than he can."

She had him there. Andrew was a soldier to his bones, West Point educated, bloodied by war, survivor of the hell called Andersonville. He knew that men had battered one another with rocks and clubs long before they learned to forge steel into swords or mix gunpowder.

His years on the frontier had reinforced that brutal but fundamental truth. In a land as vast and untamed as this, soldiers and civilians alike packed iron. A good number had dropped a man. Like Sloan...and Andrew himself.

He wasn't ready to surrender the field to Suzanne yet, however.

"You say you ache for Sloan. From what I can see, I'd say he's got the same ache. But physical want isn't enough to change what he is or bridge the differences between you."

"It certainly seems to have done the trick for Matt and Ying Li."

"You can hardly cite that pair as an example."

"No? Then how about you and Mama?" A gleam slid into her eyes. "I seem to recall her telling me that it was plain, unvarnished lust that drew the belle of New Orleans to a Yankee spy."

"I'll have no impertinence from you, miss."

Her hand whipped up in a smart salute. "No, sir!"

Much as it pained Andrew to dim the sparkle in her eyes, he'd never been less than truthful with her. "Sloan's plans for the future don't include you, poppet."

"Well, I'm glad you two settled that matter to

your satisfaction. I hope you understand it hasn't
been settled to mine.''

Which is what Suzanne intended to inform Jack
after she left the colonel to prepare for his journey
and made her way upstairs. Her intentions took a
sharp turn, however, when she rapped on the door
and entered a moment later to find him sitting on
the bed, white-faced and bare-chested. He was
struggling to get an arm into the shirt he'd asked
Suzanne to purchase for him at the sutler's store,
along with new long johns and a wool jacket to
replace his bloodied leather vest.

''What on earth are you doing?''

''What does it look like?''

The bad-tempered snarl reassured her as nothing
else could have. If he'd regained enough strength
to sit up and snipe at her, he wouldn't, he *couldn't,*
succumb to his wounds.

Clucking, she helped him pull on his shirt but
refused to fetch his boots from downstairs, where
she'd taken them for cleaning.

''You don't need them,'' she said sternly.
''You're not leaving this room.''

''The hell I'm not.''

''Do try to exercise a grain or two of common
sense, Jack. You've been flat on your back for almost a week. You haven't eaten anything but the

little we could force down your throat. You take one step and you'll fall flat on your face.''

''Then I fall flat on my face.''

He wrapped a fist around the bedpost and strained to haul himself up.

''Oh, for pity's sake! Here, lean on me.''

The moment her arm slid around him, the gentle, nurturing instincts Suzanne had nursed for the past week fled. Her hand skimmed over the bandages, the hard ribs, the taut skin. Just the feel of him against her scattered the ashes of the fear that had haunted her night and day and filled her blood with a wild, sweet singing.

This was what she'd tried to explain to the colonel, to her mother, to Bright Water. This instant, all-consuming fire was what tied her to Jack. Would always tie her to Jack.

Even when he insisted on pushing her away.

''I want you to ride out with your stepfather this afternoon,'' he said gruffly. ''Go back to Cheyenne with him and your mother.''

''I'm not going anywhere.''

''I'm on my feet. You don't have to hang around and nurse me.''

''I'm not going anywhere,'' she repeated. ''Not yet.''

''I know I owe you. You and your mother and Bright Water. But...''

''You're wasting your breath with these arguments, and from the way it's rattling around in your chest, you haven't much to spare."

"Dammit, Suzanne, I don't need you. I don't want you."

"Yes, you do."

She edged around, smiled up into his eyes. He looked so fierce, so determined to push her away.

"That's the problem, Jack. You want me, but you don't know what to do with me now that you've had me."

"Jesus!"

"Don't jerk about like that. You'll only open your wounds."

"To hell with my wounds."

He gripped her arms, as much to steady himself as to get her attention, she suspected. It was the first time he'd touched her since those hours in the canyon.

Her stomach clenched. As clear as any painting, she could see the moon-washed rock walls. The narrow slice of stars. The heat glittering in Jack's eyes.

"We need to talk about that," he said roughly.

"About what?"

"About my 'having' you, as you put it."

"Ah, yes. The colonel told me you've done some thinking about the possible consequences."

"I thought about them every time I touched

you," he growled, "but that didn't stop the touching."

"You don't need to worry," she lied. "Bright Water gave me a herb. It turns color when ground up and mixed with a breeding woman's urine. I tried it, yesterday morning. You don't have to worry about your responsibilities."

"The hell you say. You can't know this soon."

She looked him straight in the eye. "You'll have to find another reason to come back to me after you hunt down Charlie Dawes."

His fingers dug into her arms. Relief and doubt seemed to war in his eyes.

"You're bluffing," he said at last.

"Am I? Well, time will tell, won't it? Now, do sit down and eat your breakfast before you topple over."

Leaving Jack to chew over her declaration as well as his breakfast, Suzanne sailed out of the sickroom and down the hall. Her steps slowed when she spotted Bright Water in the room the two women had shared for the past few nights. Biting her lower lip, Suzanne watched the Arapaho tuck a folded garment into a calfskin traveling pouch.

"Are you really leaving?"

"I must."

Sighing, Suzanne dropped onto the bed and fingered a butter-soft buckskin shirt. The tiny glass beads shimmered in the morning light, as blue as summer, as red as the sun when it sank behind the Laramie Mountains.

"Do you remember the time your mother set us to stringing beads on threads of buffalo sinew and I dropped the bowl? The chickens pecked at them and ate half before we could gather them back up."

"I remember."

"I thought your mama would scold me for sure, but she only laughed and said she would have to watch when she cooked their eggs. I miss her."

"I, too," Bright Water said simply. "Her spirit walks with me always, as does that of my father."

Folding the shirt Suzanne handed her, she stuffed it into the pouch. The quills dangling from her sleeves tinkled with the movement.

"I see you've packed your medicines."

"All but those Jack Sloan will need. I'll leave a supply with him when I say my farewell."

"By the way," Suzanne said casually. Too casually. "If he asks you about a herb that can show whether a woman's breeding, tell him about one that turns color when mixed with her urine."

"But I have not heard of such a herb."

"Yes, you have. Just now."

She expected a smile, or even the merry laughter that had spilled from her friend during their youth. Instead, Bright Water brushed aside her traveling pouch and sat down. Her hand curled in Suzanne's, its touch strong, its warmth sure and steady.

"I think you must let Jack find his own path, my friend, even as you must let me find mine."

"How can I just stand back and let go of the people I love?"

"Perhaps you love too much," Bright Water said gently. "However much you wish it otherwise, the hawk will fly and the wolf will hunt."

20

When Suzanne watched the colonel and Bright Water ride away later that morning, a piece of her seemed to shatter into tiny pieces.

She stood with her mother on the porch of the McCormacks' quarters, her shawl gripped tight against the sharp October wind that bit into her fingers and face. She could smell snow in the air, see the first hint of it in the haze that hung over the pine-shrouded hills to the north.

As the mounted troop approached, the familiar melody of jingling bridle bits and creaking leather scraped her raw. Bright Water rode alongside Andrew at the head of the column, her buffalo robe wrapped warm around her. Suzanne managed to return her smile and wave, but wept inside as the dreams she'd brought back from Philadelphia crumpled at her feet.

"I'll never see her again," she murmured to her mother. "I'll lose her to the wind and the snow."

"Perhaps." Julia hooked an elbow through her daughter's and drew her close. "Perhaps not. So much has changed in the Territories since you and I first came out here in search of your father. There was no railroad then, remember? The Sioux and Cheyenne still warred with the whites, and the telegraph lines would be down for weeks at a time. When a troop like this one rode out then, we never knew if it would ride back. Now..."

With her free hand, she blew a kiss to her husband. Tall, square-shouldered, cavalry-proud, Andrew lifted one buff leather gauntlet in salute.

"Now we only have to count the days," Julia finished softly.

Her mother wasn't the only one who would count the days. The colonel estimated it would take two weeks to deliver Bright Water to her people, turn Parrott and his gang over to the authorities in Cheyenne and catch up with his duties at Fort Russell. Then, he and Julia had agreed, he'd return to Fort Meade to escort his family home.

The Good Lord created the world in seven days. Surely—*surely!*—Suzanne wouldn't need more than fourteen to forge something more than want between her and Jack.

She'd lost Bright Water, but she was damned if she'd lose Sloan. Hugging her arms, she puffed

short, steamy clouds into the air while the soldiers
trooped past. Richard Carruthers gave Julia a polite
salute and Suzanne a rather stiff nod. Big Nose
Parrott rode behind the lieutenant, so nonchalant in
his shackles that he flashed her a grin under his
great hooked beak.

"Take a message to Black Jack for me, missy,"
he called out. "Tell him we've got some squarin'
up to do if I don't go gettin' my neck stretched.
Which," he added with an audacious wink, "I
don't plan on doin' just yet. There ain't a jailhouse
built yet kin hold me."

When Suzanne carried both the message and a
lunch of hot biscuits and beef stew to her patient
an hour later, she found him sitting on the side of
the bed.

"The man's as slippery as a greased snake," he
commented after she relayed Parrott's remarks.
"He's already broken out of jail twice that I know
of. If the folks down in Cheyenne are smart, they'll
throw a rope over the nearest lamppost."

At the moment, the sweat sheening Jack's face
as he pushed off the bed concerned Suzanne more
than the possibility that George Parrott might escape justice.

"You're pushing too hard," she protested. "Too
fast."

"A man with two bullet holes in him can't push hard enough."

He'd kept his pants and shirt on, she noted, and had bribed someone—Sam, probably—to retrieve his boots from the kitchen. They sat beside the bed, ready, waiting. Already raw and hurting from Bright Water's departure, Suzanne wasn't prepared for the sight of those boots.

"I'm sure you think you're acting manly," she snapped. "Personally, I think you're acting like an ass."

One of his black brows lifted. "I'm done with being washed and fed like a baby."

"Indeed? Then I'll put your lunch here on the table, where you can reach it." The tray hit the table with a clatter of pottery. "Next I suppose you'll be telling me you want to dance at Matt and Ying Li's wedding."

"Are they really going through with that foolishness?"

"Yes. They're only waiting for the post chaplain to return from leave."

"I'm thinking this is more Matt's idea than the girl's." He leveled her a look. "Or is it yours? You're the one who got him started spouting poetry and such."

"Well, I didn't think he was going to spout it to Ying Li. But he has, and they've made a match of it."

"Made a mess of it, more like."

"That remains to be seen."

Losing interest in the argument, he lifted the napkin covering the crockery bowl and surveyed the thick beef stew and crusty biscuits with satisfaction.

"Keep feeding me like this," he predicted, "and I might just dance at the kid's wedding, after all."

As the days slipped by, it began to look more and more as though Jack would make good on his boast. Setting his own schedule for recovery, he increased the time he spent out of bed, until he sat up more than he stretched out. Four days after the colonel's departure, he tackled the stairs. When he finally reached the bottom step, he was drenched in sweat but grimly triumphant. Two days later, Chaplain Sergeant Renquist returned from visiting his family in Pennsylvania.

Matt arrived on the poor man's doorstep before he'd unpacked his bags. With a backlog of christenings, weddings and burials facing him, Renquist couldn't promise to conduct another ceremony until the following Saturday.

With the date fixed, Matt sought out Jack and Suzanne and found them in the front parlor of the McCormacks' quarters, along with young Samuel and his friends. The boys sat cross-legged on the floor, observing Sloan's progress with a walking stick. With each thump of the stick on the carpet, the youngsters revised their estimates as to how many more turns Sloan could take about the room before he toppled over.

Admonishing the boys to hush, Suzanne welcomed Matt and invited him to come in and visit for a bit.

"I'd better not. I left Ying Li alone with Mrs. Overton and, well, you know how they get on."

Not well, from all reports. The widow who'd taken them in at Colonel McCormack's request was a small, birdlike woman with a heart five times her size and a clutch of eager suitors already lined up to become her fourth husband. But even she was hard-pressed not to cluck in disapproval when Ying Li declared her preference for boiled fish eyes over peas, and burned incense to heathenish gods.

Even those oddities might have been overlooked if Ying Li hadn't innocently let drop that she was willing to supplement Matt's wages by performing the same services she had at Mother Featherlegs Shephard's Saloon and Hurdy-Gurdy Parlor. Word had spread through the camp with the speed of a grass fire. The indignant Mrs. Overton had taken her broom to one hopeful customer. Matt had ploughed his fist into another.

"I just stopped by to tell you the preacher's back," he announced. "He's going to say the words over me and Ying Li on Saturday. Will you come and sign the book as witnesses?''

''Of course! My mother will want to attend, too, if that's all right?''

''Me, too,'' Sam piped up.

Well versed in the niceties of military protocol, Suzanne knew better than to offer her hostess's home for a small reception. She'd already stretched the McCormacks' generosity by bringing a notorious gunfighter into the house.

''Shall I see if we can use one of the troops' messes for a small celebration afterward?'' she offered instead. ''Or perhaps Mrs. Overton wouldn't mind if we gathered in her tent.''

''Well…''

''We could raid the sutler's store for dried plums or pears for a cake. I'll mix punch for toasts, and perhaps string some paper lanterns.''

Clearly overwhelmed, Matt turned to Jack.

''Don't look at me, kid. I've tipped my glass at a sight more wakes than weddings. Best to leave this to the womenfolk.''

The dry comment brought Suzanne's head around. A shiver rippled down her spine, spoiling the moment.

''It's bad luck to talk of weddings and wakes in the same breath,'' she said, pushing to her feet. ''I'll go speak to my mother. Tell Ying Li I'll walk down to discuss arrangements with her in a bit.''

* * *

Jack insisted on walking with her.

Of necessity, their pace was slow. Suzanne kept her arm tucked in his, as much for the warmth as to provide the support he didn't seem to need. Their breath pearled on the cold air. Rays of brittle sunshine speared through dust that swirled on the breeze.

Jack looked about with interest as they crossed the parade ground surrounded by pine plank and brick buildings. Constructed only last year, Fort Meade still wore fresh paint.

"That's the headquarters," she told him, nodding to an imposing structure with the flagpole in front. "And those long, one-story buildings are the cavalry barracks."

Suzanne couldn't help noticing that the soldiers they passed showed as much interest in Jack as he did in the surroundings. And no wonder. He'd donned his flat-brimmed black hat, along with the hip-length gray wool jacket she'd purchased at the sutler's store with funds from his rapidly dwindling roll. The Colt was once again strapped against his thigh. Even the walking stick couldn't detract from the image the stories had embellished.

A red-and-white standard whipping in the breeze drew his attention. "The Seventh Cav," he read. "Custer's regiment."

"What's left of it. The regiment was considerably augmented and re-formed after the Little Big Horn.''

As they neared the stables, Jack slowed. "Is that the horse? Major Keogh's mount?"

She followed his gaze to the buckskin standing quietly in the paddock adjacent to the stables. Scars marred the golden hide; so many, Suzanne's breath caught in her throat.

"Yes," she murmured, "that's Comanche."

They moved to the split-rail fence, drawn to the sole survivor of Custer's last stand. The relief column had found him on the battlefield, head hanging, his hide pierced by twenty-seven arrows.

"Colonel McCormack told me the poor thing spent a whole year after the battle in a special belly-band sling. He's only now begun to get his strength back."

"That makes two of us," Jack muttered.

The breeze played with Suzanne's hair under the warm shawl she'd tucked around it. Brushing back the wind-tossed strands, she studied his profile.

"The army retired Comanche with full military honors," she said slowly. "He now participates only in ceremonial functions. You...you could do the same thing."

He swung her a puzzled frown. "What are you talking about?"

"I'm talking about after you settle matters with Charlie Dawes. You could retire from the field, with or without honors. Take up another occupation. Or go East, where your reputation would win you all kinds of flattering attention instead of a bullet in the back.''

"Good Lord! You're not suggesting I join Bill Cody's circus and shoot apples off someone's head?''

"No, of course not, but there are other options you might consider.''

"Such as?''

"Selling your story to the press, for one thing. Your real story.''

"I'm not letting them make more of a monkey of me than they already have.''

"All right. What about giving lectures about the West as you know it? Such speakers are much in demand.''

Amusement lit his eyes. "No, thanks. I don't see myself in a starched-up collar, making the parlor circuit.''

"Then you tell me what you want,'' she challenged, brushing impatiently at her wind-blown hair. "You said you've tried your hand at cow-punching and riding guard for the railroad. And I seem to recall something about hiring on with Wells Fargo. What do you plan to do after you find Dawes?''

Propping the walking stick against the fence, he reached up and caught a wayward strand.

"I haven't thought beyond finding him, Suzanne. I wouldn't let myself think past him."

"Try! Just this once, try to see beyond him. What comes after Dawes?"

"I suppose I want what most men want," he said slowly. "A piece of land. A few head of cattle. Blue skies in summer. A warm cabin in winter."

"No one to share the skies and the cabin with?"

His thumb played with the honey-brown strand. "I won't let myself think about that, either."

"You could have it."

She was cutting him in half. Slicing him right down the middle.

"Suzanne..."

Despite his every promise to himself, his every resolve, he gave her hair a little tug and drew her forward. With a tremulous sigh, she came into his arms, lifting her mouth to his.

The kiss was soft, gentle, so sweet it ripped the rest of the way through him. All the dreams he'd ever dreamed, every traitorous longing a man with his reputation couldn't acknowledge, seeped through the barriers he'd erected to keep them out.

Keeping her folded against him, he rested his chin atop her head. From across the paddock, Comanche regarded them steadily. He'd taken twenty-seven arrows and survived. Jack had taken his share of hits, too, but he wasn't sure he'd survive this one.

Sliding his hands up Suzanne's arms, he drew her way. "You remember I told you I sold my folks' homestead?" he heard himself say. "The money's been sitting in a bank down to Denver all these years, collecting interest. I want you to have it."

Her breath caught. "Why?"

"So you can buy yourself another hat," he said with a crooked smile. "With a whole covey of quail feathers."

"Why, Jack?"

"I'm thinking you might need it, if that business about the herbs turning color was just another bluff."

A long-suffering sigh puffed on the cold air. Suzanne studied him, tapping a toe, for several moments.

"All right. If that's the way you want to play this hand, I'll take your money and hold on to it for you. If and when you decide you want it—or me!—you can deck yourself out in your best suit, come down to Cheyenne and come beg!"

Rising up on her toes, she planted a hard kiss on his lips, then handed him his walking stick.

"Now, let's go help Matt and Ying Li plan *their* wedding."

The emphasis was slight, but pointed.

* * *

A few moments later they made their way through the maze of tents and teepees that housed the overflow of army dependents, Indian families and the inevitable entrepreneurs and hangers-on who congregated at every military post. Most of the square-shaped Shelby tents served as residences, some as shops, saloons or gambling dens. One enterprising soul had even set up an assay-and-loan office for those drifting in after trying their luck in the Black Hills. Heated by cast-iron stoves in some cases and carefully banked fires in others, the buffalo-hide and canvas residences provided adequate, if decidedly rudimentary quarters.

When Suzanne and Jack arrived at the tent Matt and Ying Li shared with the Widow Overton, the bride's eyes lit up at the suggestion of a wedding ceremony.

"Ai ya!" Displaying an uncharacteristic spurt of enthusiasm, she clapped her hands. "You will be Ying Li's good fortune woman?"

"I...er..."

"Is most important. No good fortune woman, Ying Li no can marry Matt Butts."

"Well, I'll do what I can. What, exactly, does being a good fortune woman entail?"

Suzanne soon discovered that her duties as a wedding arranger were embodied in centuries-old customs. To her secret relief, there wasn't time for the Three Letters and Six Etiquettes, but she rather thought she could manage the wedding feast, the hair-combing ceremony and the all-important dress.

"Red," the girl insisted. "Must be red, for good spirits."

Suzanne and Jack left Ying Li huddled with the Widow Overton, their differences forgotten in the all-important business of planning a wedding. Wondering where in the world she'd find the scarlet fabric the bride desired, Suzanne walked back to the McCormacks' with Jack.

"Too bad I didn't bring Mother Featherlegs's dressing gown with me."

"Yeah," he murmured, "too bad."

Her cheeks warmed, but she was too caught up in her duties to be distracted by the memories that crowded into her head.

"And a gift," she said, her brow wrinkling. "We must think of a suitable bride gift, Jack."

"I'll take care of that. You just handle the dress and the hair combing."

Luckily, one of the officers' wives on post had tucked away a bolt of cherry-colored silk, which Suzanne gratefully purchased. Even more luckily, a Chinese tailor had set up shop in a tent not far from Mrs. Overton's. Smoothing his wrinkled hands over the watered silk, he promised a fine dress.

With that important task underway, Suzanne turned her attention to the wedding feast. Both the menu and the guest list had grown considerably beyond the simple punch and cake she'd first envisioned. She was going over the menu with her mother late Thursday afternoon when Sam and one of the McCormack boys rushed into the kitchen.

"Mama, come look!" the boy panted. "There's a freight wagon coming, and the driver asked directions to our house."

"A freight wagon? Goodness!"

The flustered Elizabeth McCormack wiped her hands on her apron and headed for the front porch. Julia and Suzanne followed, as curious as she.

Sure enough, a long-box wagon drawn by four mules rumbled down the dirt road circling the parade ground. A chorus of barking dogs and curious children followed in its wake, crowding around when the driver drew to a halt in front of the McCormacks' quarters. The bandy-legged driver tipped his hat to her.

"Got a delivery fer you, ma'am."

"For me?"

He dragged a crumpled waybill out of his pocket and squinted at it. "Well, it says here to deliver it to Jack Sloan, care of Fort Meade's commandin' officer. This is the right house, ain't it?"

"Yes. Yes, it is."

The puzzled women waited on the porch while the driver knocked the pegs from the tailgate with a wooden mallet, then clambored into the wagon bed and dragged a burlap-wrapped object to the edge. Grunting, he hefted it down.

"This here is just one of five pieces," he warned, sawing at the rope securing the burlap with his pocketknife. The wrapping fell away. Women, children and the driver himself all stared in astonishment.

"What…? What in the world is it?" Mrs. Mc-Cormack gasped, her disbelieving eyes on the scaly dragon breathing wooden fire into the air.

Laughter bubbled in Suzanne's throat. "I do believe that's Ying Li's wedding present."

21

Jack and Suzanne redirected the freight driver to Mrs. Overton's tent and managed to arrive at the same time the bed did. Between bouts of tears, incredulous exclamations and beaming smiles, Ying Li thanked Jack over and over again. Matt wasn't quite as thrilled.

"How the devil am I going to get the blasted thing up to the gold fields?" he muttered to Suzanne.

"The same way Jack got it to Fort Meade, I would imagine. By freight wagon."

They stood side by side, studying the majestic piece. Assembled, it occupied almost half of poor Mrs. Overton's tent. The widow had been forced to move her belongings to the front to make room for it, which would make for cramped quarters for the small post-wedding party Suzanne had suggested and the widow insisted on hosting.

"How do you suppose he talked Mother Featherlegs into parting with it?" Matt wondered.

"She's a businesswoman first and foremost. I suspect he just offered her the right price."

Jack confirmed Suzanne's guess when he paid off the freight driver. Brushing aside the soon-to-be groom's gruff thanks, he wished him a happy wedding night.

The inevitable tide of red rushed into the kid's face. His color deepened even more when Ying Li skipped over to him, her dark eyes aglow.

"Matt Butts and Ying Li make strong sons in honorable father's bed. We fuckee..." She stopped, corrected herself. "We do dragon dance all night, all day."

That dazzling promise banished Matt's doubts. He went off to work at the quartermaster's, resigned to hauling the bed with him on his planned adventures, then spent a good part of the night before his wedding at Three Dog Saloon with Jack.

Remembering how drunk Matt had become the last time he bent a leg at a bar, Suzanne could only hope he'd exercise a bit more restraint this time. He and Jack both. Smiling at the memory of that wild night in Rawhide Buttes, she joined Ying Li for the ritual combing of the bride's hair.

"Ying Li sit here," the girl said, setting a box at the front of the tent. "Must see moon."

Despite the cold that steamed her breath and nipped at her cheeks, she bundled up in a blanket and handed Suzanne a wooden comb.

"Missee comb four times."

With her head tipped back and a curtain of wet, shining hair hanging down her back, she drew curious glances from the residents of the other tents. Wide-eyed children wandered over to watch. A thin, mangy dog sniffed around the box before Ying Li shooed it away.

Ignoring the slowly gathering audience, Suzanne drew the comb through the long, silky hair and struggled to interpret her soft phrases. The first combing, she gathered, symbolized time from beginning to end. The second, harmony from that moment until old age. The third, many sons and grandsons. The fourth, wealth and a long-lasting marriage.

The phrases might have a strange lilt to them, but the sentiments echoed those of women through the ages. A longing for harmony, for love, for a lifelong mate. Suzanne's thoughts drifted to Jack. To the way he'd held her that moment beside the paddock. To his insistence that he endow her with all his worldly goods.

They were so close, she and Jack. Only a breath or two away from admitting what was in their hearts.

Caught up in her thoughts and the ancient ritual

of preparing a bride for her wedding, she didn't notice the two men who'd joined the crowd until she caught a mumbled phrase.

"...the Chinee whore I told you about."

Glancing up, she saw a bearded, bleary-eyed watcher dig an elbow into his friend's ribs. The words were just slurred enough for Suzanne to guess the men had come from the saloon, and just crude enough for her to shoot them a glare.

"Do, please, curb your tongue."

One had the grace to look ashamed. The other, merely belligerent.

"Come on." The younger of the two pulled at the older man's arm. "We don't want no trouble."

His companion shook off the grip. "We ain't sayin' nothing that ain't true. That little Chinee done lifted her skirts for anyone with two coins to rub together down at Rawhide Buttes. From what we hear, she's willin' to do the same here."

Suzanne gave him a hard look. Although the shadows hid most of his face, she didn't like what she saw of his expression. Why didn't she think to tuck her derringer into her skirt pocket?

"Mrs. Overton," she called calmly, never missing a stroke with the comb. "Would you be so kind as to send one of your neighbors to the Three Dog Saloon to fetch Mr. Butts and Mr. Sloan?"

"Jesus," the younger man muttered. "I ain't

staying around to tangle with the likes of Black Jack Sloan.''

He melted into the crowd. After a long, narrow stare, his friend did the same.

However much Jack's reputation might worry her, Suzanne had to admit it proved rather useful in situations like this.

She was still mulling over that pertinent fact when she left Ying Li and made her way back to the McCormacks' by the light of a bright, full moon. She arrived at the house just in time to see a rider dismount and hand his reins to a waiting orderly. Even without the gold epaulets on his caped overcoat, Suzanne would have recognized him anywhere.

''Colonel! You're back!''

She rushed into his arms for a fierce hug. The joy she always felt at her stepfather's return from the field flooded her, tinged with only the tiniest hint of dismay that he'd returned to Fort Meade two days early.

''Your mother telegraphed me about your young friends' wedding. I didn't want to miss it.''

''Matt and Ying Li will be so proud to have you at the ceremony.''

''She also reported that Sloan's back on his feet.''

Suzanne bit her lip. ''Yes, he is.''

Sliding his arm around her shoulders, Andrew

Garrett walked up the front steps with her. The rich scents of his wool uniform and leather accoutrements surrounded her, as familiar and comforting as the affection he'd always showered on her.

The McCormacks' orderly met them at the door. His face wreathed in smiles, the striker greeted the colonel.

"Your missus is in the back parlor, sir, with Lieutenant Colonel and Mrs. McCormack."

"Thank you."

Handing the orderly his overcoat, hat and gloves, he straightened his uniform coat. Suzanne watched, somewhat surprised to note the sprinkling of silver at his temples. She'd never really noticed it before.

"Mother will be so glad to see you," she said, tucking her arm in his. When she would have walked down the hall with him, he stayed her.

"Do you remember asking about the pockmarked drifter who was on the stage with me when Parrott held it up?"

Her heart stuttered. "Yes?"

"When I got back to Fort Russell, I did some checking. He got off the stage at the next stop. From what I could gather, he's back in Deadwood."

Less than a half day's ride away!

"His name is Dawes," the colonel said. "Charlie Dawes."

"That's…" Suzanne swallowed. "That's what I was afraid you'd say."

She looked away, her head bent, and Andrew cursed himself for a fool. He didn't want to reach his hand into his pocket, hated what he had to do next. If he didn't love this girl so damned much, he'd bundle her and Julia and Sam up right after the wedding tomorrow, escort them home and let Sloan find his own way to perdition.

"I talked to the U.S. Marshal down in Cheyenne," he said reluctantly. "He allowed as how the territories are a bit short on deputy marshals and long on cattle rustlers and outlaws like Parrott. He also allowed as how it's time vigilante justice gave way to the courts."

Hope and caution warred in her eyes. "Does that mean he's going to go after Dawes himself?"

"Not exactly. The way he figures it, if Sloan's so all-fired determined to hunt down a man we suspect of marking coaches and worse…"

"Much worse!"

"…he might as well be wearing this."

Digging into his uniform pocket, he drew out a tin star. Suzanne stared at it for some moments before her troubled gaze lifted to his.

"I don't know whether or not he'll take it."

"He will if I have anything to say in the matter."

Andrew didn't want a lawman for Suzanne any

more than he wanted a gunfighter. Neither one could expect to live long enough to retire to a rocking chair. But her point about the violence he himself faced every time he rode out on patrol had hit home.

"Wearing a badge won't make Sloan any less of a target for every drunk or hothead who wants to prove himself a man," he admitted. "The only difference is that when he faces them down, he won't stand alone. He'll have the full force of the law behind him, as well as the citizenry. And the military," he added grudgingly.

Suzanne huddled on the humpbacked horsehair sofa in the McCormacks' front parlor, waiting for Jack to return from his prewedding revels with Matt. A flickering oil lamp with roses painted on the glass chased the shadows to the corners of the room. The banked coals in the black cast-iron heating stove did the same to the chill.

Everyone else had retired for the night, including her mother and the colonel. He'd left it to Suzanne to deliver the news about Dawes to Jack. And the tin star.

Opening her fist, she stared down at the badge. It was dented and dull, passed from one man to the next with some frequency, Suzanne suspected. Would Jack be the next to wear it? Would he want to? Men like Bat Masterson and Bill Tilghman and

Wyatt Earp had made the transition from shootist to peace officer. Could Jack make it, too?

If the colonel was right, the era of the gunfighter was fast coming to an end. Wild, wide-open cow towns like Abilene, Denver and Cheyenne were now small, bustling cities. Although they still boasted more saloons than churches and opera houses, shoot-outs in the streets were less common. Courts of law had replaced the kangaroo courts that let killers like the one who'd gunned down Wild Bill Hickok go free. Maybe… Maybe Jack would recognize that it was time to move from the gun to the gavel.

Suzanne's fingers folded over the star so tightly the edges cut into her skin. She still had it clutched in her hand when she heard his walking stick thump on the front steps. Not wanting to disturb the McCormacks' orderly, she slipped the badge into her skirt pocket and went to meet Jack at the door.

He stepped inside, bringing with him the frost of the October night. He was leaning heavily on the walking stick, Suzanne noted, and white lines bracketed his mouth, but she knew better than to comment on either.

"Still up?"

Nodding, she helped him out of his wool jacket. "I was waiting for you."

His gray eyes glinted. "Were you worried I'd

get as drunk as I did at Rawhide Buttes and rouse
the whole house?''

Folding the jacket over the stair rail, she cocked
her head. ''*Are* you drunk?''

''No, but Matt is. I left him spouting the most
god-awful poetry to Ying Li at the top of his
lungs.''

''Oh, dear.''

The glint in his eyes deepened. ''My guess is
they won't wait until tomorrow night to try out
their wedding bed. For all her peculiar ways, Ying
Li's an accommodating little thing.''

''Indeed?''

Jack might not be drunk, but he'd downed more
whiskey than he should have, trying to ease the
ache inside him at the thought of riding out the
day after tomorrow. Charlie Dawes's trail had
probably gone stone-cold by now. It could take
Jack weeks, if not months, to pick it up again. He
should have lit out after the bastard the day he'd
pulled his boots back on. He would have, if not
for the woman standing before him. Just looking
at her brought the ache back, sharper, deeper.

''Now, don't pucker up on me, sweetheart. You
know how it makes me itch to kiss you.''

One brow arched. ''Well?''

What the hell? He might not get another hour
alone with her like this, what with the kid's wedding tomorrow and Garrett due back at Fort Meade

the day after. If he was going to make any more memories to carry away with him, this looked to be as good a time as any.

He brushed his knuckles down her cheek, savoring the creamy smoothness, memorizing the curve. Curled his hand under her chin. Tipped her face up an inch or two. Her eyes held his until he angled his head and brought his mouth to hers.

The need that ate at him was like a raw wound, more lethal than any nicked lung, more painful than a bullet through the thigh. Resisting the urge to crush her against him, he slid his hand to her nape, cradling her neck while he stored up her taste and touch and scent.

She stood quiet under the kiss, letting him take his fill. It might have been two minutes or ten before he raised his head. When he did, he hurt so hard he wasn't sure he could make the stairs. To buy a little time, he reached for his jacket and drew out the crumpled yellow paper the telegraph operator had handed him when he'd sent the offer to Rawhide Buttes for Ying Li's bed.

"This is from the bank down to Denver, confirming my authorization to transfer the funds from my account to whatever bank you designate."

Frowning, she glanced down at the folded telegram.

"Take it, Suzanne. If you decide you don't want

the money, or find you don't need it, you don't have to arrange the transfer.''

Her chin came up. "I'll accept the money, if you'll accept this.''

She slid a hand into her skirt pocket. For a moment, Jack thought she intended to offer him her little derringer to carry in his boot. Maybe a likeness to tuck in his saddle as a keepsake. The last thing he expected was the star nestled in her palm.

His eyes narrowed. "Where'd you get that?"

"The colonel brought it with him.''

"He's back, is he?"

Her expression was unreadable, but Jack had a good idea what was coming.

"Yes. He arrived earlier this evening. He used his influence with the authorities down to Cheyenne. You've been appointed a deputy U.S. Marshal.''

"That right?"

"That's right.''

Folding his arms, he let the star sit in her palm. "What made him think I'd agree to letting him arrange my life for me?"

"He didn't get the idea from me, if that's what you're implying. I told you, you're going to have to decide on your own if you want to come back to me after you hunt down Charlie Dawes.''

"And I told you I ride alone, Suzanne. I always

have. I'm not dragging a posse strung out behind me when I leave Fort Meade.''

"Good! Fine! Ride out alone.''

His jaw worked. He felt trapped, caught between the single, all-consuming need to avenge his parents that had driven him for so many years and the insidious thought that he could take another road.

Suzanne was driving him to it, just as she'd tried to drive her friend to go back East and study with that doctor in Philadelphia. Bright Water had enough sense to recognize she couldn't walk in anyone's moccasins but her own. And when it came right down to it, Jack couldn't, either.

"Do you really think a piece of tin changes anything?" he asked gruffly.

"Do you think your money does?"

"It's all I have to give you, dammit!"

The fight went out of her. Expelling a ragged breath, she shook her head.

"No, Jack, it's not, but you're not ready to give me the only thing I want from you.''

It would be so simple to say the words she wanted to hear. Hell, they might even be true. He'd never loved before, never wanted any woman the way he wanted Suzanne. The tangled mix of lust and longing she stirred in him was as close to love as he'd ever expected to come.

"I'll think about the badge, Suzanne. That's all I'll promise.''

"Fair enough."

She tossed it to him. Jack caught it one-handed, smothering a curse when the sharp pin on the back jabbed into his thumb.

"As the colonel said, it won't make you any less of a target. In fact, it might just provide a nice, shiny bull's-eye. But whatever you decide, you're going to have to tell him yourself."

She started for the stairs, only to pause on the second step. "By the way, Charlie Dawes is in Deadwood."

22

Matt's wedding day dawned bright and cold and dusted with frost. He dragged himself out of the monstrous bed and righted his long johns. Shoving his feet into his boots, he stumbled to the wooden slop bucket. Ying Li was already up and huddled by the small cast-iron stove set on bricks, sipping green tea. The widow sat beside her, ensconced in several layers of shawls and nattering on about the day's festivities.

Apparently, Matt divined through the pounding in his head, the two women had temporarily bridged their differences. What was it about a wedding that got females so feathered up?

Leaning a hand against a tent pole, he let his fuzzy thoughts wander. If he'd been getting hitched back home in Ohio, his mam would have baked up a storm. His pa would have slaughtered a couple of hogs for roasting. They would have

invited all the neighbors and cleared out the barn
for dancin'. His older brothers would have planned
a shivaree for sure. Becky would be decked out in
white, not heathenish red, and…

He jerked upright, yanking in his wandering
thoughts, but he couldn't block the wave of home-
sickness that crashed over him. Memories crowded
into his aching skull, along with a searing aware-
ness of how different this day would have been if
he hadn't been so all-fired set to try his luck in the
gold fields.

Shivering in the cold air, he glanced over at his
bride. To save his soul, he couldn't tell whether
she was any happier trotting along with him than
scrubbing floors and…and doing the dragon dance
at Mother Featherlegs Shephard's Saloon and
Hurdy-Gurdy Parlor. The only time he'd glimpsed
anything approaching joy or excitement in her face
was when she caught sight of that blasted bed.

If asked, he couldn't have explained his feelings
for her. He wanted her. All he had to do was think
about what they did in the dark and his twig
sprouted straight up into a tree. And he wanted to
do right by her. She didn't have anyone else who
cared about her. Her own father had sold her off,
just like Matt's own pa sold his hogs to market.
Yet every time he envisioned strolling the streets
of San Francisco in a fancy coat and top hat, the

woman on his arm looked more like Becky than Ying Li.

With a little wrench of his heart, Matt put Becky out of his mind forever. Ying Li would soon be his wife. She... She deserved a husband who wasn't thinking thoughts of another woman.

Sighing, he dropped his hand. He'd better get dressed. He could put in four or five hours' work for the quartermaster this morning, add to his slowly re-building roll. With what he was paying the Widow Overton and the cost of supplies at the sutler's store, he couldn't afford to take a whole day off. Not if he was going to make it to the diggings before the gold ran out.

Ying Li rose to bring him a cup of tea. "Matt Butts come back, soon soon, burn incense, make offerings to honorable ancestors?"

Hiding a grimace, he gulped down the brew. It tasted like warmed-over tree bark. Lord, what he wouldn't give for a mug of thick, black coffee!

"Is most important," she insisted. "Must do, make luck."

"All right." He managed a smile. "Matt Butts come back, soon soon."

Finishing his tea, he grabbed his clothes. On his way to the quartermaster's, he stopped in his tracks, then decided on a quick detour. He'd swing by the commander's house, ask for Miss Bonneaux, have her scribble down the lines. If he was going to do this, he was going to do it right.

Across the post, Jack was in a similar mood as he struggled with the starched collar of the shirt he'd bought at the sutler's store. Damned ridiculous things, collars. Why the hell did a man want to button himself into something that scratched his neck?

He couldn't remember the last time he'd gussied up in a store-bought suit. They were all right for dandies like Bill Hickok and Bat Masterson, who never appeared in public without their watch fobs and bowler, but not for a man who packed everything he owned in a pair of saddlebags.

Hunching over, he glared into the round mirror set atop the bureau and finally got his collar to lie in decent folds over his tie. That done, he reached for the ruby-red brocade vest he'd purchased along with the black wool suit. Wincing at the pull in his chest, he eased into the vest. His countenance was grim by the time he tugged at the lapels of the coat to settle it over his shoulders.

Scowling, Jack studied the slicked-up buck in the wavy mirror. He knew damned well what was rubbing him the wrong way this morning, and it wasn't his new suit. His glance dropped to the star lying next to his hat on the bureau scarf.

He didn't like the obligations that bit of tin carried with it any more than he liked having his hand forced by a man who'd as soon skin him whole as spit. Jack had gone his own way for so long, traveled so many miles with one, driving purpose. If it wasn't for Suzanne...

Flattening both palms on the dresser, he blew out a long breath. There you had it. If it wasn't for Suzanne, none of them would be at Fort Meade. The kid, the Chinese girl, Jack himself. At least the Arapaho woman had shown sense enough to go back to her own kind. She understood, if that mule-headed female down the hall didn't, that wanting something so fierce it hurt didn't make it right.

Still scowling, he straightened and reached for the Colt. The familiar weight had settled around his hips before he remembered he'd be standing up with Matt in church in a few hours. Carefully, he rolled the leather belt around the holster and stuffed the Colt into the saddlebags he'd brought upstairs to pack his gear in.

"Shall I help you put up your hair, *ma petite?*"

Suzanne swung around on the dressing stool and gave her mother a grateful smile. "Yes, please. I seem to be all thumbs this morning. You'd think I was the bride, not Ying Li."

Gliding into the room with a rustle of skirts, Julia gathered the heavy, silken mass. She was wearing her lavender wool in honor of the occasion, Suzanne saw on a rush of affection, the one that matched her eyes. Bustled and nip-waisted, with a row of satin bows trailing from her neck to her hem, Julia Bonneaux Garrett looked more like the New Orleans belle she was than a senior officer's wife.

"You'll be a bride soon enough, Suzanne." Deftly, she twisted her daughter's hair into a series of intricate whorls. "Sooner, it appears, than later."

"What do you mean?"

"I just passed your Mr. Sloan on the stairs. I must say he looked quite handsome, if rather disgruntled. He asked where the colonel was. Pass me a comb, *ma petite*."

Suzanne's heart knocked against her ribs as she handed her mother one of the tortoiseshell combs. "Did you happen to notice whether Jack was wearing a U.S. Marshal's badge?"

Julia's hands stilled. She was already gone from her, this child who'd grown into a woman almost overnight. It seemed only months ago Julia had dressed her daughter's dolls, mere weeks since she'd watched Andrew lift a wary, wide-eyed girl onto her first pony. She'd wanted so much for Suzanne. A home. Children. A husband who'd cherish her as Andrew cherished Julia.

Swallowing a sigh, she nodded. "Yes, darling, he was."

"Oh, Mama!"

The unbridled joy in her daughter's voice vanquished Julia's doubts. Deftly, she set another comb. "We don't have much time. Can you think of anything we've left undone?"

"What?"

"Your friends' wedding. Have we left anything undone?"

"Oh." Blinking, Suzanne dragged her whirling thoughts from the personal to the practical. "What about the paper lanterns?"

"Sam and young Robert McCormack promised to string them this morning. They also begged fifty cents from me to purchase a supply of firecrackers," she warned. "The boys are taking this business of scaring away the evil spirits to heart."

"And the rice cakes? Ying Li insisted all kinds of disaster might befall if the wedding guests aren't offered traditional rice cakes."

"Mrs. McCormack sent her husband's orderly on a scavenging expedition at first light." Ruefully, Julia anchored the last comb in place. "Poor Elizabeth. She couldn't know what she was letting herself in for when she took us all in. We shall have to restock her larder and send her a particularly fine gift when we return to Cheyenne."

Teasing a few silky brown strands free to curl about her daughter's face, she smiled down at her.

"There, you look quite ravishing."

A quick glance in the mirror on the dressing table confirmed her mother's assessment. She *did* look ravishing. Thank goodness her mother had raided Suzanne's new wardrobe before rushing up to Fort Meade. This moss-green wool gown with its ruched skirt and matching cape lavishly bordered with fox was warm as well as striking. Leaving the bonnet on the dressing table, she rose and tucked her arm in her mother's.

"Shall we go downstairs now and have breakfast with our men?"

The rough pine building that housed Fort Meade's chapel had witnessed many weddings. In the mind of Chaplain Sergeant Renquist, the ceremony that joined Mr. Mathias Butts, of Ohio, and Miss Ying Li, of Canton, China, certainly numbered among the strangest.

The wedding party was relatively small, for one thing. Troopers bored with the endless round of fatigue duties usually snatched at any break in the routine as an excuse to celebrate. Ordinarily, friends of the bride and groom gathered in such crowds that they spilled out of the chapel. They also indulged in far too much hooch both before and after the ceremony, and played ribald pranks on the newly married couple in the form of a shiv-aree…sometimes with disastrous consequences. Only last year, the poor corporal who'd won the hand of a squint-eyed Norwegian laundress had spent his wedding night in the guardhouse after bashing in the skull of another trooper who'd stolen away his wife, reportedly as a joke.

Unlike those riotous wedding parties, however, the one that gathered in the post chapel that frosty October afternoon consisted only of the bride, groom and a mere half dozen or so of their associates. To be sure, those friends included Colonel Andrew Garrett, rigged out in full dress uniform, with his wife and son. The Widow Overton was there, too, as well as Fort Meade's commanding officer and various members of his family.

The groom, Renquist decided, looked nervous and somewhat the worse for wear. The great, over-size boy stood at the front of the chapel, his round-brimmed hat crushed in his hands, his hair bright as a new-minted gold coin. Beneath that shock of unruly curls, his blue eyes showed spiderwebs of red.

But it was the man standing beside the groom who held the chaplain's fascinated gaze while they waited for the bride to make her appearance. Black Jack Sloan looked just as the penny presses had described him—tall, lean, dangerous. Even the walking stick he leaned on couldn't detract from the aura that came part and parcel with the man. His unsmiling face might have been carved from granite...until the bridal party entered the room, that is.

If Chaplain Sergeant Renquist hadn't been studying the notorious shootist with such secret awe, he might have missed the almost imperceptible softening in the hard, uncompromising planes of Sloan's face. A look of longing came into his sleet-gray eyes, so intense, so fierce, so swift, that the chaplain blinked.

The awful suspicion that the gunfighter might lust for the bride darted into Renquist's mind. After all, the girl was rumored to have sold her favors to any number of men. For a horrid moment, the chaplain feared this big, gawky groom might suffer far worse than a bashed-in skull should Sloan take it in his mind to steal away the bride during the post-wedding revelries.

Then he noted how Sloan watched not the girl robed from head to toe in shocking, cherry-red silk, but the woman accompanying her. Renquist was just about to release a sigh of relief when he guessed the identity of that dainty, elegant young woman in a moss-green gown and fashionable bonnet trimmed with matching green ribbons. She had to be Colonel Garrett's daughter, the one kidnapped by Big Nose George Parrott. The one who, if the rumors were true, had spent a week or more in the company of Black Jack Sloan!

Renquist's glance darted to the colonel, standing stiff as a flagpole beside his beautiful wife. Garrett, too, was watching Sloan, and from the grim expression on his face, he wasn't real happy with what he saw.

As nervous now as the groom, the chaplain waited only until the bride and her attendant had taken their places to flip his worn Bible open to the marked pages. It was a German edition, carried from the old country by Dietrich Renquist when he emigrated to the United States after serving almost ten years in the Prussian Army, but he'd long since memorized the English translation. He recited the familiar words by rote, having said them so many times for so many couples.

Nothing in his previous experience, however, prepared him for what followed the traditional "You can kiss your bride, Mr. Butts."

The groom turned pale as a winter moon, then blushed an even brighter crimson than his wife's wedding dress.

"Kin I say something first?"

"Yes, of course."

Beet-red, he tugged a scrap of paper from his pocket.

"Miss Bonneaux told me a man who wants to court a woman should recite lines from this fellow,

Shakespeare. I mashed them up a bit the first time I said 'em to Ying Li. Thought I'd get 'em right this time.'' Clearing his throat, he read from the scrap of paper.

''The brightness in her cheek
Would shame the stars
As daylight does a lamp...''

In the small silence that followed, he stooped down and dropped a kiss on Ying Li's bright, smooth cheek. Smiles wreathed the faces of the assembled guests when he straightened and thrust a hand out to the chaplain.

''Well, uh, thank you.''

Renquist returned his hearty shake and prepared to step aside, but the bride stayed him with a worried exclamation.

''No, no! Must tie red string, drink wine!''

Renquist looked to the groom, who in turn looked to his wife. She turned to the colonel's daughter. With a nod, the elegant young woman stepped into the breach.

''Should you mind if we add a small step to the proceedings?''

''No, not at all.''

''As I understand it, we must tie a red string around two cups of wine. The bride and groom take a sip, then exchange cups and drink again. I believe this ritual ensures harmony in the marriage.''

''I expect I could locate cups,'' the chaplain said, ''but I don't have any wine here at hand.''

''We brought some with us for just this occasion. Jack, will you assist me?''

If anyone had ever told Jack that he'd one day stand in a chapel smelling of fresh-cut pine, wearing a tin star and holding two china cups while a doe-eyed female fiddled with a bit of red string, he wouldn't have believed the man. Any more than he would have believed that he'd find himself wishing he and that same female were the ones exchanging vows and sipping wine.

He'd never thought about marriage before Suzanne. Had never had cause to think about it. Looking at her now, with her hair swirled up all smart and smooth under her hat and her lashes fanned against her cheek, he let himself imagine a future. Imagine a time after Charlie Dawes.

Maybe, just maybe...

''There, they're nicely tied. Sam, do you have the wine?''

With a wide grin, the youngest member of the Garrett family produced a stoppered bottle.

''It's not plum wine,'' Suzanne told Ying Li apologetically. ''I'm afraid there wasn't any of that to be found. So we mixed together a bit of Mrs. McCormack's dandelion wine and Dr. Morganstein's Cough Elixir. It has quite the same taste, I think.''

Ying Li evidently thought so, too. Her face held the glowing happiness of every new bride as she sipped from her cup before passing it to Matt. The red string wrapped around their wrists, binding them both physically and symbolically.

On a sigh of pure sentiment, Suzanne let her glance drift from the young couple to the man standing beside them. She'd thought him handsome as sin when he first climbed aboard the stage. Seeing him now, so tall, so casually urbane in his suit and tie, she realized his handsomeness had nothing to do with his devastating impact on her senses. It was the man who set her pulse to hammering and curled her toes in her boots. It was the man she'd come to love.

He caught her gaze. For a moment, only a moment, she was sure she read in his eyes the same absolute certainty that filled her heart. A slow, glowing warmth began in her chest and hummed through her veins.

When the wine-sipping ceremony was concluded and the newly wedded couple and their witnesses had signed the registry, Jack stood beside Suzanne while the rest of the guests came up to offer their congratulations.

''Is that what you'd expect of a groom, *Miss*

Bonneaux?'' he murmured. "Red string and lines from Shakespeare?"

She hiked a brow. "A man could do worse than recite lines from *Romeo and Juliet* to his bride."

"Maybe I should hunt down a copy."

Her pulse skipped. She couldn't breathe, could barely gather her wits enough to dip her head in a regal nod.

"Perhaps you should."

Slipping a hand under her elbow, he drew her aside. "I did some thinking last night. I have to go after Charlie Dawes, Suzanne. This badge gives me the authority to track him anywhere in the territories, but even without it, I couldn't rest until he answers for what he did to my folks."

"I know."

"But when I'm done with him, I might just do what you said. Deck myself out in this fancy suit, head down to Cheyenne and beg."

"What about your worry that those around you might become a target if someone came gunning for you?"

"It's still a worry, but…" His glance flicked to the colonel, came back to her. "Between the two of you, you've convinced me it's a risk worth taking."

Happiness burst inside Suzanne, as sharp and pointed as the star pinned to his vest.

"Is that your way of saying you've developed a tender regard for me, *Mr.* Sloan?"

"No. It's my way of saying I've developed an itch that won't go away. I guess I'll have to learn to live with it."

His smile said more than he could at the moment. A dozen emotions piled on top of Suzanne's bubbling joy, not the least of which was chagrin.

"How like you to pick a time like this to tell me so! We'll continue this conversation later, when we're alone."

In a daze of joy, Suzanne indulged in a few private visions of another wedding, in another post chapel, sometime in the not-too-distant future. Her parents would be there, of course, her mother beautiful and serene as always, the colonel resplendent in his dress blues. And perhaps the McCormacks, if they wished to make the journey down to Fort Russell so Suzanne and her mother could return their generous hospitality. Matt and Ying Li, too, assuming they hadn't left for the gold fields yet. And all her friends, with the regimental band hired to play at the banquet after the ceremony.

Encased in her happy cloud, she couldn't know that her dream would shatter that very afternoon. Or that the destruction would be engineered with a string of firecrackers similar to the ones tucked in her brother's pocket.

23

The wedding procession attracted a great deal of attention as the participants made their way across the parade ground. Skirting the flagpole, the bridal couple and their guests filed past the headquarters and followed the dirt track leading to the cavalry barracks, where Troop C had generously granted Suzanne the use of their mess.

In China, Ying Li had explained, dancers bearing a long, fearsome silk dragon on sticks would have led the way to frighten off evil spirits, with firecrackers popping constantly as added protection. Bearers would have carried her shoulder-high, majestically seated in a carved chair festooned with red and gold streamers. Flutes and cymbals and paid criers would have announced to all within hearing distance that Li, of the house of Ying, had this day become a wife.

As "good fortune woman," Suzanne had done

her best to comply with all these requirements. She'd hired the regimental drummer to beat a stately tattoo. The guests all carried strips of cherry-red silk left over from Ying Li's dress. Sam and the McCormacks' oldest boy did their part by gleefully setting off strings of firecrackers.

Naturally, everyone they passed turned to gawk. Soldiers performing Saturday drill on the parade ground halted at their officers' commands. Cavalry troops putting their mounts through their paces drew rein. Children skipped alongside, and dogs barked fiercely every time another string of firecrackers began to pop.

Through the corner of one eye Suzanne caught sight of a scruffy, bearded individual among the scattering of civilians who'd paused to watch. Frowning, she recognized him from the night before. Oh, dear! She hoped neither he nor the man with him would dare repeat their rude remarks about Ying Li within hearing of the wedding party.

To her relief, the younger of the two yanked his hat down and turned away when he saw her watching him. Thank goodness! It wouldn't do for an ugly incident to occur mere moments after the marriage ceremony.

Another series of pops and a shrill, honking bray drew her attention from the crowd to a freight wagon rumbling toward the quartermaster's warehouse. The cavalry mounts were trained not to react even to rifles and pistols fired just beside their ears, but the mules drawing the freight wagon took violent exception to firecrackers sizzling and popping just a few feet from their hooves. The right leader bucked into the left, who kicked out in the bad-tempered way of mules and entangled his rear hooves in the traces. Cursing, the driver gave Sam a ferocious glare, set the brake and climbed down to untangle his team.

"No more firecrackers," the colonel instructed his son calmly as he went to aid the struggling driver. "Take the right wheeler's bridle and hold her still, Sam. I'll take the left."

Order was restored quickly enough, and the wedding party proceeded to the Troop C mess to celebrate with punch, green tea, fish soup, rice cakes and oat bars stuffed with dried pears and baked in honey.

It wasn't until after the party that disaster struck.

The Widow Overton had graciously agreed to bunk with friends for the night to give the newlyweds sole occupancy of the tent. After a final round of good wishes, Ying Li left the Troop C mess accompanied by her "good fortune woman" to prepare the nuptial chamber.

"Half hour, Matt Butts come," she informed her new groom. "Ying Li boil tea..."

"More tea?" he groaned.

"Very important. Drink tea, make dragon dance, have sons."

"I'll come with the kid to escort you home," Jack told Suzanne.

"Yes, do. Perhaps we might find a private spot to finish the conversation we began at the chapel."

He didn't try to disguise his feelings. They were right there, warm and rueful in the smile that slipped into his eyes.

"Perhaps we might, sweetheart."

Dusk was already descending, but Suzanne didn't feel the bite of the evening air as she accompanied Ying Li through the maze of tents. Hiding her impatience, she performed her designated duties.

More red streamers were required, along with the obligatory pot of tea. While Ying Li hunkered by the cook stove to steep the tea, Suzanne hung the streamers on the bridal bed and lit the required number of joss sticks. The fragrance of oranges soon floated through the tent, pleasant at first, but gradually growing so strong she moved discreetly to the front of the tent to fold back a corner of the flap.

She was dragging in a breath of cold, crisp air when she noticed a figure standing in the shadow of another tent, his hat pulled down low. She recognized him immediately. He'd watched the hair-combing ceremony last night, then observed the wedding procession this afternoon.

A shiver crawled up Suzanne's spine. This was no casual encounter. The man was there to make trouble, for what reason she couldn't guess.

"Ying Li," she called softly. "Come look and tell me if you know this man."

The girl tripped over and peered through the tent opening. "No can see."

"Over there, in the shadows. Do you recognize him? Perhaps from Rawhide Buttes?"

The new bride gave a little shrug. "All men there same same, no matter." Her brow wrinkled. "Except..."

"Except?"

"Except honorable husband," she admitted slowly, as if trying the words on for the first time.

Encouraged by this first sign of tender regard on Ying Li's part, Suzanne let the tent flap drop. Really, there was no need for alarm. One scream would alert Mrs. Overton's neighbors to trouble, and Jack would be along at any moment.

"Matt's a fine man," she concurred.

"Like Mister Jack," the girl added with a sly glance. "He and missee do dragon dance?"

"Well..."

"Do dragon dance with Mister Jack, make fine sons."

"Yes, I rather think we might."

They'd have Jack's strength, Suzanne thought with a smile, and her stubbornness.

"When missee, Mister Jack marry?"

"We intend to discuss the matter a little later, after..."

She broke off, startled by the sudden whip of the tent flap behind her. Before she could turn around, something hard and cold crashed into her temple. She crumpled without a sound.

Jack and Matt strolled through the deepening dusk. They kept to a slow pace in deference to Jack's walking stick, but anticipation put a hitch in both men's step. Smoke from stoves and cook fires curled through the deepening dusk, filling the air with the scent of frying meat.

"It won't be bad," Matt mused, "bein' married 'n all."

Jack slanted him a sardonic glance. "Who are you trying to convince, kid?"

A grin worked its way across the new groom's face. "Both of us, I reckon."

"You think I aim to follow in your footsteps?"

"Why else would you be totin' tin?"

Why else indeed?

Hooking a finger in his collar, Jack yanked at the constricting material. Damned if his whole life hadn't turned every which way but backward these past few days. A month ago, he'd been riding with

one purpose and one purpose only in mind. Now
the need to avenge his parents had taken a turn he
hadn't envisioned...one with a brown-eyed,
strong-minded female waiting at the end of it.

With a queer little catch at his heart, he quick-
ened his step.

Suzanne smelled oranges. Burnt oranges.

Joss sticks. Ying Li. The wedding.

On a haze of splintering pain, she opened her
eyes. Fear grabbed her by the throat, thick and suffocating, until she realized the snarling fangs above
her belonged to a carved wooden temple dog. A
slight movement of her neck brought the pawing,
thick-necked horse into her line of vision.

She was in Mother Featherlegs's bed. Limp with
relief, Suzanne drew in a ragged breath...or tried
to. Only then did she grasp that her suffocating
sensation wasn't due to fear alone. Someone, she
discovered, had stuffed a rag in her mouth and tied
it in place with another strip of cloth.

And her arms. She couldn't seem to get them
out from under her. Finally, she realized they were
tied behind her at the wrists.

She lay still for long moments, willing away the
agony in her temple, breathing heavily through her
nose, trying to understand what had happened. A
rustle of straw beside her brought her head around.

When the dancing spots cleared, she saw that

Ying Li's face was only inches away, hideously distorted by the cruelly tight gag cutting into her cheeks. Fear and incomprehension filled the bride's eyes. For a moment the two women simply stared at each other, then Ying Li gave a small jerk of her chin. Her glance darted to something behind Suzanne.

Still dazed and uncomprehending, Suzanne gritted her teeth and rolled over. The slight movement dragged a groan from behind her gag.

A figure appeared in her line of vision, blurred and indistinct, but definitely not carved of wood. Using the barrel of his gun, he forced up Suzanne's chin.

"Awake, are you?"

Blinking away the haze of pain, she gazed at the man hovering over her. In the flickering light of the oil lamp hanging from the tent pole, she recognized the watcher from the night before. He'd shoved his hat back so it no longer shadowed his face. It was an ordinary face, thin and somewhat pockmarked, with gray stubble roughing the cheeks and chin. She knew she'd never seen it before.

The stranger seemed to take a perverse pleasure in her confusion. A grin stretched his mouth.

"You're sure a pretty little thing."

She made a sound behind the gag, and he

dragged the gun barrel along the underside of her jaw.

"Too bad I ain't got time to take a taste of you. You 'n that Chinee whore. Be interestin' to see which one of you squeals the loudest when a man puts it to you." The cold steel traced a line down her throat. "I like it when a woman squeals."

At the look in his eyes, bile rose in Suzanne's throat. She swallowed convulsively, trying to force it back.

"Now, don't go spewin' up," the stranger snarled, digging the barrel into her throat as if to cut off the foul taste. "You'll choke on your own vomit. I seen that happen to a sod-buster's woman down to Colorado once. Damned if she didn't die right while me 'n the boys was puttin' it to her."

Suzanne went still. Absolutely still. Terror, icy cold and numbing, seeped into her veins. In her mind, she could see a narrow slice of moon hanging over red rock canyon walls, hear Jack's low voice as he described the horror of his mother's death.

Dear Lord above! This was Charlie Dawes, the man Jack had been searching for for so many years! The hunted had now become the hunter.

"Don't worry," he said with a callousness that knifed into her soul. "I'll make sure you go cleaner than she did. You 'n the whore here. Soon's I take care of Sloan. He's comin' for you. I heared him say so. Just like I heared he was comin' after me.''

Withdrawing the gun barrel from under her chin, he moved to the front of the tent to peer through the flap. The light from the oil lamp cast his shadow against the thick canvas, but Suzanne knew better than to hope he'd appear as anything more than an indistinct blur from the outside.

''Big Nose said Sloan's got some unfinished business that involves me. I don't know what that business is, but Charlie Dawes ain't letting Black Jack Sloan get the drop on him, no sir!''

A muscle worked in his gray-stubbled cheek. ''I been watching him for days, tryin' to figure out how to bushwhack the bastard without drawin' yer pa and the whole damned fort down on me. When I seen Sloan this afternoon without his Colt, I figured I weren't gonna get no better chance.''

He was right! Jack wasn't wearing his gun. Both he and Matt were unarmed. Fear clawed at Suzanne's throat as she watched Dawes lift the tent flap open another inch or two with the tip of his gun barrel. With his other hand, he dug what looked for all the world like a string of firecrackers out of his pocket.

''I still might not have chanced a shoot-out if not for these,'' he muttered, more to himself than her now. ''Soon's I heared them goin' off this afternoon, I knew how I could bring Sloan down without anyone knowin' it was me. By the time folks figure out it were gunshots they heard and not these poppers, ole Charlie Dawes will be halfway to Deadwood.''

It was just devious enough to work, Suzanne thought frantically. Sam's firecrackers had created near chaos this afternoon. Another string tossed out into the darkness would set the dogs to yelping and cause sufficient confusion to cover Dawes's escape.

Icy fear prickled her skin. She had no idea how long she'd been unconscious, or when Jack and Matt would make an appearance. Soon, she suspected. Too soon! She had to get free, had to work the gag out of her mouth, had to do something. Anything!

Clenching her jaws against the pain still hammering in her temple, she twisted her hands, pulling desperately against the strips of cloth binding her wrists. The futile effort left her dizzy. Sucking air in great gulps through her nostrils, she swept the immediate vicinity for a sharp projection she could wriggle up against and saw through her bonds. She found none.

Her ankles weren't bound. If she inched to the side of the bed and swung her legs over the side, maybe she could lunge for Dawes, knock him over or at least off balance....

So intent was she on her desperate plan that the

butterfly touch of Ying Li's fingers at her wrists startled a grunt from her. Luckily, Suzanne managed to swallow most of the sound. The gag took care of the rest.

Her skin crawling with terror that Jack and Matt might appear at any moment, she forced herself to relax her taut muscles, to let her wrists go limp and give Ying Li's small fingers room to work.

Suddenly, Dawes stiffened. Eyes narrowed to slits, he leaned forward to peer through the opening.

"That's right, boy," he muttered. "Amble on in. Your whore's awaiting fer you."

The click when he thumbed back the hammer on his revolver sounded as loud as a rifle shot in Suzanne's ears. So did the tinkle of glass when he removed the lamp chimney and tossed it aside. The open flame danced on the night air.

"Ying Li?" Matt called a moment later from outside the tent. "Can we come in?"

Frantic, the bride yanked at Suzanne's bindings. Her nails scraped away skin, gouged into flesh. The knot loosened but not enough. Not enough, dammit.

"Ying Li?"

His face grim, Dawes held the fuse of the firecrackers an inch from the open flame. Sulfur sizzled and spit.

"Reckon it's all right for us to go in?" the women heard Matt mutter.

Jack's answer came more slowly. "They knew we were coming."

"Yeah, they did."

Tiny sparks leaped along the fuse. One-handed, Dawes tossed the string of firecrackers through the tent flap.

"Well, look at that!" the new groom exclaimed. "Must be another of Ying Li's rituals. Scarin' off more bad spirits, I guess. Let's go in before—"

The rest of his words were lost in the ensuing din. A cacophony erupted, shattering the night. The exploding fireworks raised an instant, answering chorus of barks and yelps. Knowing time had just run out, Suzanne tugged at her bonds in a frenzy.

"Ungh!"

With an incoherent grunt, she slipped free. Clawing at her gag with one hand, she pushed off the bed with the other while the still-bound Ying Li struggled to her knees.

"Jack!" Suzanne screamed over the clamor. "It's Dawes! He's got a gun!"

Cursing, Dawes spun around and fired. Suzanne flung herself to the ground beside the bed, heard a muffled, agonized cry behind her. Ying Li! Dear God, Ying Li!

She was scrabbling on all fours when the tent flap flew open. Jerking back around, Dawes fired off three quick shots at the men who charged into the tent.

Matt crumpled. Leaping over his body, Jack swung his walking stick with bone-cracking fury. The gun flew out of Dawes's hand and the two men went down. They thrashed around in the confined space, snarling, grappling for a hold. The din outside drowned their grunts and Suzanne's panting gasps as she dived for Dawes's pistol.

Rage drove Jack, hot and murderous. He'd waited for this for so many years, envisioned Dawes pale and sweating as he faced his executioner. Yet at this moment, all Jack's fury, all his fear, was for Suzanne. If Dawes had touched her, if he'd hurt her or Ying Li...

Hooking a leg behind Dawes's knee, Jack used the leverage to roll upright. His fist slammed into the face he'd carried in his head all these years. Once, twice, again. Bone crunched. Blood spurted.

"Ungh!"

Dawes's elbow dug into Jack's ribs, hard, right where the bullet had gone into his lung. Everything went black. For a moment, the tent spun around him.

That moment was all Dawes needed. Bucking like a crazed wild horse, he dislodged his attacker, scrabbled for the gnarled oak walking stick and smashed the knob into Jack's skull.

Struggling to his feet, Dawes swung the stick

again. He was bringing it down with all the force in him when Suzanne fired at point-blank range.

The last firecracker popped.

The chorus of barks and yelps continued, until finally that, too, died away.

Suzanne didn't hear the silence, *couldn't* hear it over the roaring in her ears. The stink of gunpowder seared her nostrils, blurred her vision. Blinking to clear her burning eyes, she spun toward the bed.

"Oh, no! Dear Lord, no!"

One glance, one touch confirmed the small, still figure lying in a pool of blood on her wedding bed was dead.

With Dawes's six-shooter still clutched tight in her fist, Suzanne edged around his body and dropped to her knees. Jack's groan told her he was recovering from the savage blow to his head. Matt...

Matt died in her arms.

Shaking from head to toe, Suzanne rolled him over to check his wounds. He'd taken a bullet through the throat, another through the heart. Convulsions racked him even as Suzanne grabbed a fistful of skirt and petticoat in a futile attempt to staunch the blood. All she could do then was hold him.

The awful shudders ceased. His eyelids fluttered,

came up. Confusion blanked his blue eyes. In a torturous effort, he gurgled out a single word.

"Becky?"

Her heart breaking, Suzanne rocked him in her arms. "I'm here," she whispered. "I'm here."

His eyes closed. With a long, rattling sigh, he was still.

Tears streaming down her cheeks, Suzanne held him tight against her breast, rocking back and forth, until Jack reached down, eased the boy from her arms and took her into his.

24

They buried Matt and Ying Li in the Fort Meade cemetery. The post carpenter nailed together raw pine boards for the coffins. Prisoners from the guardhouse were detailed to dig the graves. Huddled together for protection against the biting wind that carried light swirls of snow, they leaned elbows on their shovels and waited impatiently for the services to conclude.

The few mourners who gathered at the graveside had tied white handkerchiefs around their arms, since Chinese custom dictated that as the color of sorrow. Chaplain Sergeant Renquist said the words over them in a bitter mockery of the ceremony he'd performed only the day before.

His nine-year-old face solemn, Sam set off another string of firecrackers.

"To frighten away the evil spirits," Suzanne murmured, grieving for the generous-hearted Romeo and his unlikely Juliet. "So they might make the journey to the next world safely."

Chinese burial customs, she'd learned in the brief hours since she'd participated in Ying Li's wedding rituals, weren't all that different from those of the Plains Indians. Both peoples believed in the long journey to the afterlife and offered symbolic gifts of food and precious objects to the departed to ease their way.

Julia Bonneaux Garrett stepped to the graveside. Slender and elegant in her lavender wool gown and fur-trimmed coat, she opened her fist. Bits of crumbled rice cakes drifted down onto the raw pine boards.

"To sustain you on your journey," she murmured.

Her husband joined her. Rigged out in his dress uniform once again, the colonel rested a hand on his sword and dropped a wad of greenbacks onto the coffins. They'd no doubt disappear into the pockets of the grave-diggers, but at least Ying Li's gods would be appeased.

With a wrenching ache, Suzanne added her contribution. She'd searched the post library for a dimly remembered verse until she found the bard's declaration to an unknown love and copied it in flowing, embellished script. The poem fluttered down as she recited the lines.

"So long as men can breathe,
Or eyes can see,
So long lives this,
And this gives life to thee."

She'd included the same lines in the letter she'd written to Matt's parents back in Ohio. In that letter, she'd enclosed a brief note for Becky. It was, she thought, the most difficult missive she'd ever had to compose.

Swallowing to ease the ache in her throat, Suzanne stepped back and hooked her arm in Jack's. He'd said little after the shootings last night, even less this morning. Worrying that he'd injured himself more than he'd admit, she studied his stony profile.

Bruises purpled the side of his face. His knuckles were raw, his eyes as gray and cold as the snow-laded sky. He stared down at the pine coffins for a long moment before lifting his gaze to stare at the distant mountains.

A fresh, piercing grief lanced into Suzanne's heart. Jack blamed himself, she knew. He'd warned her repeatedly that anyone who walked or rode in his shadow faced as much danger as he did. The badge he wore wouldn't protect him or anyone with him.

He was going to ride out. Alone. She sensed it with everything in her. And this time she couldn't, *wouldn't* even try to stop him. She'd curl up with her misery and die before she let another creature like Dawes use her as bait to lure Jack into a trap.

Finally, Suzanne had come to accept the truth of Bright Water's gentle observation. She loved too much. Too hard. She had to let go.

"Jack..."

"Hold on a minute."

Shaking free of her hold, he limped to the grave. His jaw tight, he tugged at the leather ties anchoring the Colt's holster to his thigh.

Suzanne's heart jumped into her throat. Stunned, she watched him fumble under his gray wool jacket and unbuckle his gun belt. Slowly, deliberately, he wrapped the cartridge belt around the worn leather holster. It landed atop the coffins with a thud that sounded as final as death.

Turning his back on the past that had haunted him for so many years, Jack reached for the future he'd never imagined he'd have.

"I'm thinking it's time to start looking for that piece of land we talked about," he said quietly. "Maybe buy a few head of cattle, build that cabin..."

"I...I think so, too."

"Marry me, Suzanne." He lifted his hand, brushed his knuckles down the curve of her cheek. "Tomorrow, if you can see past the sorrow of today."

''Oh, Jack!''

The tears fell freely now. Joy overlaid the hurt in her heart.

''I don't think Matt and Ying Li would want us to wait until tomorrow. As she'd point out, it's…it's all same, no matter.''

Extracting a promise from the astonished Chaplain Sergeant Renquist to meet them in the chapel come sundown, Suzanne tucked her arm in his.

25

A fresh dusting of snow glistened over the parade ground when Colonel and Mrs. Garrett bid farewell to the McCormacks and came down the front steps of the commanding officer's quarters. Bundled in a warm beaver coat, Julia insisted on riding the gelding her husband had procured for her instead of traveling via wagon, as did their son. Sam was already in the saddle and ready for the long trip back to Fort Russell.

The colonel's charger and the gelding waited patiently, their breath steaming on the cold air. They were tied at the mounting block next to a big roan and a chestnut wearing the Black Hills Stage and Express Line brand.

Jack stood beside the roan, with Suzanne at his side. As the colonel approached, Jack held out a gloved hand. In his palm lay the tin star.

"I won't be needing this."

Andrew pocketed the badge and met Sloan's look head-on. He still didn't like the man, although he supposed that might come with time. Maybe.

"You sure you two don't want to ride back to Cheyenne with us?" he asked Suzanne.

"No. We'll take the long way, through Rawhide Buttes. I left a string of debts I've yet to make good on, remember?"

Her glance tipped to Sloan. A small, intimate smile curved her lips. "Some of my debts are rather more urgent than others," she murmured.

Conceding defeat for one of the few times in his life, Andrew consigned the daughter he loved as much as life itself to Sloan's care.

"We'll see you in Cheyenne."

After a fierce hug from her mother, Suzanne watched the small cavalcade wheel and start across the parade ground. A part of her shivered, realizing they took with them the life she'd known up to now. Yet the larger part was filled with a bursting, blooming happiness.

Giving her love free rein, she smiled up at the man watching the riders with a grim expression.

"Don't worry about the colonel. He'll come around. My mother and I are both convinced the baby will mend matters between you two."

"Baby?"

His glance whipped down to her. Disbelief chased across his face, followed in close order by uncertainty and something perilously close to exasperation.

"Dammit! I knew that business with Bright Water's herbs was a bluff!"

Mischief dancing in her eyes, she pursed her lips. "Indeed?"

Her laughter vanquished him. Grinning, Jack wrapped his hands around her upper arms and drew her close.

Suzanne wasn't sure what she expected at that point. A repeat of the vow he'd made last evening to hold and cherish her for the rest of his days, perhaps. Or more of the whispered words of love they'd exchanged in the dark, tangled together in the bedclothes in the McCormacks' upstairs bedchamber. What she didn't expect was the sardonic hook to his brow.

"Are you ever going to tell me what the hell was in the hand you folded that night at Mother Featherlegs's Saloon?"

"A good poker player never reveals her strategy," she returned primly.

"One of these days, *Miss Donn*—" he caught himself just in time "—Mrs. Sloan, I'm going to call your bluff."

Flinging her arms around his neck, she rose up on tiptoe and brushed her lips to his.

"I hope so, Mr. Sloan! I sincerely hope so."

USA Today bestselling author

CARLA NEGGERS

Susanna Galway was only trying to find a place where she could get away from everything when she bought the isolated cabin in the Adirondacks. With her usually perfect marriage hitting a rough patch, it seems the idyllic spot to hide from fears and secrets—and from the man she loves. But Susanna is unaware that she, her daughters and her mother have been followed into the mountains— by her husband, Texas Ranger Jack Galway, and by a murderer intent on ruining their lives.

THE CABIN

"The Cabin kept me up all night.
No one does romantic suspense better!"
—Janet Evanovich

On sale January 2002
wherever paperbacks are sold!

Visit us at www.mirabooks.com

MCN845

Between friendship and love...

Loving

Jessie

Dallas Schulze

Growing up, Matt Latimer was always around when
Jessie Sinclair needed him most. Now he's returned to their
tiny hometown, and Jessie needs him for the most important
decision of her life. She wants a baby. Suddenly the lives of
Matt and Jessie and others in the small California town
collide in unexpected ways. Jessie must choose between
what was and what might still be, between past heartbreak
and the promise of new love, between what was lost and
what is still waiting to be found.

"Schulze delivers a love story that is both
heartwarming and steamy."
—*Publishers Weekly*

*Available the first week of January 2002
wherever paperbacks are sold!*

Visit us at www.mirabooks.com

MDS791

An incredibly gripping novel from bestselling author

DIANE CHAMBERLAIN

When eight-year-old Sophie Donohue fails to return from a camping
trip, her frantic parents mount a desperate search...a search made
more critical by the fact that Sophie is sick with a serious illness. As her
mother, Janine, refuses to give up hope that her daughter is alive, Sophie
finds refuge in a remote cabin with a mysterious woman. A woman who
holds Sophie's fate in her hands, but who knows doing the right thing
for the little girl will mean sacrificing her own daughter.

THE COURAGE TREE

"A suspenseful family drama...this page-turner will please
those who like their stories with...many twists and turns."
—*Publishers Weekly* on *The Courage Tree*

On sale January 2002 wherever paperbacks are sold!

MIRA®

The unforgettable sequel to *Iron Lace*

RISING TIDES

Aurore Gerritsen left clear instructions: Her will is to be read over a four-day period at her summer cottage on a small Louisiana island. Those who don't stay will forfeit their inheritance. With a vast fortune at stake, no one will take that risk. Suspicions rise as Aurore's lawyer dispenses small bequests, each designed to expose the matriarch's well-kept secrets. Family loyalties are jeopardized and shocking new alliances are formed. But with a savage hurricane approaching, tensions reach a dangerous climax. And the very survival of Aurore's heirs is threatened.

EMILIE RICHARDS

"...a multi-layered plot, vivid descriptions, and a keen sense of time and place."
—*Library Journal*

Available the first week of January 2002 wherever paperbacks are sold!

MIRA®

Visit us at www.mirabooks.com

MER888

If you enjoyed what you just read,
then we've got an offer you can't resist!

Take 2
bestselling novels FREE!
Plus get a FREE surprise gift!

Clip this page and mail it to The Best of the Best™

IN U.S.A.
3010 Walden Ave.
P.O. Box 1867
Buffalo, N.Y. 14240-1867

IN CANADA
P.O. Box 609
Fort Erie, Ontario
L2A 5X3

YES! Please send me 2 free Best of the Best™ novels and my free surprise gift. After receiving them, if I don't wish to receive anymore, I can return the shipping statement marked cancel. If I don't cancel, I will receive 4 brand-new novels every month, before they're available in stores! In the U.S.A., bill me at the bargain price of $4.24 plus 25¢ shipping and handling per book and applicable sales tax, if any*. In Canada, bill me at the bargain price of $4.74 plus 25¢ shipping and handling per book and applicable taxes**. That's the complete price and a savings of over 15% off the cover prices—what a great deal! I understand that accepting the 2 free books and gift places me under no obligation ever to buy any books. I can always return a shipment and cancel at any time. Even if I never buy another book from The Best of the Best™, the 2 free books and gift are mine to keep forever.

185 MEN DFNG
385 MEN DFNH

Name	(PLEASE PRINT)	
Address	Apt.#	
City	State/Prov.	Zip/Postal Code

* Terms and prices subject to change without notice. Sales tax applicable in N.Y.
** Canadian residents will be charged applicable provincial taxes and GST.
All orders subject to approval. Offer limited to one per household and not valid to current Best of the Best™ subscribers.
® are registered trademarks of Harlequin Enterprises Limited.

BOB01   ©1998 Harlequin Enterprises Limited

MIRABooks.com

We've got the lowdown on your favorite author!

☆ Read an excerpt of your favorite author's newest book

☆ Check out her bio

☆ Talk to her in our Discussion Forums

☆ Read interviews, diaries, and more

☆ Find her current besteller, and even her backlist titles

All this and more available at

www.MiraBooks.com

MEAUT1R2

Merline Lovelace

66784   THE HORSE SOLDIER   ___ $5.99 U.S. ___ $6.99 CAN.

(limited quantities available)

TOTAL AMOUNT $_____
POSTAGE & HANDLING $_____
($1.00 for 1 book, 50¢ for each additional)
APPLICABLE TAXES* $_____
<u>TOTAL PAYABLE</u> $_____
(check or money order—please do not send cash)

To order, complete this form and send it, along with a check or
money order for the total above, payable to MIRA Books®, to:
In the U.S.: 3010 Walden Avenue, P.O. Box 9077, Buffalo,
NY 14269-9077; **In Canada**: P.O. Box 636, Fort Erie, Ontario,
L2A 5X3.

Name:_____
Address:_____ City:_____
State/Prov.:_____ Zip/Postal Code:_____
Account Number (if applicable):_____
075 CSAS

*New York residents remit applicable sales taxes.
Canadian residents remit applicable GST and provincial taxes.

MIRA®